Andrew is an ancient immortal with dark history. Edmund is a human sailor with a desire for both adventure and violence. Together, they build a love that could last centuries...if ghosts of the past don't drive them apart.

Escaping Exile

Andrew is a vampire, exiled to an island as punishment for his bloodlust. During a storm, a ship crashes off shore. After rescuing a sailor from cannibals, Andrew becomes fascinated with his new companion, Edmund. Fascination turns to passion, but as cannibals creep closer—and as Andrew's hunger threatens—can this vampire keep his human alive long enough to explore their newfound love?

Escaping Solitude

Recently returned from exile, vampire Andrew and his beloved human sailor Edmund move to New Orleans where they search for an Elder who can make Edmund immortal. A frantic letter from London propels them overseas, but an accident puts Edmund's life in jeopardy. Only an Elder can save him, if they can find one in time.

Escaping Mortality

An Elder saves Edmund's life at sea. Now a vampire, he can stand by Andrew's side forever, but they must first visit Edmund's ailing mother in England. The Elder shows an ominous liking to his new sire, while Edmund's mother's friend threatens them all. Andrew will do anything to keep Edmund by his side, but his most dangerous adversary may be Edmund himself.

The Escape Trilogy

Sara Dobie Bauer

A NineStar Press Publication

Published by NineStar Press
P.O. Box 91792,
Albuquerque, New Mexico, 87199 USA.
www.ninestarpress.com

The Escape Trilogy

Printed in the USA
First Edition
May, 2019

Print ISBN: 978-1-950412-61-7

Warning: This book contains sexually explicit content, which may only be suitable for mature readers.

Table of Contents

To all the Johnlock and Charmie shippers who inspire me every day.

And to Chris, my nasty boy.

ESCAPING EXILE

Chapter One

THE CRACK AS the hull breaks echoes across the beach, into the woods, and inside my head as I try to sleep. I was just beginning to dream of New Orleans. I almost smelled whiskey and muddy streets—*almost*. Instead, I jolt awake, still surrounded by the fresh flowery scent of this blasted tropical island in the middle of... Well, I don't know really. That's the point of exile.

I pull on a worn linen shirt. For the first few months here, I slept with my clothes on in case the cannibals came knocking. They never did. I think they knew this strange white man would make a disgusting meal. As if they could smell death on me. I wonder if eating my flesh could actually kill them. Wouldn't mind offering a bite if only for some entertainment. I haven't watched a human die in ages, but now, here we go: a shipwreck. There's bound to be death in abundance tonight.

It's not raining when I step outside my house. Yes, I have a small house on a tropical island in the middle of the ocean, overrun with cannibals and all manner of man-eating beasts. Michelle wasn't that cruel when she sent me here. She did provide me with a home. *Congratulations, you heartless bitch, you gave me a house in which to spend eternity alone.*

I didn't even mean to kill that last human back home in Louisiana.

Or maybe I did.

A leathery leaf to the face brings me back to the present as I stomp in tall boots through thick foliage. Despite the lack of rain now falling on my island, a flash of lightning illuminates the beach ahead long enough for me to see them—the natives who've managed to steal so many meals from me.

The irony would make me crack a smile if not for my ever-growing bitterness. I once considered capturing a cannibal, but then, they might come hunting me and I'm not half as strong as I once was. And I don't think Michelle means to leave me here forever. I must wait out her overblown sense of justice.

From where I stand, sheltered behind a fence of palms, I see remnants of a great ship washing to shore. Thunder cracks as a man screams. My focus darts toward the dancing orange light of the native's torches, and I see but outlines of their naked bodies as they tug and pull on a creature wrapped in white fabric. I squint and identify a man in his sleeping clothes. Dinner is served.

My gaze skims the beach, but it's mostly detritus and dead men. Dead men are no good to me as their blood is most certainly not part of my unique diet. Oh, but then, there's a scent on the wind. There is something alive nearby, and it's bleeding. The smell of blood mixes with the salt of the sea and bitter stress-sweat.

I hone my senses to find the source of blood, but it's been so long. Once a master, my hunting skills are now out of practice. I take a step back into the jungle and move to my right, away from the dancing torches and the man's screams, and almost trip over a body. Out of practice is apparently a gross understatement as he was near me this whole time.

Unlike his soon to be devoured compatriot, this man is fully clothed in a coat and trousers. His hair is dark, and he wears black gloves. He's but a shadow on the sand as I lift him and carry him farther into the woods.

Finally, a meal they won't steal from me.

SAFELY INSIDE MY little house, I lay the man on the floor and poke at the fire until it roars like the thunder outside. Now, it rains. The ocean storm falls heavy, rocks on the roof, and an animal howls nearby, woken wet from its slumber.

I peel off his soaked clothes as the wound on his head continues to bleed. Unconscious, it's a wonder he wasn't pulled away by the current to die in the arms of some mythical mermaid. As I look at him in the firelight, I realize he is indeed a wonder. Perhaps it's been too long since I've felt another man's skin, but perhaps not. This injured sailor might be beautiful.

Looking at his hairless face, I would have guessed him barely a man. The thick muscles of his chest, arms, and legs dictate otherwise, as do the calluses on his hands. Not only is he a full-grown man, but he's also a man who works hard. He is lean with hair the color of the ocean on a moonless night—and if I don't stop his head bleeding, my curse of nothing but dead flesh could continue.

"Don't die," I say to him. It's the first I've spoken to a human in ages.

I move him, naked and dry, to my bed and cover him in blankets before wetting a cloth and wiping his wound. It's a sizeable gash high on his forehead. The dark creature inside me wrestles at the sight of his blood, but I woo it with promises of *later, later*.

I hold the rag to his head and realize I have no bandages. It's not as though I need them. I'll just have to sit here then. I perch on the side of my bed, and my thumb touches his bottom lip. Like a sunrise, this man is becoming more beautiful by the minute. I want to ravage him. I push the blankets away enough to run my hand over his chest. An angry scrape mars the pale skin, and I bet my guest will be covered in bruises by morning. The sea is not a gentle mistress. I know. I've tried to escape my exile by swimming out into white waves to no avail. The crushing currents always bring me back.

A log pops in the fire as the rain continues. My house now smells of smoke, mud, and *him*. I climb farther into the bed and recline at his side. I still hold the cloth to his head as I wrap him in my arms and run my nose up the side of his neck.

I think Michelle would be angry to see how happy I am.

Chapter Two

HE HASN'T MOVED come morning, but he's not dead. His heart beats beneath the palm of my hand. He would smell different, too, if he'd died in the night, like meat gone sour. Outside, the sun tries to escape the clouds to no avail, although it doesn't rain anymore. The jungle is quiet, resting after the storm.

I take care to further clean his wound, now that the bleeding has stopped. The day warms quickly. Through my open windows, humid air rides breezes that should be a relief and are instead suffocating with wetness. I pull his blankets down and run my fingers over his shoulders and arms. My sailor is such a lovely thing—but I was right. His torso is painted in shades of purple already. He'll be sore when he wakes up. If he wakes up. He has to wake up.

Before I know it, I've been staring at him for hours with my hand on his flat stomach, and I feel a desperate need to know the color of his eyes. I want to hear his voice. I want to make him come. All of these sudden, frantic yearnings wash over me, all because it's been too long. A man like me should not be alone for so long, not when I so enjoy the company of others—but I am being punished. Maybe I deserve punishment. Maybe I really did mean to kill that whore in New Orleans.

I should scour the beach for remnants. Boats carry so many supplies, and I need...who knows what for my guest? I can't leave him, though, not unconscious.

Unmoving in my bed, he can't fight back. He couldn't even call for help. If the cannibals found out I had a healthy young man in my house, they would never leave us in peace.

In the sunlight, my sailor is a contradiction. He's not a privileged weakling with clean fingernails, but he's not a roughened brute either. He's nothing but muscle and skin, but he's got the face of a man I might see wearing a woman's frock in some back den off Bourbon Street. He is elegant, and if only he'd wake up so I could taste his tongue.

I barely notice the falling of night, but here we are in the dark again. My fingers have mapped almost every inch of him by now as his bruises continue to spread. I've about resigned myself to never hearing him sigh when he gasps awake.

He sits up and sucks air into his lungs as if he's spent the past two days drowning. I keep my hands on his shoulders and see that his eyes are light—some shade of gray or bright blue like the sea.

"You're all right," I say.

"Bollocks," he gasps. Then he chokes, and I hurry to get him water from the large rain bucket outside. He gulps down a cup before wiping the back of his hand over his mouth and staring up at me. "Where..." His eyes glaze over. "The ship!" He tosses the blankets back and stands with no concern for his nudity. I'm there to catch him when he almost falls over.

"You need to sit." I push him back onto the edge of my bed and sit in the chair nearby.

He winces and bends forward. "Christ, I hurt everywhere. I..." He squeezes his eyes shut.

I now know not only the color of those eyes but also the sound of his voice: velvet with a touch of smoke. I want to hear that voice calling my name. Also, he's English, which truly does make me wonder where the hell Michelle found this ridiculous island for my exile. Where in God's name are we? My sailor will probably be just as confused as I when he realizes I'm American, but he seems too confused by other things at the moment to care.

"Where am I?"

I want to laugh but don't. "Your ship crashed on the reef last night. I found you on the beach."

"I was on deck," he says without looking at me. "Mapping the stars." His tongue pokes out to lick his lips. "There was a noise, and then... My head, I think..." He reaches for his forehead, but I grab his wrist to stop him.

"Don't. You have an open wound."

"Oh. That explains the hammering in my skull. The rest of the crew?"

I shake my head. "I didn't find anyone else."

He covers his face with his hands and says with vehemence, "Fuck."

The word from his mouth makes me smile. I've always found the British to be a charming, self-deprecating people, but of their propriety, I have been less than enthused. My sailor seems on the more colorful spectrum. And his comfort with nudity is a welcome relief. If I had my way, the man would never wear clothes.

He lifts his head. "We must go to the beach."

"It's not a good idea."

"Why not? I might be able to find—" He shrugs. "—anything."

"I fear the natives might be too fond of you."

He groans. "Not cannibals again!"

I chuckle, surprised.

"Considering their brutality," he rants, "it's amazing these creatures survive. I once saw one take a bite out of the other during an argument. And they were friends! Suppose you don't like your neighbor? Well, show up and eat their children!"

I laugh, and it's akin to floating on a warm tide.

"Oh, my head."

I lean forward in my chair as his face crumples in pain. "Why don't you lie down?"

He collapses onto the pillow. "I don't even know your name."

"Andrew."

"Andrew," he says, and his voice shakes. "Thank you."

Before he dozes off again, I push coils of black curl behind his ear. "And you? What do I call you?"

"Edmund," he whispers as he slips away, and I sit by his side as he wrestles through dreams.

Chapter Three

BY THE NEXT morning, I'm considering not killing him, no matter what the dark creature might say, no matter how it begs. Fact is, I believe Michelle is due for a visit sometime soon. She comes to see me—I think annually—to gloat and remind me *why I'm here.*

Yes, yes, the killing—yes, I recall. How could I forget?

I hadn't touched a human in ages until Edmund washed up on my beach. Now, he's here in my bed, and I'd like him to remain if only to hear more of his ravings. He's fearless, I think, and just a bit callous. How else can I explain the lack of empathy for his dead comrades? He's a man of the sea, accustomed to losses big and small. If I were to kill him, he might not even struggle—although I like that part, the struggling—and Edmund looks strong. At least, he will be once he's healed. I will keep him alive to heal. I hope to see his body without all the bruises, but maybe I can also show Michelle how good I am, how I've kept a human without hurting it. Maybe she'll let me go back.

Even with the sun up, Edmund still sleeps. During the night, his quiet whimpers and sighs acted as a beacon to my long neglected cock. Several times, I talked myself out of rolling him over and taking what I wanted. Several more times, I touched myself instead of touching him because that's what I really want: the freedom to *touch* and turn his quiet dream whimpers into stuttering shouts.

I am guilty of killing humans, but not before overwhelming them with pleasure.

Once again, I'm tempted to leave as he sleeps to find food since I require so little, but I'm scared to leave him alone. Now that I know his name, I would be shattered if the cannibals took Edmund. I would attempt to kill them all, my weakened state be damned. So I wait, but it's not long before his eyes blink open. I pretend I haven't been staring.

"Oh, God, it wasn't a dream," he says.

"No."

He rests his forearm across his eyes. "Mum always said I'd die at sea."

"You didn't."

"They'll think I did, though." The trim muscles in his abdomen shift as he leans up on his elbows. "Did your ship crash as well?"

I nod. "In a way."

"How long have you been here?" He eyes the surrounding area: a sparse living space, washbasin, some books and clothes. "Long enough to build a house apparently."

I want to tell him it doesn't matter how long I've been on this damn island. It doesn't matter because he's here with me now, and I want to fuck him until we're dumb with it. I want to have this beautiful creature until my crazed brain hallucinates the whole of Mardi Gras. I almost believe his skin could take me home.

"I forget your name."

I look up to see him watching me. "Andrew."

"Andrew. How long?"

"I don't know how long I've been here."

"Have other ships crashed?"

I nod. "A few."

"But no survivors."

I stare at him to see if he's as smart as his proper enunciation makes him sound.

"Ah," he says. "Cannibals."

"You were halfway up the beach when I found you. You must have dragged yourself from the water."

"I don't remember that." He runs his hand through his hair, oily with sweat and saltwater. He hisses when one of his fingers touches his wound, and I leap from my seat.

I pull his hand away. "Don't hurt yourself, Edmund. I must find you a bandage."

"We *must* go to the beach," he says. "Please."

BEFORE WE GO outside, I give him some of my clothes. Although mine are too big, Edmund's are still wet. They'll never dry in this sweltering wet hell of a furnace. He's not a little man by any means, my sailor, but I've met few brutes that rival my size. I think it's a symptom of these modern times. When I was born, men were expected to not only survive the wilderness but protect their families too. Men now are so soft in their fancy waistcoats, working behind desks while their women sit at home and sew. Not that I'm complaining. Modern men are much easier to seduce.

I wonder how Edmund will respond once he figures out what I am, what I want. He is friendly, and I believe he trusts me already, but will he struggle against my advances? Will he try to make me stop?

Ahead of me on the path, he freezes. Ah, the ocean has come into view. Emerald water surrounds white beaches as far as the eye can see. All signs of a storm are long since gone, replaced by the heat of tropical sun. I hear the waves and his breath, and despite the nearby flowers, I smell only him. Edmund is quickly invading all areas of my brain. Already, he has replaced the overpowering scent of the sea. His are the only eyes I remember—alert and gray—and his bruised flesh is the only skin I've ever touched.

The boy in New Orleans is barely a memory. A young prostitute, he seduced me with soft kisses. I killed him because I wanted to know what a sweet soul tasted like, but I don't think I'll kill Edmund. I must show him to Michelle.

I trust the coast is clear, because Edmund steps free of the foliage and out into the sun. The makeshift bandage I cut from the bottom of a shirt resembles a turban on his head as he walks toward the water.

When a great ship breaks, one thinks massive chunks of wood might remain. However, the ocean is a hungry bitch. There's little evidence of Edmund's ship beyond pieces of wood. As he wanders the water's edge, I keep close and smell for natives, but all I sense now is death.

We come upon a torn apart corpse. Red sticky ribs cook in the sun, but I recognize the white fabric. This is the screaming man from two nights prior. Edmund turns away from the body. He covers his mouth with one hand and places the other on my shoulder. When he coughs, his whole chest lurches. I know his body wants to be sick, but his stomach is empty—although this is not the opportune time to mention his need for food.

I drag him away from his dead friend. "What were you looking for?"

"My journals," he says. "Silly."

"What do you write in these journals?" I continue leading him by his elbow. The less time he spends out and about, the safer he'll be.

"I'm a naturalist. I travel the world looking for new species. I find more comfort in nature than other humans. Which is preposterous to you, I'm sure, trapped out here with only nature. You probably sang a 'Hallelujah Chorus' when I woke up, and what sort of company am I? I'd rather talk to trees." He must expect me to be offended, because he stutters. "Not that I...I mean to..." He stops walking and puts his hand to his face, possibly to cover the wet redness of his eyes.

Not so callous after all then.

Chapter Four

FOR SOMEONE WHO studies species, Edmund is quite interested in killing them. When I tell him there's a lagoon by my home—our home—he shakes off the melancholy from the beach and builds a net out of moss. He says he learned the trick from a man on the ship they called Samuel, although that wasn't his real name. Samuel was African, Edmund says. They were friends, he says. Then, he shakes his head and keeps working on his net.

As we wander off into the jungle toward the lagoon, he asks, "Do the natives not come to this side of the island?"

He asks more than his question might have me believe. "No," I say.

He squints into the sun. "You said the natives might be fond of me, but would they not be fond of you, as well?"

"They haven't bothered me so far." I've been dead much too long.

"Perhaps they think this side of the island is cursed."

I smile. "Perhaps."

Edmund tries to hide the way he winces when he walks, but I remember the bruises on his body. He should be resting, but I allow him this taste of freedom. At least he still wears the bandage on his head, even though I can see it's soaked in sweat as we pass beneath towering palms as old as God.

It's not long before the lagoon comes into view, but it's the sharp mountain that catches Edmund's attention first. He halts. "It's like a finger pointing to the sky." Then, he sees the water, a shocking blue that makes him blink with its beauty. "So we're not in Hell after all."

He's been walking the island barefoot, so all he does is roll up the cuffs of his too-long breeches before tiptoeing into the clear water. He gestures for me to stay back, and we wait. I've never seen a human so still. He reminds me of the white egrets I've observed hunting in long grass. The only discernible movement is the ever-so-slight up-down of his chest as he breathes.

Then, he moves. The net made of moss and reeds disappears below the surface. When he pulls it back up, a fish the size of my forearm thrashes with enough vehemence to almost knock my injured Edmund over. He laughs, and the low rumble is delightful enough to eat.

I have a small knife back at the house. He guts the fish and cooks it as the sun begins to set. He sits on the floor to eat and looks up at me in my chair. "There's plenty for you."

"No, thank you, Edmund."

"But you need to eat."

I fold my hands over my stomach. "Later. Your ship, where were you headed? I mean to ask, where do you think we are?"

He sighs and swallows. I don't like how the reek of fish covers the scent of him. "We were headed to Brazil."

"That's a long way from home for an Englishman."

"Home is wherever the creatures are. England's boring anyway. Horses and dogs and foxes. *Birds.* Nothing new. Nothing interesting." He sucks one of his fingers. "I assume we're somewhere off the coast of South America."

It wasn't my America, but it was close—another of Michelle's little jokes, taunting me with almost but not quite.

"Where was your ship headed when you wrecked here?" he asks.

I'm distracted when he licks his lips. "Uh, New Orleans. It's my home."

"I've met men from there before. They don't talk like you. Most of them were Creole. French. You're not." He shoves at the bandage on his forehead with the back of his sticky hand.

"I come from all over."

He smiles, a flash of white in the firelight, as if he's heard this before. Being a traveler, he surely has. It's the usual story of criminals and cowards. "Not to bring up bad memories, but did you have a wife? Children?"

"I had no one. And you—wife, kids?"

He chuckles. "Who would want to marry me? Yes, my family has money, but I would never be home. London is a filthy prison, and the bars are made of people, crushing you, boxing you in." His brows lower. "I suppose I'll never see it again." He takes another huge bite of fish, followed by a gulp of water from the stone pitcher I use for washing.

I lean forward in my chair. Even though I detest fish, I want to lick the juice from his chin. "You don't seem upset about that."

"I don't think I am. I always thought I'd end up this way, stranded or murdered by cannibals. I never expected to become an old man, not the way I've lived."

"How old are you?"

"Old enough to die, although death doesn't really care about age. That man on the beach was only twenty. It was his first time out with us. He wanted to go on an adventure." He puts down the remaining fish and chews his bottom lip. "What did you do before you came here, Andrew? Did you have a profession?"

Yes, I seduced and murdered lovely things like you. "I was a soldier once."

"Should have guessed. Built like a brick shithouse, you are."

I snort, which makes him laugh.

"Did you enjoy being a soldier?"

"I did. I was good at it."

He wraps his arms around his knees. "Good at killing people?"

My gaze falls to the floor. "It was a bit more than that. Oh God, you're not a pacifist, are you?"

He shakes his head. "Impossible in my line of work."

"A lot of violence in naturalism?"

He smacks the side of my knee. "You tit. No, I mean exploring. It's kill or be killed sometimes."

"You've killed before?"

He looks away from me toward the window—sun gone and night dark. "Yeah. And you?"

I don't mean to chuckle, but it happens.

He smirks. "Of course."

"How do you feel?" I gesture to his head.

"Better now that I've eaten." He lifts the front of his shirt and stares at his chest. "Jesus. I look like a fucking watercolor."

He's good at making me laugh.

He stands—unsteadily. I rise to help him but drop my hands to my sides instead. If I touch him now, I doubt I'll stop.

"Where shall I sleep tonight?" he asks. "I'm not hoarding your bed again."

"Yes, you are."

"Andrew, Christ, I'm not an old woman. I can sleep on the floor."

I do touch him then, once, a sudden shove to the center of his chest that sends him tumbling backward onto grimy sheets and pillows.

"Oh, you bastard," he says up at me, but his head already tilts back on the pillows, revealing his long, pale neck. The skin there looks soft as sun-bleached sand—probably just as warm too.

With humans, I've found skin is the most obvious indicator of age. The older they get, the thinner the skin, like decaying silk. Edmund said the dead man on the beach was *only* twenty, but my handsome sailor can't be much older. I can picture him at eighteen, boarding his first ship in London and never looking back.

I spend hours watching him sleep, but like a storm across the ocean, the nightmare comes quickly. His voice rumbles over a single syllable—*no, no, no*—over and over again. Fingers claw at bed sheets, and the bandage doesn't stand a chance against his flailing.

I kneel beside him on the bed and pin his shoulders down. He fights with fists as if I'm the monster he sees in dreams. I should be. I say his name, and when he doesn't respond, I climb in bed and pull him to me. He pushes against my chest. My God, he's powerful, but still, I hold on. With one hand, I cradle the back of his head, tangling fingers in his sweat-soaked hair. I press my hand into his lower back as I pull his body against mine.

I shush him and kiss near the cut on his forehead. I press us together and hum until he stops mumbling, stops fighting. He coasts back into a peaceful slumber with his hands curled in the front of my shirt. His exhales tickle my throat in warm puffs.

Belatedly, I notice I'm hard as a rock. If he wakes now, he'll feel me pressed against his hip. I wonder what Edmund would do if he knew how badly I want him. I hope to find out as soon as his bruises begin to fade.

Chapter Five

I RARELY DREAM, but when I do, it is of one particular night in New Orleans—the night of that final slaughter, that final stolen soul. Without a care in the world, I left my favorite brothel, as I had long before learned to never kill where I sought repeated pleasure.

I lit a cigar in an alley off Gallatin Street and ambled noiselessly through crowds of drunken swine. I wanted a meal; of course I did. After sex, I was always hungry back then. With the scent of whores still clinging to me, I walked as though invisible through the masses until I heard a gentle tittering like piano notes.

I faced the direction of the noise and spotted him immediately, a young, joyful male prostitute being awkwardly seduced by a short man with a beard. I tilted my head and watched them converse. The hairy man pawed at the young beauty and began digging in his pockets as the whore watched and waited.

He couldn't have been much older than eighteen—if even that old. He wore his blond hair to just above his ears, and with a good bath, it might have even glowed gold. As it was, days of sweat weighed it down, although no amount of dirt could soften those cheekbones or the pout of his lips. His malnutrition only added to his appeal, as did his small stature. I could easily have picked him up and carried him wherever I wanted if I'd been so inclined, but a nearby alley would do.

Before the bearded man could make his play, I stepped up behind him and blew smoke in the air. The whore's dark gaze found me. Forgotten was the silly little man bartering.

"If you'll excuse us," I said.

The would-be client started and turned. As soon as he saw me, he scuttled away like a spooked beetle.

I didn't touch my conquest, no, not in the open—not in New Orleans, where love between two men was only acceptable in certain circles.

I tossed my cigar and stepped closer. "Do me the honor of your company?"

The whore stared at me, probably marveling at my height and wondering how much damage I might do.

"I'll be gentle," I said and smiled. Few could refuse me back then, when I dressed in expensive suits every day and glowed, well fed. "You will find I pay well."

I caught him admiring the silk of my waistcoat before he nodded, grabbed my arm, and tugged me into an alley. In the darkness, I backed him against a wall. I had to lean over to reach his mouth. I kissed him once, twice.

"What is your name?"

"Azrael," he said.

"Like the angel?"

He blinked those large eyes up at me until I kissed him some more. His mouth tasted sweet, reminiscent of mulled wine. His tongue poked and prodded at my mouth. Inexperienced, then, new to the streets and a little bit innocent.

I kissed him harder until he gasped in surprise. I lifted his small body onto the top of a barrel that smelled of beer, but as I moved ever closer—slipping fingers beneath his coat—I smelled only Azrael. He was sweat and dirt and sex...and something sweet like a pastry. He lurched forward when I sucked his tongue into my mouth.

"Hush," I whispered. "Are you afraid of me, Azrael?"

He shook his head. I still remember the way those filthy blond locks stuck to the sweat of his forehead.

I unbuttoned his breeches and reached inside. He made a sound of disagreement, but I shushed him some more.

"But, sir, I should—"

I cut off his need to please me by tonguing the side of his neck.

He was so easily coerced off the barrel. I turned him around and instructed him to rest his hands on the wall. I pushed his breeches down, and his shoulders tensed, his body sadly accustomed to rough treatment. Yet, I, the monster, was nothing but gentle.

I petted and caressed until my whore actually sighed in pleasure. He whimpered and begged eventually, and that was how I wanted him—my delicate Azrael—begging for it.

Our fucking was long and slow. He was so small, my embrace sometimes lifted his very feet from the ground. When I reached around and worked his cock, he went practically limp against me, overwrought with sensation. I like to think I made him forget he provided but a service. Instead, I hope I made him feel adored.

He came with a surprised shout. His muscles still clenching around my girth, I set my fangs free and bit hard as my orgasm blotted out all sound but the beat of his young heart.

So sated on sex, it took Azrael a moment to realize I was feeding. Once he noticed my teeth had broken his skin, though, he panicked. He tried to push against the wall, back against me, but I had him trapped in my embrace. Before he could scream, I covered his mouth with my hand and drank faster, faster.

God, he tasted like one hundred merry Christmases. No, his blood wasn't rich like that of the aristocracy. He was an impoverished boy of the streets, not a pampered brat. Still, he was the best meal I'd had in weeks—innocent and struggling and so desperate to live and begging against my palm as he sobbed and I drank and drank and drank.

I swallowed his very soul. His death was a bright light between my eyes. My head soared as he finally went limp and I dropped his body on the ground. I wiped my mouth.

"An angel indeed," I said. I left his corpse to rot but at least pulled up his breeches and straightened his clothes.

I hailed a carriage and rode back home floating on the freedom of the kill. Holding someone's life in my hands? It was a thrill I have never forgotten—and will seemingly never live down.

When I walked back into my coven that night, Michelle waited at the bottom of the grand steps. She looked me over and sniffed. Her face twisted as though she tasted every bit of sex and every bit of murder.

She pointed, and they descended on me, faceless immortal villains I once thought friends. And that was only the beginning of my hell. It was fitting. After all, Azrael was the archangel of retribution.

Chapter Six

A WHISTLE WAKES me. Not a whistle—a bird.

I'm back on my island and smell nothing but Edmund, sweat, and fire. I feel him in my arms, warm and small. Edmund is not small, but he feels that way in his sleep as if lack of consciousness lessens him somehow. Sometime in the night, we moved. I now have my front pressed to his back, my arms completely surrounding him. His hair tickles my nose, and I open my eyes to see the sun streaming through the window. Peaceful breaths escape his parted lips as I roll away. It would not do to have him wake practically tied to the bed by my embrace. However, my left arm is trapped beneath his head, and my shifting does indeed wake him.

His breathing changes, and he sighs. Probably realizing my intimate proximity, he says, "Andrew?"

"You had a nightmare." As if that explains everything. I'd put money on him never waking up on his ship with another man wrapped around him, bad dreams or not.

"Nightmare? I never have nightmares." He rubs his eyes but doesn't shove me away. "Well, I never *used* to." He sits up and stretches his arms overhead. "I could murder a cup of tea right now."

With the scent of him farther away, I realize something's wrong. Did a bird's morning cry wake me, or...

I tackle Edmund to the bed and cover his mouth.

"Don't make a sound," I whisper.

It was indeed a whistle that woke me, and I didn't smell the invaders earlier because all I smelled was Edmund. I smell them now, though, the cannibals. They are blood and filth and murder—and they are close, closer than they've ever been to my house before. I never should have let Edmund go to the beach. I never should have let him fish. The breeze probably carried the scent of his blood for miles in every direction, right to these monsters that hope to swallow his screams and devour his flesh.

Pressed together as we are, I feel his heart pumping blood at a panicked pace, especially when we hear the natives speaking in their foreign tongue. They speak and whistle to each other, but they must be at least twenty feet away. Perhaps they fear coming any closer to the home of the dead thing that walks among them? God, I hope so. Starved of human blood, I'm weak—too weak even to defend my Edmund.

His heart continues to thump against me as I remove my hand from his mouth and wait. His chest rises and falls, but his breaths are silent.

I smell them moving away more than I hear them. Once the breeze is again perfumed by only ocean and Edmund, I exhale and lean back, but Edmund, eyes wide, shoves me away and tumbles onto the floor in his hurry to escape. The vehemence is surprising considering he woke up minutes earlier with a man in his bed and didn't bat an eye.

But the look in his eyes.

Oh, no.

"You have no heartbeat," he says. "How is that..." He stands and picks up the knife by the fire, cleaned of fish guts. "You don't eat. You have no heartbeat. You're of no interest to cannibals. Wh—what are you?"

I hold my hands out in front of me. "I'm not your enemy."

He chuckles and searches for words. "Damn it, what are you, Andrew?"

"Something very old."

"Christ, crocodiles are old!" He holds the small knife out in front of him. "Tell me."

I sit on the edge of my bed. "My people called me *upiór*. In your modern English, I suppose the word would be vampire."

He laughs and stares at me. It's not long before he stops laughing and says, "Loogaroo."

"How do you know that word?"

He has the audacity to roll his eyes. "I've been around the world. You think I don't pick things up? In South America, they hung aloe vera plants to ward her off, keep her from..." He reaches for his neck.

"I haven't."

"But you want to drink my blood."

"Yes."

He drops his arm and the knife with it. "Then get it over with."

"No."

"If you're hoping to fatten me up first, it's not gonna happen, mate. Why don't you go after one of those well-fed cannibals?"

I shake my head as the room pulsates with his near hysteria. "I refuse to become a thing hunted."

"Like me?" he croaks.

I close my eyes.

"Bollocks." His footsteps move toward the door. "I'm catching a fish and setting traps."

I look up at him in the doorway. "Traps?"

"Yeah, traps." He picks up his net and holds the knife. "The natives won't be getting close again without us knowing. And I'd rather you kill me anyway. Fuck." He shakes his head and leaves.

I WAS ONLY on the island a few days when I first came upon a cannibal. Ever since those damnable sailors dropped me at my paltry shack, I had been wandering, seeking a village or human contact—seeking a way back to civilization. After two days, I'd found no sign of intelligent life until I came upon *her*.

I smelled her before I saw her: decay. I half expected to stumble upon a long-dead corpse, but then, there she stood, setting what looked to be a trap. A man of the city, I knew nothing of surviving on an island. I still don't really.

She stood up straight when she saw me, her skin painted in blue-white mud. Her breasts hung heavy, evidence of child rearing. Most of her tattered hair sat coiled on the top of her head, held there by what looked like tiny bones. She bared her teeth at me, so I returned the gesture in kind.

We circled each other. With a knife in her hand, she sniffed at me. She studied my once-fine clothes, now hardly rags, and I studied the pulse point on the side of her long neck.

I was starving, true, but something about this terrible creature made my stomach turn. I could imagine it: the sourness of her blood—not dead but close. Her soul would be rotten too. I suppose she thought the same of me as she sniffed again and shook her head as if to clear the area of my undead reek.

She snarled like a mad beast, and I hissed in return. I did not hide my fangs from her, no, because I wanted to live. If I could scare her enough, send her running, hopefully the rest of her tribe would leave me alone. Because of course, she was not alone. No, I sensed the others on her, layer upon layer of darkness and death. True, I was an evil thing, but so was she. So were the children she had birthed. These were murderers.

I've often wondered if evil sours the blood. In New Orleans, I killed all sorts before my exile, but my favorite meals were innocents like Azrael. The tainted blood of street thugs and drunken thieves never tasted as good as that of a young manservant in a fine house or a male whore, new to the streets.

The creature on the island, she was evil.

I stank of evil too. I must have, what with all the killing I'd done over the centuries. Add to that my status as a walking corpse, and the female cannibal wanted nothing to do with me. We slowly backed away from each other that day, focus never shaking.

I bowed to her before she disappeared into thick foliage as if to say, *I shall not pass here again.* She ignored my gesture and ran off, silent. And so I knew of them, and they knew of me—and we left each other well enough alone.

Now, Edmund has changed everything.

I'm not sure if he knows I'm watching him, but I linger close by as he hunts, eats, and then gets to work. With the cannibals moving so bravely into my territory, I won't let Edmund out of my sight. I don't know what he's doing, but then I've never hunted in the jungle. When I was human, I hunted high plains and mostly in snow. This humid land of leathery leaves and fertile black soil is beyond me.

Halfway through the day, he removes his shirt. His skin glistens, soaking wet, as he weaves reeds into what resembles a rope. His bruises are getting better, but at one point, he winces and bends over with his hands on his knees. He's in pain and tiring easily; I see it in the laborious way he moves, but I won't offer help. I don't expect it would be welcome anyway.

He works into late afternoon. He hangs his makeshift rope and large leaves all around the house. I think he's built foot snares, which I never used myself but have heard about. When he collapses, I move quickly enough to catch him. I hold him close and whisper his name.

"I knew you were there," he says, eyes half-shut.

I've forgotten so much about being human, but I do remember one thing. "You haven't had water all day."

"Water?" he mutters. "What's that?"

I carry him back to my house and stand him next to the washbasin.

He weaves but steadies himself by grabbing its edge. "Shit. I couldn't fight you off if I wanted to."

"You will not need to fight me off." As soon as I say it, I wonder if it's true. I don't think I'll accept no from him—not with the way his skin feels, the way he looks and laughs in the face of a murdering beast. He is a beguiling amalgam of brave and frightened, brilliant and insane.

Several times, I fill the pitcher. He drinks from it first, and then I fill the basin. I soak a soft cloth and squeeze it over his head. Clear droplets move from his scalp, down the dark edges of his hair.

"Do you need to sit?"

"More," he says.

I pour water over his shoulders this time. The water at his feet runs brown with dirt and old blood from the wound on his head.

He slumps to the floor and rests his arms on his bent knees. "I wasn't trying to kill myself, honestly." He pushes wet hair out of his face. A single droplet hangs from the tip of his nose, and I want to lick it off. "It felt good to work. My African friend, Samuel, he taught me how to lay traps. Not that I ever needed to. He caught all of our food while I wandered around, 'playing with my animals,' he used to say. He, um, he didn't understand my fascination. He thought the animals of interest were the ones that could kill you, and they were only interesting because you needed to know to avoid them." He smiles. "Funny, that. I'm not avoiding you. I'm sleeping in your bed. How long do you think I have anyway, before you kill me?"

"I won't kill you, Edmund."

He still has that little smile on his lips. "I have an idea."

I sit on the floor a couple feet from him. "Should I be pleased or concerned?"

His voice is tired when he speaks, drunk on exhaustion. "I almost died a couple years ago in Brazil. I accidentally touched a blue poison dart frog. A witch doctor saved my life, but the whole time I was in my fever, I kept thinking, *But it was so beautiful.* Once I recovered, we stayed there for months, because I couldn't get enough of studying those deadly little things. Now, I'm trapped here with you." That gray-blue gaze of his finds me. "Let me study your species."

"What?"

"I want to learn everything about you. Let me, or I fear I might go mad, waiting to die."

I think of Michelle. When she comes to check on this exiled villain, will she be Edmund's rescuer or destroyer?

"But I am a scientist," he continues. "Maybe if I fill my days with the subject I love, I will survive longer. With your permission, of course."

"How will you study me?"

"Talk. A lot of talking. Something I can't usually do with frogs."

"*Usually* implies you have spoken to frogs, though."

"It can be very quiet alone in the jungle."

"I know."

He tips his head in acknowledgment.

"What else? How else will you study me?"

"Physical examination. A few pokes and prods."

"I don't bleed."

His eyebrows shoot up.

"Did I just make your day?"

He grins, wide and wicked. "More like my bloody year." He leans forward, kneeling right in front of me, and puts the palm of his hand flat against my chest. "How are you put together?" He's talking to himself now. "No heartbeat. How has your brain not rotted out of your head?"

Despite the morning he had, he's willing to be close to me. I think of that poison dart frog that almost took his life and realize Edmund might be perfect.

Chapter Seven

MY SAILOR IS not just a scientist but also a survivor. First thing in the morning, after a night spent sleeping side by side, he starts asking questions—but not the questions I expected. I thought he would immediately want to know when I was born, my age, my diet, and whatever other scientific details he might need to properly categorize my "species."

Instead, after he eats yet another fish caught with ease, he says, "Have you ever tried to leave the island?" He pauses. "Christ, do we even know if we're on an island?"

"We are on an island." I walked all the way around it once, careful to avoid my neighbors, who long ago decided they wanted nothing to do with me. "And yes, I've tried to leave. The current is too strong."

He pauses midchew. "You tried swimming?"

I shrug.

"Madman," he says. "Wait, are you amphibious?"

"I don't *need* to breathe."

His mouth hangs open for a moment before he shakes his head. "What about making some kind of raft? If we got past the reef, maybe we could make it to the mainland."

I shrug again. Edmund is the sailor. I don't know a thing about water.

Once he's done eating, he starts talking about a regular food source. He says "for both of us" and eyes me meaningfully. I furrow my brow, but he must notice how

I look at him. How could he not? He observes the world around him and undoubtedly has since childhood when he was a precocious little boy with bright eyes; the image is so vivid, I can almost picture him running down tall, grassy hills in England. I picture him other ways, as well—adult Edmund, muscular and grown, panting beneath me. God, do I ever picture him.

He sets up more traps, for animals this time. I've fed on all manner of wild beast during my exile, but I don't want him to watch. I assume he's going to want to watch as part of his study of me, but I don't want him to see me with my teeth in some lizard's throat. There are strange-looking deer creatures here, too, and my mouth waters at the thought of catching one. Although I can go weeks without feeding, I'm hungry, and Edmund's proximity is making it worse.

"We're going back to the beach," he says. No question. He takes charge of his situation.

I follow him to the water, and there are more remnants washed up today. Apparently, the sea did not swallow everything. I help him drag a few boxes farther up the beach, away from the crashing waves. Another storm is coming. I sense it in the way the wind blows cool in my face, the way the air hangs heavy with moisture.

He manages to open the first box and immediately hoots like a very large owl. He turns around and hugs me, laughing. It's a quick hug, only long enough for me to pat him once on the back.

"What are you so happy about?"

"Rum!"

"What?"

"Twenty bottles of rum! Miraculous that they survived the storm. God must be feeling guilty," he shouts to the sky. His happiness is thicker than the wet air and tastes to me of honey.

In the other boxes, he finds some useless, wet charcoal and salted pork. He smiles so hard, I imagine his face must hurt. Then, in the next moment, his knees go out from under him, and he ends up sprawled in the sand.

My instinct is to run to him, make sure my Edmund is all right, but he mutters to himself, "I'm not going to die here. I'm not going to die here," and stares at the ever-darkening sky over the deep-blue sea. I leave him be.

I THINK, *NO man is more content in this moment than my Edmund*, which is when I finally think to ask his surname.

"Baines," he says. Edmund Baines is the happiest man I've ever seen.

The rum helps, as does the full belly of salted pork. Although I could join him in drinking—vampires are rather fond of alcohol, really—I don't. I'm enjoying watching him too much. He sits with me by the fire, sipping from his bottle, as the rain falls like small pebbles on the roof. Thunder rumbles occasionally, but it's nothing like the night of the wreck. That storm was a shout, while this is a quiet murmur.

"Is Andrew even your real name?"

"Think I'd give you a pseudonym?"

He snorts. "I don't know."

"Andrew is not actually my real name."

Now he laughs, and oh, how darling. I have to stop myself from leaning forward and tasting the rum on his tongue.

"My name was Andreas, but I brought it up to date when I moved to America."

"And when was that? Wait!" He looks around our little house. "Paper? Pencil?"

"You want to record all this?"

"It's what I do."

I have both of the items he requests—gifts from Michelle on one of her visits. Perhaps she wanted me to write about my guilt, but I don't remember guilt right now. My entire lengthy memory has been wiped clean by the face of this man who looks so young when he laughs.

He balances the paper on his knee and writes something as I sit across from him. "When were you born?"

"The year was 1036."

I expect him to write, but he doesn't. He just stares at me.

"I don't think there's a wrong answer to that question."

He stares a bit longer before writing. "No, I guess not." He clears his throat and drinks more rum. "Where were you born?"

"Norway. I was a Viking, and I died in battle in 1066, fighting the British actually."

Wind rushes against the side of the house as rain splatters across the roof. The fire dims for but a moment before rushing back to life, and Edmund blinks at me.

"Edmund?"

"You...died?"

"Well. Not for very long. An Elder brought me back."

The paper is forgotten. He tosses both his hurried notes and pencil to the ground and leans his elbows on his knees. "What's an Elder?"

I mimic his pose. We're little more than six inches apart, and it would be so easy to finally kiss him, but I don't want to scare him away—not when he's so happy right now.

My silence is apparently annoying, because he repeats, "Andrew, what's an Elder?"

"A very, very old vampire, born possibly before time itself. There used to be many. Now, there are only rumors. A new vampire hasn't been born for centuries."

"Well, how did this Elder—" He smirks. "—birth you?"

"Not sure really. I remember the sounds of battle, a sudden shove forward into the mud, and nothing. When I awoke, a wrinkled old man stood in front of me and said that he had given me eternal life in exchange for my service."

"But you need blood to stay alive."

I nod. "I was ravenous for it at first. I don't know how many I killed. There were stories about me in villages. They called me Red Death."

Edmund leans back suddenly.

"I'm not like that anymore. I barely need to eat to stay alive now, but I am much weaker without human blood."

He remains leaned away from me. "Human blood is better for some reason?"

"For some reason." I look down at my hands. "I think it's to do with the soul. When I drink human blood, I drink not only the blood but also the life. The intellect. The passion. Maybe even the memories. Not very scientific, I know, but it feels accurate. There's an intimacy with human prey that I don't get with, say, a rabbit."

"Intimacy?"

I can't help but look at him. "Very much so."

He jumps at the flash of lightning outside and smiles before sipping rum and rubbing his eyes. "The Elder, the one you were meant to serve, where is he now?"

"Oh. Sadly, he killed himself ages ago."

"I think you might kill me," he says.

"I will not."

"A part of you wants to. I see it sometimes."

Yes, the dark creature. Its sharp claws tap against my skull whenever Edmund gets too close, but I won't let that part of myself touch him. Not unless he asks—and he might, if he's out here long enough. If it's years before Michelle comes back, Edmund might go mad from the loneliness. Or, when the time comes that my fantasies fly free, when I have him pinned to my bed, he might prefer death to the pleasures of sin.

I wonder how many of these thoughts play across my face when he says, "There it is. The part of you that wants to hurt me."

I shake my head as he misinterprets. I don't want to hurt him—again, unless he asks. I want him mindless with desire. I want his skin against mine. I want him whispering my name, moaning, groaning. He'll forget every woman who ever touched him as I use my fingers and mouth to take him apart until he begs for things he never knew he wanted.

"Christ, Andrew," he whispers. He stands and turns his back to me.

I think, fleetingly, how stupid that is—to turn his back on a predator. Then, I remember he trusts me. "Ask me more questions," I say, because I can't think of anything else.

He glances over his shoulder. "How can I kill you?"

A chuckle bubbles up inside me. "You can't."

He spins around and sits. After drinking a hefty gulp of his precious rum, he starts talking as if we're old friends. "Well. You say that, but I once got in a knife fight in Tortuga, and..."

I don't believe in a heavenly power, but I thank whoever is listening that this dazzling creature lived long enough to find me.

Chapter Eight

THE RUM MAKES him snore, but I fall asleep eventually, amused by the so very human sound. I wake to the sun, faced away from him, but don't dare move because I feel him behind me. The crown of his head leans against my spine, and one of his hands curls over my hip.

He sighs. "You're awake."

"Yes."

He pulls his hand back. His whole body rolls away as he stretches. "God, my throat aches."

"You were snoring."

"I do that when I drink." He yawns behind me. "Hope I didn't keep you up."

I'm up all right. I want to laugh at how *up* I am, and all it took was the light touch of his hand on my hip. My control is slipping. Dangerous, dangerous.

I remain in bed as he goes through his morning routine. As he pulls his shirt on and walks toward the water basin, I notice something I had not previously. "You have a scar."

"I have several." He splashes water on his face and runs his fingers through his sleep-mussed hair.

"The one on your back." It's long and angry and curved.

"Electric eel." He looks back at me, hair heavy and wet. "That was a bad day."

I follow him all morning as he checks his animal traps, all empty so far, and walks back to the quiet lagoon nearby. I don't even pretend to look away when he removes his clothes for a swim, although I don't join him, too tempting. He asks questions like bullets about my species...

"I thought your kind were nocturnal."

"I enjoy the night as much as the day."

"How many of you are there?"

"I really don't know."

"Have you heard of two vampires being mated for life?"

"Absolutely not."

He laughs at what I imagine is my horrified expression. "So you run around shtupping everything in sight?"

"I do have some standards."

He floats on his back in the crystal-clear water, trim chest and stomach revealed. He closes his eyes and bobs up and down with his deep breaths. Then, he disappears below the surface. His feet kick once, hard, like a fish fin. A moment later, he's ten feet away. Edmund swims like a merman, made for the sea.

Later, he walks to the water's edge and stands there, dripping, with no attempt at modesty. "So nothing can hurt you?"

I try not to stare. "Not that I know of."

He steps out of the water and brushes water droplets from his skin. "Well, do you age?"

I consider this and try not to consider the thatch of black hair between his legs surrounding an impressive cock. "I was thirty years old when I died. Do I look thirty now?"

"Last night, I could almost see you picturing it, picturing us."

I shiver when his lip touches my earlobe.

"The expression on your face was so hungry, I turned away to hide my own excitement. Imagine my surprise: trapped on an island with a creature of similar taste."

I'm going to come from just his hand and his voice if I don't put a stop to it.

"Did you enjoy my show today? Waking to my touch? Watching me bathe? I thought I might drive you mad with lust."

"Oh, God…" I press my nose against his neck. Then, I open my mouth and suck his skin. "I want you. God, I want you."

"You can have me." He pulls back enough for me to see his smirk. "As many times as you can manage."

My cock feels cold with the absence of his touch. "I won't stop if I start."

"Promise?" He smiles.

I lunge forward and kiss him as if he's a ripe peach. I'm sucking and biting and licking as my hands reach beneath the material of his breeches, cup his ass, and shove the fabric down. Then I tear his shirt open and drag the offending item from his shoulders. We're both naked when I shove him on the bed and immediately press our cocks together. He about bucks off the bed as I start rutting. This will be over much too fast, but damned if I care. I need this. I need *him*, his sputtering and begging, reaching to grab me—but I trap his wrists and pin his arms above his head as I continue to grind against his hot skin.

Beneath me, his eyes are shut, his mouth wide as he groans. I suck on the side of his jaw. "Fuck, you're beautiful," I mutter. "So fucking beautiful…"

He comes, his seed wet and warm between us. I let go of his wrists and hold tight to his hips. I thrust once, twice, and I'm coming, too, in a way that halfway makes me think I'm indeed alive again. I can't hear, can barely see, when I fall forward and crush him beneath me. He gasps when I force my arms beneath his body and squeeze him tightly against my chest. He wraps his legs around my waist and rocks his hips until I wince with oversensitivity.

"Stop," I say.

He's completely out of breath. "You'll find that's rather...hard to make me do."

I let go only long enough to lean down and lick at the white stripes on his stomach. I taste the difference between us. He is salty-sweet, an orchestra of flavor, while I am a single, sullen note. His muscles twitch beneath my tongue as I keep licking.

"That's bloody gorgeous."

I look up, and he's leaned on his elbows, staring at me. Beads of sweat shine within the curls of his sparse chest hair, and his cheeks are a shade of pink I've never seen before. His bottom lip is red and puffy as if he's been bitten—by his own doing or mine, I'm not sure.

He curls his fingers in my hair. "Smother me again."

I wrap my arms around him as his legs surround me. We bury our faces in each other's shoulders, and I hear nothing but his pulse.

Chapter Nine

IT'S NOT LONG before he begs for more, which makes me again consider the youth of my new lover. Men of a certain maturity don't have this kind of stamina—even I have yet to recuperate from our first harried go—and although I am still uncertain as to Edmund's actual age, I have to conclude young.

"I want to take you in my mouth," I whisper against his lips.

His heart gives a jump. I actually feel its lovely beating when I kiss his chest. He tastes of sweat and the sea.

I'm halfway down his stomach when he says, "Wait." The sun is still high, streaming through the windows, so his face is a mishmash of light and dark.

"What is it?" I ask.

"Your teeth," he says. "In order to eat the way you eat, they must be sharp. Or am I mistaken?"

I think of his scars. My Edmund is reckless but not dumb. I can't help but grin up at him, not only because of the nervous wrinkle between his eyes but also because I'm incapable of anything but joy with his body beneath me.

"Do not look at me like that." The quirk of his lips belies the seriousness of his words.

"Like what?"

"As if I'm a curious child. A man's cock and balls are no laughing matter. Show me your teeth."

I laugh with my mouth against his hip, but he tugs at my hair until I shift up and rest by his side. It doesn't take much for my teeth to change. When I was a young vampire, centuries ago, I had little control over them. If I was hungry, they happened. If I was angry, they were there. Now, my true teeth only show when I choose, so I choose to show Edmund.

I smile at him.

"Christ." He reaches his hand out between us and stops. "How sharp are they?"

"Sharp." I've torn throats out before. Several, in fact, but I don't feel the need to share such details.

He still looks nervous.

"I can control them." I kiss him. To prove my control, I suck his bottom lip into my mouth, fangs once again hidden.

He makes a sound like a lion's purr.

"You love danger, Edmund. Admit it."

"Yes, well, not around my dick," he says, but he doesn't stop me when I kneel between his spread legs and kiss his inner thighs. His fingertips play across my bare shoulders. "Promise you won't hurt me."

I might be lying, but I make the promise anyway.

I admire his anatomy. His cock is like the rest of him: long and lean, although darker in shade. I lick up the underside of his shaft before wrapping my lips around the head of his cock.

He grunts, and I glance up to find him staring at me, lips pressed together tight.

I push the foreskin back and lick his slit. "Make as much noise as you want. In fact, if you even try to stay quiet, I will make this go on forever." I flick my tongue out and tease his tip, which makes his abdomen leap. The breath vacates his lungs.

I envelop the entire length of him in my mouth until his cock presses against the back of my throat, and a deep, drawn-out moan fills the room like pipe smoke. He squeezes my shoulders and then the sheets as a fountain of cuss words erupts from his throat.

"You're going to be the death of me," he says.

I bob my head up and down a few times before stopping. I press my open tongue on the underside of his dick, just below the head, and move it in waves.

"Oh, fucking fuck..."

He quickly comes undone. All of his muscles—an extensive array—seem to clench at the same time as he shouts my name and comes down my throat. Oh, this is better: drinking right from the source. It's not his blood, but it might as well be, the way I lap up every last drop. I run my hand up the center of his sweaty chest and to his throat. I tickle his Adam's apple with my thumb as he twitches beneath me. He presses his palms against his eyes.

"Jesus." It's almost a prayer.

He's too wrecked to reciprocate right away, so I feed him small slices of salted pork and sips of water as we rest together into late afternoon.

"Have you had many lovers?" I ask.

"Dunno. What constitutes many?"

I have no answer to that, so instead of speaking, I gobble up the sight of him naked and half wrapped in bedclothes.

"I suppose I've had my share. I was very popular as a society boy in London, but I always preferred the more...unique." His smile doesn't lighten his eyes as usual. "Like Samuel."

"The African on the ship was your lover?"

"I knew he'd been banished from his village, but I didn't realize why." He brushes his fingers against my arm. "At first, he wanted to teach me basic things—ways to stay alive, find food in the wilderness. Then, it became more. Small touches, innocent innuendo." He smiles a true smile now. "It was almost laughable, watching him test my limits. I think he was waiting for me to shove him away, but I never did. Do you want to hear about this?"

"Yes." Something about the thought of my sailor with another man makes me angry—but incredibly hard.

"After months of Samuel's fumbling, he snuck into my room one night. He had me on my stomach before I could even speak." Edmund presses a kiss to my cheek as he tickles below, finds my excitement. "We fucked with my face against the pillow to stifle my screams. I could have woken the whole ship."

My mouth drops open as he strokes me.

"That's how he always was. He called me his pet. Some nights, I wouldn't even hear him sneak in. I would simply wake with his fingers inside me." He licks his tongue between my parted lips, and my hips thrust forward.

"I think I could come just from listening to you say filthy things."

His pace increases on my aching cock. "I had two men at once in China. Two huge brutes tossing me around. They treated me like their possession, passing me back and forth all night. I was limp with pleasure, sore for days. I think they even loved me by the end."

"I want to murder all of them."

As I come, I hear him say, "I believe you."

Chapter Ten

FELIPE WAS MY friend in New Orleans—at least, I thought he was—and we used to share humans. Well, "share" is not the correct word. More so, we used to battle over them.

Felipe and I were of a different ilk. Both ancient immortals, he was a bit of a ponce, and although he was quite pretty, he enjoyed pretty men just as much as me. Most of the time, he inhabited Michelle's bed as her devoted lover, but on occasion, he came out with me to high-class New Orleans soirees. There, our battles would begin.

I remember in particular one night at the birthday of a famed barrister's wife, Mrs. June. We arrived to wish her a *"bon anniversaire."* Oh, it was prime hunting. Felipe, as usual, wore too much lace, his hair falling free around his pointed face. I stayed by his side as we sauntered to and fro with champagne and admiring smiles.

He stopped and grabbed my arm. "My God, look at that one."

I knew immediately to which man he referred: a tall, slim gent with auburn hair and lips the shape of a heart. He spoke to the lady of the house, but as soon as he noticed us watching, his attention lingered before looking away and feigning interest in whatever the aging birthday *femme* had to say.

Felipe tugged on his cuffs and adjusted his hair. "I would eat him alive."

"Wouldn't you just?" I sipped my bubbly.

"Come now, don't pretend you don't want to have that fantastic creature in bed. Jesus, his mouth alone is sin incarnate."

I glanced down at Felipe before looking back up at said stranger whose pale cheeks had turned a delightful shade of pink—although he was doing a winning job of pretending to listen to Mrs. June.

Felipe turned his back on the enchanting young man and faced me. "Let's make a wager."

No one made my eyes roll like Felipe with his silly games.

"It will be entertaining."

"I'm sure," I muttered.

"First to touch his cock is the winner."

"Jesus..."

Felipe offered that dark-eyed smile of his—half charm, a quarter mischief, and another quarter murderous. Of all the vampires I'd known, he was least trustworthy, which is why I never should have been surprised that spending time with him aided in my exile.

"So," he continued. "Will you accept my wager?"

"What's the prize?"

"You mean beyond touching his prick?" He shrugged. "Pride."

Thanks to the unending funds of our coven, saved for centuries, we had no need for making money. Felipe knew my belongings were sparse, beyond my extensive wardrobe, too big for Felipe anyway. Pride was all we had to offer each other anymore.

I nodded my assent, and I swear Felipe's eyes flashed red.

To talk to our prize, we moved ever closer to the belle of the ball. As usual, Mrs. June wore a low-cut gown that almost flashed her bosom in an effort to appear sensual and young. Her age, though, was made all the more apparent, standing beside the youthful red-haired man who didn't have a line on his face. His green gaze darted from us and back to her.

Felipe bowed first, and Mrs. June crooned at his arrival. Older ladies loved Felipe, possibly because he resembled a china doll they wanted to dress up. She raised her gloved hand to me, and I kissed it.

"My good sirs, this young man is new to our fine city by way of Boston." She had a loud singsong voice that echoed like opera.

His name was Mr. Deville—although he was quick to say "just Cameron"—and his accent was so unlike the familiar Southern lilt to be practically foreign. Fairly quickly, Mrs. June swept off in her myriad skirts to mingle with other guests, which left Felipe and me alone with the tall delicacy that had apparently moved south to manage his father's shipping business on the Louisiana coast.

"How long have you been here, Cameron?" Felipe's elbow brushed against the born-and-bred Northerner's too-thick coat.

"Only a week. I still get lost every morning on the way to work."

Felipe laughed at this.

I sipped my champagne, smiling. "And what do you think of our grand city?"

His eyes brightened slightly at the sound of my voice. Egad, I practically had this battle won, and it had barely begun.

"New Orleans is different than Boston. There's something mesmerizing about it." He paused. "The gardens are beautiful."

Felipe leaned closer. "Aren't they?"

"Have you seen the garden here?" I asked. "Mrs. June has an impressive green thumb."

Cameron cleared his throat and looked at his shoes. Shy, then? How delightful. "I haven't, no. I haven't seen the garden."

"But you must," Felipe purred. He wrapped loose fingers around Cameron's forearm. "We'll show you."

He nodded his assent and looked up at me from behind a fringe of light eyelashes. Poor Felipe would have to take desperate measures to win his attentions as our new friend apparently had an affection for overly tall men with rugged jaws and blond hair.

We made our way past guests and down candlelit halls. Felipe still held to Cameron's arm, but the crimson beauty kept glancing back at me. Outside, no moon shone on the lush gated garden. The only light came from a few flickering torches, which threw dancing shadows over flower and leaf. Sweet gardenia and the scent of Cameron's blood mixed in the night.

"Told you it was luscious," Felipe crooned. God, he was laying it on thick.

"Yes." Cameron's hand reached out, fingers touching the edge of a rose.

I listened for other occupants, but finding none, I made the first advance. I stepped up close behind Cameron and kissed the side of his neck. He whimpered immediately.

Felipe's teeth flashed in the semidark. "Well, wasn't that a lovely sound? Are there many garden trysts in Boston?"

"No." Cameron leaned back against me, so I planted kisses behind his ear.

Felipe moved closer and rested his palms on Cameron's chest. "You aren't a virgin, are you, darling?"

Cameron's head drooped forward as I ran my nose up the back of his neck.

"My goodness, you are."

I looked up in time to see Felipe lick his lips, and I was fully prepared to tell my little friend to go the fuck away when he reached a fist forward and wrapped his hand in Cameron's hair. He tugged Cameron's head up roughly, and the young man shouted in complaint.

"Didn't anyone ever tell you that sodomites burn in hell?" Felipe smiled and bared every bit of his razor-sharp fangs.

I stifled Cameron's cries with my hand and held tight when he tried to back away, flee, and tell the whole city that two polite society gents were actually monsters.

Panic made him flail, but I held on tight and glared at Felipe. "What is the matter with you? Are you utterly mad?"

Recognizing my unnatural strength, Cameron slumped back against me. His warm tears tickled the hand that covered his mouth.

Felipe laughed. "A little. I also did not want you to win."

I shushed Cameron, more out of self-preservation than compassion. It would be easy to kill him, but how many people had seen us leave together? I was not prepared to flee my favorite city thanks to one vampire's idiotic pride.

"What do we do with him now, you fool?"

Felipe crept closer, and Cameron renewed his fight, especially when Felipe again revealed his fangs and petted the poor boy's head. "Take him home. Play with him. Make sure he's never seen again."

The sound of Cameron's hysterical screams threatened to escape my palm, so I bit into his neck and drank. He froze as soon as my teeth broke his skin. I turned away so Felipe couldn't watch—I knew how much he liked to watch—and drank until Cameron was too weak to stand. I dropped him in the dirt and shoved Felipe so hard, his feet left the ground as he flew backward.

"Did you mean to kidnap him all along?"

Felipe shrugged, brushing at his arms as though dirty. "My yearnings can be so fickle. Yes. No. Does it matter? He's coming with us now." He came closer and knelt by Cameron, whose fingers flexed and dug in the dirt. "I do believe I'll make him my slave."

"He wanted me."

"Yes, Andrew, but you don't keep humans." He stood and tapped me on the shoulder. "Now. Let us clear our reputations, hmm?"

Felipe was the king of subterfuge. He tied Cameron's cravat higher on his neck, tighter, to hide my bite mark. Then, we called for a robust servant. In the grand hall, we excused Cameron's drunkenness to Mrs. June and put him in a carriage—destination, our coven. We made sure to wander the party to prove our innocence and, eventually, with vampire speed, rushed home to find Cameron unconscious in our foyer and a very angry Michelle.

Felipe waved at me before scooping Cameron into his arms. "Andrew's idea. After all, you would forgive him anything."

I shook my head as Felipe disappeared upstairs with his new toy.

"Someday, it will be too much," Michelle said. "You will go too far."

Looking back, I wonder at how much Felipe played me, how much he made me seem the villain. I didn't mind being feared, especially by other vampires, but I should have foreseen my end. I should have expected my exile.

For his part, poor Cameron killed himself two months later. No one ever arrived on our doorstep looking for him. Felipe would have left his body to rot, so I took responsibility. I dug up a recently buried corpse in Saint Louis Cemetery and added Cameron's to the plot to ensure his body would never be found. So many years later, his family probably still searches for him.

I suppose no one searches for me, but after all the monstrous things I've done, maybe I do not deserve to be found.

Chapter Eleven

EDMUND SPRAWLS ACROSS me, half conscious. I kiss his forehead, still too awake myself. "Who was the first man to touch you?"

He chuckles warm breath across my neck. "Why, so you can hunt him down and tear his head off?" He moves closer and tangles our legs together. "He wasn't a man. We were boys."

"Now, I really must hear."

He runs his hand across my chest, and I hum at the attention. "There isn't much to hear. We were fourteen, and he was a boy at school. Messy kisses and sloppy hands in a broom closet." He laughs. "I recall I had yet to grow, but Thomas—that was his name—had to have been six feet tall already. I didn't care. I was so thrilled. I balanced on the edge of a shelf to be able to reach his mouth."

I give his shoulders a squeeze.

"We ended up rutting against each other on the floor. I suppose that was the first time I realized how much I enjoy having someone's weight on me. We ruined our breeches, and Thomas split my lip in his fervor." He leans up on his elbow, and whatever tiredness I suspected is gone. Visiting the past has awakened my sailor. "Impossible to separate us after that."

When he says no more, I ask, "What happened to him?"

"Oh, I suspect he's married by now. He shunned that deviant side of himself eventually."

I sit up beside him and cup his face. "How could anyone turn his back on you?"

"Not everyone is as morally reprehensible as the two of us."

"Thank God." I suck his lower lip and let it go with a pop. "The entire world would be nothing but blood and orgies."

He snickers. "Now you. You tell me about your first."

"It was a very long time ago."

"I imagine. But you do remember, don't you?"

I twist my finger around a lock of his hair. Filthy as it is, I am amazed it still feels so soft. "Yes. I remember. Of course I do. I was too busy fighting battles to be forced into providing offspring. The thought of being with a woman..." I shudder, and Edmund laughs.

"My God. A lover of men, through and through."

"Yes. Would you believe I wasn't a sensual person until my twenties at least?"

"No." He shakes his head.

"It's true. I didn't know that kind of pleasure until, well...until I was old enough to die."

"We are always old enough to die."

I chuckle my agreement. "He was a keeper of horses. Younger than me and smaller. They sometimes called him a witch, the way he could calm even the maddest stallion— and maybe he was. He certainly cast a spell on me. We kept everything secret. And then, he died of a strange illness. I took many lovers after him."

Edmund touches my lips, and I suck his fingertip into my mouth. "Making up for lost time?"

I kiss the tip of his finger as he pulls it back. "No. Burying the memory of him perhaps. Losing myself in the bodies of others, on and off the battlefield. Either I was killing or fucking."

"Like a wild animal."

I move closer until Edmund falls onto his back, and I linger above him. "I believe you are the wilder of the two of us." I lean down and kiss his neck. I kiss and lick until he shivers and sighs.

"I was very tired not ten minutes ago."

"Tired now?" I suck at his collarbone, and his chest expands with breath.

"No. Not tired."

I straddle his hips and drive him happily mad, one lick and one nibble at a time. His skin tastes salty like the ocean, and his grasping, scraping hands would draw blood—if I could bleed.

Chapter Twelve

THERE IS NOTHING innocent about my Edmund. As he climbs a palm tree, seeking a few high-flying coconuts, I smile at my own naiveté. To think, I'd once fretted over scaring him away—the poor, bruised sailor who knew only the gentle touch of women. Laughable. Edmund is more of a beast than I, and yet even in the blindness of passion, he's smart.

We've spent the majority of the past day and night pleasuring each other, but he hasn't let me fuck him. He hasn't given me that part of himself, no matter how much my fingers wander, no matter how many times I've begged. No, he will not allow me into that part of his body I so soundly seek.

I suspect he considers fucking the epitome of his value. Somewhere in his psyche, he thinks I will kill him once his most intimate heat has surrounded me. I won't. I could never kill Edmund, not now. I would even die for him, give up my gift of eternity for him.

If I told him these things, I doubt he'd believe me. He would think me playing him like some mid-Eastern trader. He does trust me—too much maybe—but not enough to give me everything. Not yet.

"Careful," he shouts.

I step back as a coconut falls with a heavy thud onto the moist forest floor. Then, I look up at Edmund. He has rigged some huge jungle leaves into a harness that allows him to rest his feet on the trunk and balance without falling. The man is full of strange information. I almost love him for it.

He even caught a wild boar this morning. I asked him not to kill it, and he didn't question me. The filthy creature remains tied up near our house, and I hope to find a way to feed without Edmund watching—but that's not likely. He'll want to watch me feed as part of his species study. I don't so much mind showing him my increased strength after consuming blood, but I'm still embarrassed by the idea of letting Edmund see what a monster I am. I don't imagine he'll be scared, but, God, he makes me want to be human again.

He's only halfway down the tree when he leaps, lands, and rolls.

"You remind me of soldiers I once saw in Japan."

He tucks two coconuts under his arm. "Never been."

"So you haven't been everywhere."

He smiles and kisses me, his hand on the back of my neck.

Then, I smell them and curse myself again for allowing Edmund's scent to blind me to our surroundings.

I whisper, "We need to move."

He freezes, focus darting to the thick surrounding foliage. "Which direction?"

"Behind you. Run."

He drops the coconuts and takes off barefoot. I follow close behind and hear only one native voice, shouting something in their barbarian tongue. Edmund runs as fast as he thinks. He's adept at avoiding hanging leaves and roots alike. Even I struggle to keep pace, but I still feel presences around us like dark spirits in a wood. No one knows this damned island better than the cannibals. Still, we aren't surrounded. The natives are behind us at least, so Edmund and I keep running until we see our precious lagoon, sharp mountain at its opposite end.

He stops at the water's edge. "They'll lose my scent if I'm underwater."

"But—"

He points to a shadowy spot. "Get them to go away. They've no interest in you."

And if he drowns?

"I'll be fine." He must read my expression. "Just hurry the fuck up." Fully clothed, he dives in and starts swimming. As soon as his head disappears beneath the surface, I hear a twig snap.

There are four of them, all men, and they're not as well fed as Edmund once joked. Skin painted in dried mud, the natives are short but broad. Their rib cages, covered in nothing but skin, heave from exertion.

I press my fangs out and smile.

Four pairs of hands tighten on pointed spears, but they make no move to come closer. They probably think me a demon, and my great height has intimidated men from Paris to Timbuktu.

I wave my hand, gesturing behind them. I hope they understand I want them to go away—need them to, in fact. Edmund will soon have been underwater too long.

When they don't move, I hiss. Their eyes widen as they mumble between each other. I take a warning step forward, and finally, they scatter into the woods like an earthbound flock of birds.

I back into the warm water, still watching for any sign they might return, but already, their horrid scent has moved away. The stench of rotting flesh is but a memory when I reach Edmund and drag him up by the front of his soaking shirt.

He gasps in a huge breath of air as I hug him to me. I push his wet hair from his face and kiss his cheeks. "How long can you hold your breath?"

He still swallows air in great gulps. "I guess we found out."

My Edmund doesn't even argue when I carry him home.

Chapter Thirteen

THE CANNIBALS KNOW he's here, and I don't know what to do about it. It's only a matter of time before they come to kill us both. I think Edmund realizes as much. He's more subdued tonight as he guts some fish by the fire. He doesn't talk as he usually does. He doesn't tell me any of his mad stories or about yet another rare species of butterfly he found when he tripped through a spiderweb in India.

I need to be as strong as possible for him. "Edmund. I must feed."

He stops working on the fish. "Can I watch?"

I nod. It's time for him to see me for what I am—not only his lover but a dark creature, as well.

Outside, the wild boar grunts and leaps forward and back as we approach. Despite being tethered to a tree, this beast is ruthless. It will not die without a fight. I think of Edmund with his poison dart frogs, knife fights, and electric eels. He's been chasing death his whole life, and he finally found me.

I hold the struggling beast to my chest. It squeals and kicks as I bite down hard into its back. The hair is coarse, rank with filth, and the skin is hard to break—but I break it. Blood spurts into my mouth as the animal continues to flail against me. Its blood is sour but palatable. It's nothing like Edmund would taste. I lose myself in the warm, red liquid and drink and drink until the boar's heart stops beating. I throw the dead carcass away from me and don't even bother wiping the blood from my face. I turn around.

He kneels at the base of a tree with his back leaned against it. His fingers cling to the bark, and his eyes are wide. He stands when I draw close but still clings to the tree as if it might protect him.

Edmund shouts when I grab his arm—too roughly, as the beast's blood flows through me. I still might be too weak to kill a tribe of cannibals, but I'm powerful enough to control one human. I shove him into our house, and he almost tumbles from the force of it. He spins to face me, shoulders tense. I lick my lips and grin before rinsing the horrid scent of slaughtered boar from my face.

I move toward him and tear his shirt. He shoves me backward, but I latch onto his wrist, spin him around, and pin him to the wall. His elbow to my ribs knocks a gasp from my chest, and I laugh. It puts enough space between us for him to punch me hard. Christ, the man knows how to hit. When the haze clears from my eyes, he stands in front of me, gaze darting to the door, to me, and back again. He has nowhere to go.

"I'm sorry I hit you," he says.

"Trying to sweet-talk me, Edmund?"

He stares at me.

"Are you frightened, now that you've seen me feed? I'm as bad as the cannibals, wouldn't you say?" He doesn't stop me when I push him backward with my hand on his chest. He trips into bed, and I tear off his breeches and the remainder of his shirt before climbing on top of him and lifting one of his legs over my shoulder. I push one finger into him, and his head falls back, mouth wide. I thrust in a second finger, and his eyes shoot open, pain wrinkling his features.

"Andrew—"

I shove my tongue into his mouth to stop him from speaking.

I curl my two fingers and caress inside of him. I can practically hear his cock filling with blood as I pump my fingers in and out. Edmund's chest turns red and blotchy in the firelight as he scrapes his fingertips against the sheets. I add a third finger, and within seconds, tears escape his closed eyes. My fingers inside of him, I grab a handful of his hair and pull until his head tilts back at a painful angle. I bite the side of his neck—no fangs but still hard enough to leave a mark. He tries to pull away from the pain, but I have him pinned with my body and with the fingers that fuck him.

I run my tongue over what will soon be a bruise, and he whimpers, pushing weakly against my shoulders. "I thought about this," I say. "I spent hours thinking about this—whether or not you would fight me when I fucked you."

He shivers when I push my fingers extra deep.

"I thought I would take you anyway, even if you fought. I needed you." My hand is cold when I remove my fingers from his body. I kiss the side of his face and pull away. "But here we are, and I can't." I lean on the edge of the bed and cover my face with my hands. "You should be frightened of me, Edmund. I've done horrible things."

The bed shifts behind me. I expect another of his brutal punches, but instead, he rests his hand on my shoulder. "Horrible things, hmm?"

"Yes."

"If you don't fuck me right now, I'm going to agree with you."

I swivel my head around so fast, it almost hurts. "What?"

He chews his lower lip. "I'm quite mad, you know. Part of why I left London, in fact. My mother wanted to send me to some home to fix me because I like men. Because I only feel alive on the edge of a knife. I'm filthy rich, did I tell you that? I'm supposed to be a duke, as my father before me. The seventh Duke of Wilshire. Instead, I play pirate because I'm miserable with the calmness of life. You asked me if I've killed, and I have. I like killing things. Well." He looks away. "I could never kill a caterpillar, but I don't mind killing men. When I saw you with that animal outside, it was like looking in a mirror. I don't know if I'm more frightened of you or of myself."

I don't reach out to touch him—even though he's so close, I feel his heat.

"If we fuck, will you kill me after? Will you be done with me?"

"No." I shake my head. "I don't think I'll ever be done with you."

"In love already?"

I am so far beyond love with this kindred spirit. Love is too meek a word.

I show him how I feel with a kiss—a violent gnashing of teeth and tongues. My sudden approach must have injured his lip, because I taste Edmund's blood, rich and metallic. He is no wild boar.

He pushes me away just long enough to turn around. He rests on his hands and knees in the center of the bed and presents his tempting ass to me. "Please, Andrew."

I practically shred my clothes. When I lean forward and lick at his hole, he makes a surprised *oh* sound. His arms go out from under him, and his spine curls as he shoves the side of his face against the pillow. I continue to lick and suck the part of his body I've already roughly prepared until his voice cracks beneath the volume of his moans.

"Am I being punished for some reason?" I feel more than hear the rumble of his laugh, his voice muffled by linen.

I kneel on the bed behind him and run my hand up and down his spine. I've wanted this since I rescued him on the beach, and now, I prolong the moment. I admire the angry scar on his back, the way his muscles seem to struggle beneath his skin. He is so strong but so pliant for me—a beguiling cocktail of humor and darkness, brilliant yet idiotically drawn to death.

"Do I need to tackle you and ride your cock, you awful man?" Each word is coated with his panting breath.

I push into him with the tip of my cock. The hot grip and Edmund's relieved groan are almost enough to make me come. I clutch his hips and hold him steady as I take a few deep breaths, then I keep pushing. He sputters a long line of mixed vowels and consonants, but I'm beyond speech. Fully seated inside him, I bend forward and rest my body across his back, arms around his ribs. I rise and fall to the rhythm of his breath as he intertwines his fingers with mine.

I thrust once, and he practically sobs. Again and I inhale the scent at the back of his neck and smell the beach after rain. My cock twitches inside him. Christ, I'm too close.

I freeze. "What's your favorite animal?"

"What?" He sounds frantic.

I press my mouth against his upper back. "Favorite animal. Tell me."

"Uh...gah...uh, I don't have one. There's too many. They're all... They're all fascinating. What are you—"

"Choose one." I press open-mouthed kisses to his scalding skin.

"Sharks because...I can never get close enough to study one. They're...a mystery to me. Sailors used to call them sea monsters. Did you know that?"

"Not mermaids?"

He chuckles. "No. Sharks are beautiful, but...not like that. Not like mermaids."

"You speak as though you've seen a mermaid before."

He must think I'm distracted, because he tries to shove himself up from the bed and me with him. I hold tighter and press down harder, which makes him choke on a laugh.

"You're torturing me, you know."

I roll my hips forward, and he shouts. I've calmed enough to thrust into him, and this time, I don't stop. This time, I lean back, grip his hips, and fuck him until even the pillow can't stifle the litany of curse words intermingled with my name.

"Oh God, oh God, oh God," he says.

I take hold of his hair and pull his head back. I wrap my other arm around his chest and drag him upward until he sits in my lap. The upright angle pushes me even farther into him, and his entire body shakes in my arms. A sound escapes him, a howl of pleasure-pain. With his back against my front, his knees on either side of mine, I press up and up. I keep him pinned to me with one hand on his chest as my other wraps around his cock.

"Andrew," he mutters and comes. Warm liquid covers my hand as his muscles contract around me and wrench an orgasm from my body. I growl and bite into his shoulder with my human teeth. He doesn't make a sound, just wilts against me as I hold us together. I lick salty sweat from his back. His head falls forward, and I imagine he feels as I do—unmoored and floating. I'm a ship lost at sea, and Edmund is my compass. As long as I hold to him, I am not lost. This exile now feels less like a punishment and more like a reward, especially when he rests his hands on mine.

I leave the bed long enough to wet my discarded shirt and wipe us both clean. I add another log to the fire before resting on top of the bedclothes beside my Edmund.

He opens his eyes, just barely. "Why are you really on this island?"

"I killed one too many people."

He squints in question. "You're a loogaroo. Isn't that what you do?"

I push sweaty black hair from his forehead. "In the past. Modern times would have us more civilized. Drinking but not killing. You asked me once if there are many of my kind. I don't know, but I was part of a coven in New Orleans. A club, of sorts, where vampires and humans joined together for...I believe the word would be orgy."

Edmund smiles. "Of course."

"We weren't supposed to kill the humans, but I was never good at self-control."

"You are with me," he says.

"You're different."

"How so?"

I run my fingers across his chest. My brow furrows when I realize. "I'd like to keep you."

"I am happy to be kept." He kisses my forehead. "So this island is your punishment."

"Yes. The leader of my coven, Michelle—she's even older than me. She exiled me here."

He blinks, and some of the sex haze lifts from his eyes. I see the moment he is fully functional, intellect engaged. "How did you get here? Did you not fight back? Could you not have escaped?"

I think back to the long-ago day in New Orleans, after I'd killed that sweet whore with no remorse and come home to an ambush. "There were too many of them. They subdued me and locked me away. I don't know for how long. By the time Michelle came for me, I was too weak to fight back. I was starving. That was before..." I follow a trail of sweat down his chest with my finger. "I had to learn to live on less once I arrived here. In New Orleans, I used to eat daily because I could. I can now go a week at least. Longer. The worst part was being tied up in the bottom of some infernal ship, mad with hunger. Next thing I knew, I woke up here." I glance around our shack. "Loneliness has been my punishment...until you. Although even Michelle does me the honor of the occasional visit."

He leans up on his elbow. "She comes here?"

I nod.

"So she could take us back. To the mainland, I mean."

"If she chooses."

"Fuck, I might not actually die on an island."

Like a churning ocean wave, a bad feeling smothers me. Michelle will adore Edmund. His bright eyes will charm her. She will laugh at his wry humor and appreciate his intelligence. Most importantly, she will see the way I love him. Oh God, she will take him away. She will punish me with his absence. Oh my God.

"Andrew?" He touches my face. "What's the matter?"

I hug him hard against me.

He takes a breath as if to speak but says nothing when a snap and a shout come from outside. Edmund pushes me away and lurches upward. "One of my traps." He stares at me. "The man-eating bastards are here."

He's right. I smell at least twenty men and women outside. The light from the native torches dances against the windows as my sailor pulls his clothes back on. He almost falls over in his hurry, as though clothes will protect him from being eaten alive.

"Andrew," he whispers. "Get up."

"I can't protect you from them. I have not enough strength."

He stares at me, breath coming ragged and hard. His panicked pulse drums in my ears. "What if you drank from me?"

"No." Now, I stand. I move toward the window and see their torches come ever closer.

At a metallic scrape, I turn to find him with my small knife pressed against his forearm. "I will not be eaten alive by cannibals."

I hold my hand out. "No, Edmund."

"This is what's happening now, whether you like it or not."

"I might not be able to stop."

He sighs and smiles softly. "Then, don't."

He cuts hard and deep, and blood bubbles from the wound. I sweep forward and lift his arm to my mouth. I drink heartily, sucking his skin into my mouth. He doesn't pull back. He doesn't fight me. He stands as I drink until he can stand no more, but I catch him before he hits the floor. I cradle him in my arms as I continue to consume until his heartbeat slows, quiets. I want to keep going. His blood is rich and sweet, but I want to devour his very soul.

I stop before I kill him. Only just. Strength flows through me as I leave Edmund curled by the fire and step out into the humid night in nothing but my skin and my beloved's blood. I resemble one of them now, the barbarians. We are the same, and the dark creature in me grins.

The first man to attack, I twist his head from his spine. The second: I tear his heart from his chest. I soon lose count as spears pierce my flesh, but the only blood that flows from me belongs to Edmund. What I consumed of him, they steal, so I steal some more. My fangs rip flesh, and I gorge myself on blood that tastes of terror. It's not like the innocent boy in New Orleans. I don't feel their wild souls as they die. They're empty inside, made vacant by murder. Good thing I don't believe I have a soul to lose.

Soon, everything is quiet. Discarded torches sputter out in the sand. A female creature moans, so I chew her throat until I hit spine. Waves crash against the shore. I've never heard the ocean from this far away before, but I blame the blood. I could fly back to America right now if I wanted.

Then, Edmund whispers my name.

I rush inside, and he hasn't moved. He still rests on his side in front of the fading fire. I tear fabric from a shirt of mine and wrap the deep cut on his arm that has mostly stopped bleeding. Then, mindless of the gore, I lie down behind him and tug his body against mine.

"My beautiful sailor," I whisper into his hair.

He murmurs but soon falls asleep again. His heart beats as I kiss his neck and behind his ear.

"I love you," I say. "I love you, I love you..."

Chapter Fourteen

BEFORE I EVEN open my eyes, I know she's here, because suddenly, the house smells of New Orleans—of smoke and incense and whiskey and all the wicked bits of modern humanity. A week ago, I would have bathed in that scent, but now, all I want is the man in my arms, sweating with the heat of a well-fed vampire and the still-sputtering fire.

Michelle lingers in the doorway. Her eyes, a beguiling shade of purple, take in the scene before her. I'm sure I left her quite a different scene outside. Over the scent of my lover, there is rotting flesh. Flies buzz. The presence of death might as well be an actual person in our midst. A very large person.

"Care to explain yourself?" she asks. I've never been able to place her accent, a strange mixture that is sometimes Irish and sometimes Creole.

I sit up and pull Edmund with me. He falls limply across my chest, but even half-awake, he still clings to me—and I cling back. "You won't take him from me."

Michelle doesn't smile. She eyes Edmund like one of those damned dead cannibals. "Hmm, would that finally teach you to behave?"

"I have nothing left to learn."

She crouches in front of us, and her long, green velvet skirts spread like water. "You have one thing still to learn: how to live without something you love."

Edmund's grip on my shoulders tightens and releases when he wakes. I look down as his eyes open. He looks up to see me covered in blood, but it's the sight of Michelle that makes him jump.

He notices the well-dressed woman with the long white hair and says, "Bollocks!"

She is high class and cleanliness. I am a filthy, murdering piece of offal. Yet, he's actually afraid of her, bless him.

"It's all right," she says calmly, but he ignores her.

"Andrew. What the hell happened last night?"

"You need food." I never intend to let him go. "Michelle, would you be so kind as to get Edmund some salted pork?"

"Of course," she says as if she's oh so amicable.

Edmund moves away but not very far. He falls off my lap and onto the ground at my side, giving only a fleeting glance to the makeshift bandage on his arm.

"I'm alive." He laughs and looks up at me.

I smile back at him.

He takes the piece of meat Michelle extends to him. I'm surprised when she joins us on the ground, but I suspect she wants to be close to the mystery of my human.

"Thank you," he tells her. "I apologize for screaming at you when I woke, but I didn't expect to... Well, I guess I thought I'd be dead when I woke. Which doesn't make sense, because I suppose you don't wake up when you're dead."

"Andrew and I did," she says.

Edmund takes a long, deep breath. "Oh. Right." He swallows a piece of pork and blinks at me. "Andrew, did it rain blood last night?"

Michelle has the gall to chuckle, but I drop my chin to my chest and close my eyes.

The whole world goes quiet when Edmund presses his nose against my cheek and whispers, "Thank you."

With my eyes still shut, I reach up and tangle my fingers in his hair. I hold his face close to mine, because she's going to take him away. I know she will.

Her voice cuts through our calm. "Edmund, is it?"

"Yes, miss." His face moves away from mine, but he holds my hand tightly.

"Would you like to go home, dear?"

He squints at her pale, perfect face with the small nose and wide eyes. I think I know that look of his. He appraises her as he would a new species—one laden with poisonous skin. "I won't leave without Andrew."

Christ, I don't know if he's bluffing. His steady heartbeat gives nothing away. Of course, if Michelle wanted him to leave, she could make him. Or she could kill him. I'll die if she does. Immortality be damned, I will drop dead, erase myself like the Elder who birthed me.

Michelle smiles. The tips of her fangs touch her bottom lip. "Do you love him, Edmund?"

He laughs once, quickly. "I hope to spend the rest of my reckless life with this madman, but I fear you won't let me."

I linger somewhere between joy and horrible grief because what he said could seal my fate. I'm ecstatic my feelings are reciprocated, but this could be the perfect eternal punishment, taking him away. Michelle finally has the means to break me. She thought sending me into exile would make me an example? No, this—robbing Edmund from my grasp—is the true torture she has sought.

"You believe I would kill you?" she asks. She brushes her long fingernails rhythmically against the fabric of her dress as though music plays where it does not.

Edmund smiles. "Oh, yes. I think you'd rather love to."

Her fingers stop moving as her head tilts to the side. "You are a very dangerous thing to love, aren't you?"

"Terribly," he says. "As luck would have it, though, I think Andrew can handle me."

She doesn't even honor me with a glance, but my Edmund does not wilt beneath her scrutiny. If anything, he sits up taller.

"I look forward to getting to know you better, Edmund." She stands. "Congratulations, Andrew, your exile is over."

"What?" I practically choke on the word.

"You have not only spared a human from your own tendencies, but you protected him from outside threats, as well. In the many years of our friendship, you have never loved anything. Now, you do. Cherish it." Her purple gaze takes in our bare surroundings. "We sail for New Orleans. I'll give you a moment to collect what you will."

Edmund whoops and tackles me to the floor of our home—the four walls within which we fell in love—but the house is only walls. We will take our love with us. And rum, apparently. Once I've collected changes of clothes for us both and a healthy portion of salted pork for Edmund, he grabs two jugs of alcohol and winks. I follow my sailor out into the sun where Michelle stands amidst corpses.

God, it is carnage out here. I tore these desperate natives limb from limb and barely remember any of it.

Edmund covers his mouth and nose with his hand. "Holy Christ."

"Close your eyes and climb on my back."

He does as instructed, and I carry him past the worst of it. The feeding flies hum like an orchestra warming up.

We walk for a while, Michelle leading the way in her long green gown. Eventually, the thick foliage thins. I see the beach at the same time I see our ship. The smell of tropical flowers and fire floats through the air—and Edmund, of course. I could recognize my beloved's scent from halfway around the world.

BY THE TIME the sun begins to set, we are far, far away from the island of my exile. It disappeared as I stood with my arms around Edmund's shoulders and my nose in his hair. He tried to hide the way his eyes watered, but I kissed his tears until he laughed.

Now, I stand on deck and watch him. He sits up near the bow, balanced on the back legs of a chair with his feet resting on the rail. He's already consumed one jug of rum, and he is the picture of contentment as sea breezes ruffle his hair. He scratches at the whiskers on his cheeks, and I can't wait to have him clean-shaven again. I don't imagine Edmund would appreciate being called pretty, but God knows he is.

Michelle appears like an unexpected bit of fog. "And what will you do with him now?"

"Love him."

"But what of England? What of his home?"

I shrug. "I could live in England. Then again, I doubt Edmund will want to live anywhere but the sea. He'll want to keep moving."

"He'll age," she says. "Faster than you might think."

"I will find him an Elder." I look down at her. Michelle is powerful, ancient, and cruel, but she is smaller than me by almost two feet.

She scoffs. "All the Elders are dead."

"They can't be. I don't believe it. And if anyone can find something on this huge earth, it's my Edmund. He's a naturalist. He hunts curiosities."

He takes a sip of rum and runs his hand over his mouth.

"Does he know of your intentions?"

I chuckle. "Honestly, my intention only just occurred to me."

"And if he doesn't want to become like us?"

"Then, I'll die with him."

Her hand touches mine. "My God, you mean it."

I step away and smile. "Good night, Michelle. I look forward to catching up in the morning. I'm sure I've missed things during my exile. How many Mardi Gras have come and gone?"

"Four," she says.

"Hmm. Well." I nod to her and turn my back. Although there are several willing blood slaves on board this vampire ship, I focus all my attention on the only human I want—*my* human. I approach quietly and put my hands on his shoulders. He tilts his head back to look at me, the cheerful haze of rum in his eyes.

He grins. "Hello."

I kiss his nose, which makes him snicker and snort. "Drink much more rum, and you'll fall overboard. Get a chance to see your elusive shark very close up."

"Oh, you wouldn't let me fall."

"No. Come to bed?"

"Only if that's an expression for something much more exciting."

I pull him up by his biceps and am tempted to throw the lunatic over my shoulder. Instead, I drag him behind me below deck and into the dark, quiet, and rather opulent quarters Michelle must have deemed worthy of two men newly in love. I stumble out of my boots as Edmund now does the dragging. He kisses my neck and walks backward—my bright, barefoot sailor—until his knees hit the bed, big enough for both of us and then some. He falls back and pulls me with him.

"I will never tire of your weight on me," he murmurs through rum-soaked kisses. He tastes sweet and spicy all at once.

I show him I feel the same by pushing the collar of his shirt out of the way and nibbling his collarbones. I shift a bit off his lap to give me space to rub my palm between his legs. His hips buck forward when I tease his hardness. He groans, and I smile against his throat.

"Carry on that way, and the whole ship will know what we're doing."

"As if they don't already. Fucking vampires. I bet they can hear the blood pulsing in my cock."

I realize he's right. I not only hear his blood but also feel it. I rub at him through his worn clothes. "I can't wait to see you in a proper waistcoat and breeches. The moment we disembark, I'll find the best tailor in New Orleans. You'll be the most beautiful creature that filthy town has ever seen."

He shakes his head, eyes squeezed shut. "Don't think about that. Think about right now. Take me apart."

I shove both our clothes off. I kneel, and he spreads his long legs out on either side of me. I plant one hand by his head and lean forward to kiss him. I slide my other hand down his shaft, farther, farther, until I press against his hole. His body welcomes me inside even as the muscles of his chest and stomach clench.

"An...drew..." My name has never sounded so long.

Unlike the first time we made love, we watch each other as we fuck. When I first press into him, his arms and legs tighten as though they might break my bones. He shoves his face into the crook of my neck.

"All right?"

His hair tickles my ear when he nods. "You feel bigger this way. As if you weren't big enough already."

I run a hand over his hip. "Relax."

Warm breaths puff against my face, and then he tells me to move. It sounds more order than suggestion. I give him what he wants. Gently. I slide in and out as the ship rocks back and forth. I'm an extension of the sea, and Edmund loves us both.

The tension in his body soon lessens, replaced by a languid grip and repeated grunts. I don't know if he's aware his mouth hangs open—at least, not until I stick my tongue inside. He purrs into my kiss before pulling away long enough to speak.

"Anytime you want me like this? Anytime, you can have me."

I rub our noses together. "God, I love you. There will never be anyone else."

He smiles. "What on earth have I done to you?"

I swivel my hips, and his eyes shut.

"Have I made you a tame beast?"

I lick the mouth-shaped bruise on his neck. It feels like I marked him a million years ago. "Tame? Never." To prove it, I pin his arms above his head and slam my hips forward.

"Ah! Jesus."

"Don't even try to say you're not ready for me now. Your body's begging for it."

"Yes."

It doesn't take long for him to come with a shout that Neptune on his throne at the bottom of the sea probably heard. I torture him by not letting myself go. I continue rocking into him, altering angles and speeds, until he begs me to come. He says he can't take anymore, but I smile to see his cock half-hard again.

"I think I might be able to get you to come again like this."

He shakes his head, at my mercy. "I'll go blind, I swear."

He does come again, and his shout is more pain than pleasure. His whole body shivers after, so I finally take pity on my wrecked darling. My orgasm makes me see stars. I feel every pulse of pleasure all the way to my fingers and toes as I suck his scent into my mouth and say his name like a litany of everything good in the world.

The only part of him that moves is his chest heaving up and down. "I thought...you said you...weren't going to kill me."

"You're strong enough to live through Armageddon," I say as I use a piece of our discarded clothing to clean him.

He twitches when I get near his cock. "Don't even think about it."

I laugh and climb back into bed where my Edmund wraps himself around me like a long, warm piece of rope. I study him. The wound on his forehead is almost just a memory as I run my hands down his healing body.

"I never expected I'd have you," I say. "When I first took you back to my house on the island, I considered killing you."

"I figured as much."

"Then, I considered forcing myself on you. I was so lonely, and you were so lovely."

"You did neither of those things."

"No." I rub my chin against his cheek. The dark creature has not stirred in days.

"To think, I forced both sex and blood on *you*."

I squeeze his shoulders. "You forced nothing."

Edmund yawns. "What's it like in New Orleans?"

I click my tongue. "Dirty. Stinking. Beautiful. Bewitching."

"I'll have to write my mother," he mutters.

"Yes. And I have already planned our next adventure."

"Mm." He's slipping off to sleep.

I kiss him before he does, one more taste of his tongue. He's snoring within minutes since he always snores when he drinks. I close my eyes and do think of the future. I picture the way Edmund will look in silk and crisp cotton. In my mind, I see him tipping his hat to giggling girls on Bourbon Street. But I also see him buried in books, learning the legends. Together, we will find an Elder, and I will love my sailor forever.

ESCAPING

SOLITUDE

Chapter Two

IN THE MORNING, Edmund skips the pastries but drinks tea, although he says it doesn't taste right.

I call him a snob.

"No. I'm British, you tit." He demands we visit a proper teashop.

First, though, we must get clothes. I drag him past the spectacle that is New Orleans, even in the morning. Already, the streets crawl with sailors, businessmen, women of class and of ill repute. In the four years I've been gone, everything has grown. Buildings are higher. Streets are busier. Gardens are lusher—and the men. Oh, the men. There are so many men. Old, young, fat, thin, handsome, ugly, *gorgeous*. I smile at my Edmund in his worn breeches, linen shirt, and coat that doesn't fit. No one compares to him.

His gray eyes flit back and forth over everything as though devouring my city with his gaze. Lips parted, he sucks sea air into his lungs and almost falls over his own feet when he passes a grand theater playing *Faust*.

I chuckle.

"You're laughing at me."

"You've always made me laugh." I turn down Bourbon Street. If I keep staring at Edmund, I'm liable to stumble, too, but his enthusiasm drips from his face like afternoon sweat.

We step aside as a horse carriage passes. Women on a balcony wave at Edmund and I, and Edmund waves back. They continue to shout at us as we walk, so I grab his arm to keep him moving.

"This city oozes sex," he says. "And it's not even lunchtime."

"Wait until the sun sets."

"Must I?" He elbows me as I steer us toward St. Anne Street.

Tucked quietly away from boisterous Bourbon, I see the sign for "Peters Clothier" in swirling, black script. Either the old man is still alive or someone has bought out his business. Either way, the shop will have what we need.

A tiny bell rings when we walk inside. The air around us feels dry, unlike the late summer damp of outdoors, and smells cool, clean, with just a touch of earthy eau de cologne. I know that scent, so I'm not surprised when Peters—with his fluffy white muttonchops and bright blue eyes—pokes his head around a pedestal filled with fabric.

He puts on a pair of wire rim glasses and squints. "Andrew? I thought you were dead. Shame to lose such a good customer."

"Not dead."

"Good. Come in and spend your money."

He never was one for conversation.

Peters remembers my favorite fabrics—the deep blues and purples I used to wear before my exile. He probably even remembers my measurements. I go first so that Edmund can wander around and find fabrics of his own choosing. I have no idea what colors he prefers or, frankly, if my sailor has a sense of style at all. I have so much learning to do, but luckily, I also have time.

Once Peters and I have gone through the familiar rigmarole, I order two suits: one black and one gray, along with a variety of waistcoats and cravats. Peters offers to show me corsets—apparently they're all the rage for men nowadays—but I refuse. That'll be the day...

I buy a sensible suit off the rack so I have something nice to wear until the old man finishes with my order. Standing in front of the mirror, I run my hands down my sides and hips. It feels so good to be clean and properly dressed after years spent sweating and filthy on an island.

I find Edmund bent over some deep crimson, patterned silk. "That will look perfect on you," I whisper.

He smiles and rubs the fabric between his thumb and forefinger. "I haven't worn a bespoke suit in a very long time."

"Well, the time is now."

With pieces of fabric in hand, we return to Peters. I tug the coat from Edmund's shoulders and give him a little shove. My aging tailor goes right to work, measuring, writing notes, and mumbling to himself.

"This one doesn't require a corset," Peters says to me. "Broad shoulders, and I can nearly fit my hands around his waist."

I almost say "I know" but stop myself. I'm out of practice at keeping secrets.

Peters grabs Edmund by the chin and stares up at him. I see Edmund in the mirror's reflection, staring back.

"New around here?"

"Yes," Edmund says.

"The girls are going to love you. That red is perfect with your coloring, but I've got something else too. Been saving it for the right gent." Peters hustles away toward the back of the shop as Edmund again touches the red fabric he chose on the table nearby.

It takes all my resolve to not nuzzle my face in his hair. "What color suits would you like?"

"One black and one green. Those were my colors in London."

"Two suits. Waistcoats, cravats—"

"I don't wear them."

"Hmm?"

"I don't wear cravats." He winks at me because he knows how much I adore his neck and he plans to have it out for show on the decadent streets of New Orleans for everyone to see.

I bite hard on my bottom lip to keep myself from biting his.

Peters returns. "Here we are." He carries what appears to be liquid silver over his arm but is actually a swatch of fabric.

I hear the sharp intake of Edmund's breath. Then, he moves, reaches out to touch. "You brilliant man."

Peters actually appears to blush.

"Where did you get this?"

"An Italian trader. He brought it over from Catanzaro. I reckon it'll go with your eyes."

Edmund chuckles. "Oh, you're good, aren't you? I'll take it."

Like me, my sailor is forced to choose a suit off the rack before we depart, but something about the cut of current fashion fits him perfectly. The black suit might as well be tailored, and instead of traditional breeches, he chooses trousers that go all the way to his ankles.

"I do believe he's going to be even more fashionable than you, Andrew." Peters winks, and I think my tailor is not only onto us but *one of us* if the way he studies Edmund is any indication.

I buy a tall hat; Edmund does not. We promise to return in two days' time for our orders as we step out into midday. The city is fragrant, ripe—and loud. As we walk down the streets, it's just as I imagined on that ship days ago: my Edmund in a fancy suit, smiling at the people we pass. He still wears a bandage on his arm, but other than that, any evidence of the shipwreck, the cannibals, is erased. He is a wealthy man of leisure with callused hands and scars. He is a scientist who studies monsters—and loves them.

We make several stops as the day wears on. Edmund writes letters to his mother and to the trading company. He requests we walk the harbor and wants to see both cemeteries and museums. He chooses to lunch not at a fancy restaurant but at a small seaside inn that promises the best pasties on American soil. By the time the sun sets, I have become reacquainted with the city that I love and Edmund has learned it brand new.

On several occasions, I reach out to hold him but stop. I want to wrap my arms around him. I want to taste his smile or perhaps nibble on that exposed neck. Instead, I spend the day treating him as friend not lover, but my need to take, touch, fuck...well, my need will have to wait a bit longer because I have plans.

After dark, I lead Edmund to the back of the French Quarter, away from the society folks and their theaters. I tell him to stay close on Gallatin Street, but Edmund laughs at me.

"I'd rather you not get stabbed," I mutter.

"Andrew, do you know how many knife fights I've survived in my life? This one arse—Jesus, where were we?—some island off the coast of Africa, I think. He had a sword the size of my arm. I thought I was done for, but then, some native shot him in the face. I had brains all over me."

I snort and laugh because only Edmund could talk about a man's head exploding and sound mildly annoyed instead of disgusted.

"Where are you taking me, anyway?"

I grab his hand and tug him down an alley. Rank with the scent of rotting garbage and probably a dead body or two, nothing but a flickering gas lamp lights our way. We need not go far. Below the gas lamp is a red painted door. I knock—the special way—and the door opens.

The sweet scent of sex replaces that of refuse. Sex and incense and opium smoke. I tug Edmund to me and kiss him hard on the mouth because we're safe here. Here, men dress as women and women dress as men. Mouths and hands wander wherever they may, and services are purchased.

I sent a note earlier to the brothel's Irish madam, May, who I spot as soon as we enter the candlelit bar. She saunters toward us, wide skirts flowing, and exhales sweet smoke toward the ceiling. "Andrew. Thought someone had finally killed you." She wears too much kohl around her eyes, half her pale face painted black. With the hand not holding a cigarette reeking of hashish, she grabs Edmund by the front of his coat. "My, my, where do you find such pretty things?"

"Deserted islands, my lady," he says, studying her face.

Her smile reveals crooked teeth. "Haven't thought to search there." She glances at me. "Your room's ready, Andrew. Rum and the rest. Pay when you're finished. And if there's time, I wouldn't mind the pleasure of a drink with your pretty British thing. I could use some news from the old country."

I put my hand on Edmund's shoulder and squeeze. "Perhaps, although Edmund is going to be very tired after tonight."

May's words are tinged with smoke as she exhales. "Aye, he certainly is." Her skirts billow as she turns and walks back to the bar.

Very little has changed at my favorite brothel. The wood floors are still stained and creak as though they might break. The hallways still glow gold with dancing flame. And my favorite room, at the back of the second story, still waits quietly. I press Edmund against the door and kiss his neck. I kiss and suck until his fingertips dig into my shoulders.

"Bed," he mutters.

I hum and kiss his jaw.

His hand must turn the knob, because the door opens. I suck his lower lip into my mouth and walk him backward farther inside. Then, I stop. I pull away, and when he reaches for my lapels, I *tut-tut*. I shake my head and gesture with my chin toward the bed.

He glances over his shoulder, and there they are, kissing in the largest bed in the brothel: the beauties I requested. It was with shock and relief when I learned earlier that my two favorite whores were not only still alive but also still working. Being a New Orleans prostitute did not guarantee a long life, especially for men catering to men—yet, here they are, my powerful Haitian and pale Creole treat.

Edmund lets out a long, slow sigh and leans his back against my chest. I wrap my arms around him as the men in bed stop kissing each other and turn to stare at us. Danys stands first, brushing away the tangled sheets to reveal his dark skin and thick, corded muscle. He is a *gens de couleur libres* who arrived in America a decade ago on a weatherworn Haitian vessel. In New Orleans, he could have found respectable employment on the docks, but he chose instead to feed his baser instincts and fuck for money.

Then, there is sweet Gabriel—or Gabriela, depending on the night. I requested he play the part of a man this evening for Edmund. Where Danys is thick and stocky, Gabriel is small and thin. He plays a woman well and doesn't even need to don a blond wig, as his hair is so long.

Gabriel watches from the bed, smiling, as Danys approaches and studies my sailor. *"Ki jan bèl,"* he says.

"Sorry?" Edmund asks.

Danys's dark eyes crinkle when he smiles. "How handsome." He runs his thumb over Edmund's bottom lip. "Gabriel, bring some rum."

I've always had an affinity not only for Danys's island accent but also for his bossiness in bed. True, I generally enjoy being the boss—especially with Edmund—but it can be nice to let someone else take control occasionally.

Edmund chuckles and leans his head back against my shoulder, running his hands over mine. I accept his silent command and kiss his neck.

Of course, Gabriel is naked as he walks over with a bottle. He gives it to Edmund who takes a long gulp before passing the bottle back. *"Regardez."* He runs a hand through my sailor's dark curls. "I think I'll call you *mon chat noir.*"

Danys laughs—a deep vibrating noise—probably because, if anyone in the room is a "black cat," it's him.

"Would you give us a moment, gentlemen?" Edmund asks, and although their eyes linger, Danys and Gabriel do give us some space as they pass the bottle of rum back and forth. Edmund turns to face me. One of his eyebrows lifts, and his lips press together.

"What's the matter?"

"You won't hurt them," he says.

"God, no."

He chews his bottom lip.

"Edmund?"

"You once said you would murder any man who ever touched me."

Ah, yes. *That.* I do vaguely recall some such statement tumbling from my lips in a moment of passion on the island. I also, however, remember the thought of my sailor with another man making me incredibly hard. Despite these two opposing feelings, such inklings could exist side by side, so I placate Edmund with my conclusion: "I would murder any man who touched you without me watching. And no other vampire than me—ever."

He smiles, but his amusement does little to hide his blush. "So as long as I put on a show, you don't care?"

I kiss him once. "As long as I'm the encore."

"I fear there might not be much of me left after these two."

I lick into his mouth, and he moans. "There's always more of you left." I shove him in the chest, and he takes two stumbling steps backward before Danys rushes forward to catch him. As soon as Edmund is in his arms, Danys attacks his ear with his mouth. Edmund leans back into his embrace as Gabriel unbuttons his waistcoat, and soon, Edmund's new suit is strewn across the room.

In bed, he's as pale as Gabriel with muscles more akin to Danys. I'm happy to see the last of my sailor's bruises from the shipwreck have finally begun to fade. They are nothing but light yellow galaxies on his back and ribs.

The whores' lips are everywhere. Gabriel licks at Edmund's nipples as Danys swallows his cock. Edmund clutches to sheet and hair—anything he can grab—and makes the pleasure-pain noises I so adore. I pull up a chair and sip rum, watching as these so talented men take my lover apart.

Edmund comes while panting into Gabriel's mouth. The pleased look on Gabriel's face makes me think the sound of his shouts tastes sweet. Danys kisses his way up Edmund's body, making Edmund jump when he bites at the straining tendons of his neck. Danys covers Edmund's mouth with his, kissing roughly as he grinds his own engorged flesh against Edmund's hip.

I've requested they show no mercy.

With Edmund still floating in a postorgasmic haze, Danys rolls him onto his side. Gabriel kisses him in that sweet way he does, but he also guides Edmund's hand to his prick. Half alert, Edmund moves his hand up and down Gabriel's cock until he has Gabriel whispering quiet pleas in French.

Behind him, Danys reaches for a small bowl on the side table and coats his fingers in oil. He bites at Edmund's shoulders as his fingers caress his hip and then move lower. I do wish the candlelight was a bit brighter for this, but I recognize the noise Edmund makes when Danys's fingers press inside him. It's the noise he made when I pinned him to our bed on the island and fucked him with my fingers until I thought he might sob.

"Oh...God..." Edmund groans, eyes squeezed shut.

Danys sucks on Edmund's ear and whispers, "*Dous mwen.*" *My sweet.*

Gabriel and Danys move together on the bed as if they've done this before—probably have, although not with me. They shift and turn until Edmund is on his stomach, panting into the pillowcase. Gabriel pushes his hair out of the way and kisses his forehead while Danys takes him from behind.

At first, Edmund gasps. His hands claw at fabric until Danys wraps his arms around him. Then, Edmund sighs. He accepts kisses from Gabriel that leave his lips wet. When Danys pulls him up onto his knees, Edmund rests on his elbow and finally looks at me. His light eyes are dazed, glowing, as he accepts every thrust Danys offers.

Gabriel, such a slight thing, makes his way below them both. Edmund runs his hands through Gabriel's long, blond hair and kisses him before taking hold of the whore's cock. Oil from Danys must have tumbled between them, because Edmund's hand shines in the light as it moves.

The three of them build a wave of motion. I rest my hand over my own desperate cock as I watch the man I love being fucked as he pleasures another. Both Danys and Gabriel seem lost in Edmund. Their eyes are shut tight as their hands and mouths wander over him. One might think him a sorcerer, the way his skin so enthralls.

Danys leans forward and speaks against the back of Edmund's neck. "Me after you, *dous mwen.*"

Edmund smiles at this, but his mouth drops open when Danys wraps his fist around his already spent member. Of course, Edmund is hard again already. His youth is insatiable.

Gabriel comes first, clutching to Edmund's shoulders. Perhaps the lovely sight of that pretty blond pushes Edmund over, because he joins soon after, followed by Danys who groans, long and deep, before crushing both Edmund and Gabriel below him.

They are a candlelit pile of sweet-smelling, sweat-soaked skin. When Danys and Gabriel immediately start rubbing on Edmund like hungry cats, he turns to me and grins.

WE HAVE TO send for more candles—and rum—before they've finally finished, the three of them jumbled together side by side in bed. Danys is glued to Edmund's back. He kisses Edmund's shoulders as Edmund and Gabriel brush noses and tongues.

My Edmund took Gabriel earlier. It wasn't like Danys's powerful thrusts from behind. No, Edmund took Gabriel face-to-face, hands roaming, eyes wandering, *gently*. It had never occurred to me that Edmund might enjoy sex both ways, not as if I would offer. I will always be the one climbing on top in our relationship, but it was still beautiful to watch—two pretty things fucking.

"Let us keep him, Andrew," Gabriel begs.

Danys hums his agreement against Edmund's spine.

I sigh and stand, sore from the waist down. I've gone from hard to harder to soft and back again a dozen times. "I think not."

Gabriel pouts. Edmund, smiling, kisses him on the chin.

"Sadly, it's time for the two of you to give us some privacy, although I must say you were worth every penny."

Danys sits up and stretches his neck from side to side. "Let us stay and watch?"

Edmund chuckles as he rolls onto his back. He's covered in love bites.

"No." I gesture to the door. "Come on. Out."

Gabriel gives Edmund one last lingering kiss before he stands. *"Mon chat noir."*

"I should probably learn French," Edmund says.

The lovely whores whisper their goodbyes to us both as they wrap themselves in robes and leave the ever-darkening room. We could again do with more candles, but I suppose my eyes have already seen. Now, it's time to feel.

I lie beside my love and run my hand over his abdomen.

He smiles at me. "Thank you. That was..." He whimpers as though that one delicate sound sums up a night of endless pleasure.

"Yes. It was."

He wraps one leg over mine and rubs his naked body against my clothes. "Take these off."

I do as he requests and climb back into bed with him. The entire room smells of sex and sweet smoke from the bar downstairs. When he kisses me, I taste the other men. I lick the flavor from his mouth before moving to his neck. I spot a particularly dark bite—I watched Danys apply it hours before—and suck hard. Edmund gasps. His immediate response is to push me away, escape the pain, but then he shudders and draws me closer.

"Was that all right?" he pants. "What we did...was it...?"

I shush him. "It was beautiful. You're beautiful. But remember: you will never come here without me."

His eyes are shut. He's about to fall asleep, but he still has the energy to smile. "It wouldn't be half as fun without you watching."

I roll him onto his stomach.

He mutters a questioning, "Andrew? I don't think—"

"I won't." Even my insatiable Edmund can't take any more. I reach out for what's left of the oil and coat my neglected member. I thrust between the cheeks of his muscular ass and come in less than a minute. He sighs below me as my dead seed coats his back. I lean forward, hungry, ready to feed on this beguiling creature below me. My fangs distend to the tune of his lazy heartbeat and all I can think is "Kill...kill...kill."

I draw back with such vehemence, I almost tumble from the bed. I cover my mouth with my hand and stare at his familiar back, marred by an electric eel. This is not some nameless whore; this is Edmund, the man I love...and I almost just killed him.

Jesus, when did I last eat? Our final night on the island? But that was ages ago. True, I can go long periods of time without eating, but not after the temptation of today, surrounded by so much human flesh. The dark creature I've kept away from Edmund's throat has returned.

I must feed.

THANKS TO MY long-standing loyalty to May, she allows me to buy Danys until morning. He promises to sleep beside Edmund until I return—and, frankly, protect him. Under normal circumstances, Edmund can protect himself. However, he's been fucked into next year and was snoring when I left. I don't dare leave my exhausted lover alone in a dangerous brothel, but no sane person would attack Danys. I hear he once killed a man with a broken champagne bottle.

Although the night is black, the streets outside still ring with shouts and the muffled sound of back-alley trysts. The alleys of my New Orleans have always been sanctuary to a man like me: a sodomite and murderer. I'm indeed starving. I let it get bad this time, desperate. I'm out of practice, accustomed to nothing but lizards and small birds for four whole years. Now, surrounded by the lush aroma of humanity, I've allowed myself to become a danger to the thing I care for most. I must be more cautious—for Edmund.

Most street corners are empty or occupied by half-conscious, mumbling drunks, and although I consider the ease of an inebriated attack, I keep moving. The gas lamps flicker as I pass, but no one pays me any mind, except...

There are a few young men up ahead, hidden in shadow. They talk and laugh among themselves, and I hear the click of coin. As I approach, they freeze. Their darting eyes take in the sight of me—an imposingly large figure with blond hair and a new suit.

"*Bonsoir.*" I smile without showing my fangs.

"*Monsieur.*" A tall, skinny boy steps forward in greeting, but he's not the one I want. I want the boy in the back with the shy eyes and black hair. I point and gesture him forward. He ducks his head and takes my hand before pulling me away from his friends and into the dark.

Away from the street, I press him against a wall and nose up his neck. He reeks like the grabbing hands of other men. His fingers gently brush down the front of my suit, but he makes no move to seduce me. He stands, shoulders tense, as I continue to breathe him in.

I'm reminded of Edmund—or what I expected of Edmund—when we first met. I thought my advances would disgust him. I thought he would be shy, scared even. How wrong I had been the day Edmund instead seduced *me.* I grow hard just thinking about the first moment he touched me. I must make a noise, because the boy in the alley nods against my shoulder.

"Do you want to kiss me, sir?" he asks.

His mouth is too small. His mouth isn't...

Edmund.

God, what's happening to me? I rub my hand over my face.

"Sir?"

Now, I'm back in that alley from four years ago. I'm back in the moment when I killed that other prostitute just to taste his sweet soul. I used to love killing things.

"Are you all right, sir?"

"No, I..." I stare into his wide, nervous eyes. It would be so easy to just lean down and take a bite. I wouldn't have to kill him, just drink until he passed out. Simple. So why aren't my fangs cooperating? Why am I not hungry anymore? I press a silver coin into his palm. "Thank you."

In the darkness, his face twists into dark shadow. "That's all, sir?"

"Yes. Thank you. Be on your way."

The young streetwalker takes off with his coin. I'm sure they'll have a good laugh at the beast of a man who couldn't do the deed. I don't have time to care. I hurry back up Gallatin Street, down the familiar alley, and let myself in through the red door. The bar is still crowded with people, so I merely wave to May as I pass.

I take the steps three at a time and don't knock before entering the room. There's only one candle lit, but the dancing light is enough to show Danys in bed, leaned up as if ready to attack the interloper. He relaxes when he sees it is I. Edmund doesn't move at all. I climb into bed behind him and lift him onto my chest, my nose in his hair.

"Mm...Andrew..." he mutters but does not wake.

Danys reaches out and squeezes my forearm. "You love him?"

I nod. "Sometimes it feels like too much."

Chapter Three

HIS HAND GRABS for my thigh when the carriage hits a violent bump. He smiles up at me and sighs. "What am I to expect?"

"I'm not sure what you mean."

"Well, am I to be paraded around your coven like some rich society girl?"

"Well. Not like a *girl*." I try not to stare at him, but what's the harm? He is mine, after all, and he's wearing one of the perfectly fitted suits we picked up from Peters that afternoon. The red silk vest is stunning, as Edmund foresaw. He's just shaved. Odd that he shaves every day. I wonder if he did so all those years sailing or if this is Edmund on land, different from the sailor and more the London socialite he was before he left it all behind.

"Are you being daft on purpose?"

I smile and fold his hand in mine.

"My mother used to parade me around at all her parties in an effort to find me a wife." He says the word with such revulsion, I laugh. "Can you even imagine me at a high society soiree? It's no wonder everyone thought me mad. You're not supposed to say what you're really thinking at those things, you know, but God, I always did. It became an amusement. I was so damn bored once, I seduced a baron and sucked him off in his own washroom. He chased me around the rest of the season hoping for a repeat performance."

I laugh so hard, I snort, which makes Edmund look at me and grin.

"I'm serious, Andrew, how do you want me to behave?"

I don't want him to behave at all, but I've been careful with him today. My stomach aches with emptiness, so sexual congress would be more dangerous than fun.

He taps the top hat between us—mine. Just as Edmund doesn't wear cravats, he doesn't wear hats, I suspect to not ruin his hair. I also suspect my sailor is incredibly vain. From the everyday shaving to the way he instructed Peters to "take it in a bit more around the hips" to the way he oils his black curls, Edmund knows he is handsome, and he exploits those good looks. I'll have to keep him close at my coven, pretty thing.

I watch the streets of New Orleans pass outside. "Just be you, my love."

"Dangerous advice." He leans over and sucks my earlobe.

My fangs throb.

The carriage stops on the edge of the French Quarter, away from the murderers and thieves. Actually, standing in front of a grand mansion that houses a vampire coven, perhaps that assessment is inaccurate. There are murderers aplenty.

I pay the driver as Edmund steps out onto the road. When I turn around, I find him standing there, grinning up at the façade. The manse is indeed impressive, especially since I haven't seen it in years. It's three stories with a huge, wraparound porch. White Doric columns seem to support the whole thing, and candles burn in every window.

"Does God live here?" he asks.

I put my hand on his shoulder and guide him down the flower-lined front path. He pauses to study a huge crimson blossom.

Compared to Edmund, I think the rest of us see the world in black and white.

A human servant opens the door and bows when we enter. From the grand front foyer, I already hear the sound of a string quartet. The echo is ghostly, floating around the high ceilings. Enormous pieces of art hang from every wall, and the floor is freshly waxed. I smell crawfish and butter—food to keep our human guests strong throughout the night of revelry. Edmund falls into step at my side as we walk farther inside, down the hall and toward the lamp-lit back garden. However, the lush greenery doesn't bring comfort; it only reminds me of my island exile. Edmund grabs my hand as if he understands, and then...well, I'm not sure what happens.

Edmund moves quickly. He's a flash of black fabric before everything stops, and I realize he's pinned someone, face-first, against the wall. He, in fact, holds that someone's arm at an unnatural angle, and that someone winces in pain. It takes a moment for me to recognize Felipe, my old *friend*.

"I've heard I have a lush ass," Edmund hisses, "but grabbing is just rude."

Felipe looks the same as always, his dark hair tied at the back of his neck. The shadows beneath his cheekbones are practically ghoulish, but his eyes shine in the dim light. I see a flash of teeth when he laughs. "My, my, Andrew, you've bagged a strong one. However do you manage him in bed?"

"He manages," Edmund says.

"Let go of me, child."

"Promise to behave?"

Felipe presses away from the wall and spins using every bit of his vampire strength. Edmund falls back against my chest, and I catch him just as Felipe bares his fangs. "Do not forget the monsters with which you play."

In the face of one such monster, Edmund's heart rate doesn't even jump. He leans close to Felipe and whispers, "Don't touch what isn't yours."

Felipe licks his bottom lip, fangs still out for show.

Pride courses through me, because not only is my sailor strong, but he's also brave. I love the way he laughs in the face of destruction.

"Gentlemen." Michelle's crystal clear voice cuts the quiet. Felipe, always her pet, turns at the sound, and there she stands, long, white hair piled on top of her head. Her gown is pale lavender. "Edmund." Her face brightens when she says his name. She holds her hand out, and he steps forward to take it. "It's so good to see you." She means it. I can see it in the way her eyes crinkle. "You look wonderful."

He bends and kisses her hand. "Nothing compared to you. You put all the flowers of the world to shame."

She smiles, as does Felipe. The way he watches Edmund—as though torn between feelings of homicide and sex—I want to kick him. He'll never touch my boy. Never.

"And Andrew." She beckons me closer, so I go. She kisses me on the cheek. "When have you last fed? You look exhausted. Scared of another exile?"

Edmund ignores the veiled threat. "Damn it, when did you last feed?"

"I..." No part of me wants to explain that the only blood I can now stomach is Edmund's. "I'm still getting used to being back."

Felipe chuckles. "Goodness. He is a changed man, Michelle."

She hums. "He is indeed." Her eyes dart to Edmund as if she can read my thoughts. "Let's join the party, shall we?" She extends her arm to Felipe, and he jumps to take it, leading her back toward the foyer and the grand staircase.

"What a cock-up." He nods toward their retreating backs. "Who the hell was that?"

"Felipe. He is Michelle's occasional lover and devotee, although he'd never turn down something like you."

"Oh, good, I've been here five minutes, and I already made someone hate me. That might be a record."

I shake my head. "He doesn't hate you. He wants to fuck you."

"Not happening." He lifts his arm. "Shall we?"

Instead of taking his arm, I crowd him against the wall and swallow any further questions with an openmouthed kiss. He welcomes my tongue into his mouth and moans while grabbing at my lapels. "I adore you," I say. "Felipe's face when you crushed him into that wall was invaluable."

He smiles but glances away. "He felt...stronger than you."

"Yes. Well."

"You need to eat, don't you?"

I kiss his forehead. "Later." With my hand on the back of his neck, I guide him to the staircase. He ducks and smiles under my attentions.

Together, we climb. I continue guiding him down the candlelit hall. The music is louder up here, as are the voices, the laughter. When we step into the double doorway that leads to the grand ballroom, Edmund's eyes widen.

"Fuck me," he mutters.

"Once we get home, yes," I say.

He rolls his eyes but only wastes his gaze on me for a moment, because attractive vampires and humans in varying states of undress are everywhere. I doubt even experienced Edmund has ever seen a ballroom like this, decorated with couches and overflowing beds. Servants rush around with trays of champagne, oysters, and absinthe. I give my sailor a little shove inside, and he grabs two champagne flutes from a passing tray before handing one to me.

I see Michelle and Felipe up ahead, waiting for us, so I tug Edmund's arm to get him moving. A woman in nothing but feathers pauses long enough to give him the once-over, and he spins to watch her retreating back.

"Have you ever slept with a woman?" I ask, surprised I've never asked before.

"Several," he says, finishing his first glass of wine and already reaching for another.

"Really?"

"I assume that means you haven't." Two young men rutting against each other distract him.

"No. I've never slept with a woman."

He laughs at me before wrapping an arm around my shoulders. "So I have done something you haven't!"

I sling my arm around his waist and speak with my lips against his forehead. "I'm fairly positive you've done several things I haven't, you madman."

We catch up to Felipe and Michelle who recline on a grand, red couch against the back wall. Michelle pets the empty space at her side. "Edmund, you will sit beside me."

He does as told, although he eyes me first. I grudgingly sit next to Felipe.

"What do you think of New Orleans?" Michelle asks.

His bright eyes take in the high ceiling, painted black, and the brightly lit chandelier. "It's beautiful and, uh, perfect. For a man like me."

Felipe shouts, "What kind of man are you exactly?"

"Wouldn't you like to know?"

Felipe puts his hand to his chest as though scandalized and whispers to me, "He is a bit of an ass."

"You didn't exactly make a winning first impression."

Felipe shrugs and tugs at his lace cuffs.

"Do you like our soiree? Perhaps you and Andrew would enjoy a bed of your own, hmm?" Michelle puts her hand on his forearm. "I would love to see more of your skin."

He quickly looks at me, and I just barely shake my head.

"No. Thank you," he says.

She runs her fingers through the side of his hair. "Shy?"

He chuckles. "They remind me a bit of cannibals, the way they devour each other."

Michelle hums. "Perhaps, but no one ends up dead in the morning."

"Not anymore," Felipe mutters.

"How old are you, Edmund?"

I sit up a bit straighter at her question, because through all the madness that has kept us alive, I still never thought to ask.

He leans forward to snatch another glass from a passing tray—pale green absinthe, this time. "Does it matter?"

"You're a puzzle, you see. You look very young, but I don't think you are. You are worldly. Experienced." She touches his cheek. "Hmm?"

"I'm twenty-eight," he says.

I cuss. "You are not." Jesus, I'd once guessed him no more than twenty. He seems so damn young when he laughs.

Ignoring the others, he stands, crosses to me, and straddles my lap. My hands immediately reach beneath his jacket and run up the back of that red, silk waistcoat. He presses his nose against mine. "Have I lost my allure since I'm so very old?"

I laugh against his mouth. His warm breath smells of black licorice. "No. Just surprised is all." I kiss him and taste the Green Fairy on his tongue.

"Are you sure you two do not want a bed of your own?" Felipe asks. I glance at him, and he's licking his lips while staring at Edmund's mouth.

Edmund slides to my side, eyes back on the party. We both ignore Felipe's question.

I don't know if my sailor has noticed, but blood play has begun. Vampires have started to feed, in the midst of fucking. Blood drips down chins and onto dark sheets. I've never explained this to my darling—that blood and sex are often intertwined within the bounds of my immortal culture. The only time I've fed from Edmund, actually, was when he forced it upon me, and there was nothing sexual about it. It was kill or be killed, back on our island of exile, and the addition of his sweet blood made me strong enough to protect him from man-eating monsters.

I watch, rapt, as a male vampire with long, black hair breaks the skin of a pale, redheaded wisp of a boy and drinks deeply.

Edmund grabs my chin so hard it hurts and forces me to look at him. Dark eyebrows drawn together over stormy eyes, he glares at me. I've never seen him angry before—but what provoked the fire in his gaze?

"Come." Michelle stands. "I think it's time Edmund saw the library."

The library? Why...? Oh. But I haven't—

"A library in this place?" He stands, anger gone, and even folds Michelle's arm over his. "Show me."

Her entire face lights up at the sight of his enthusiasm as she guides him away from the orgy and toward the dim hallway off the back of the ballroom. I am quick to follow, although Felipe does not join us. He actually joins the black-haired beauty and his young human instead.

Michelle explains as we walk, "I've been compiling the history of our people for centuries. Every bit of vampire knowledge is stored here."

"Best hope there's never a house fire."

She pets his arm, and Edmund glances back at me as if to check I still follow.

A rather large vampire—even by my standards—hovers beside the library's double doors. When he sees Michelle, I hear the metal clink of keys as he turns and begins the process of unlocking several deadbolts.

"We keep it locked when we have parties. The last thing I need is some wayward drunk disturbing my collection."

The doors swing open, and the room glows clean and white as candles dance behind glass lanterns. Staring at the two-story library, stacks and stacks of ancient texts and scrolls, Edmund looks as though, this time, he's walked into an orgy of centaurs and unicorns.

I smack him on the back. "Breathe."

He sucks air into his lungs.

Michelle touches my elbow. "Is he all right?"

I chuckle. "Edmund is a lover of knowledge."

As if to demonstrate, my sailor takes several steps forward and begins poking at bookshelves. "It would take years to even begin to catalog all the information you have stored here." He runs his fingers down book spines and even leans forward to sniff a few. He laughs like he's smelled something particularly sweet, even though his nose is probably filled with dust. "Andrew, I'm sorry. I'm leaving you for a library."

I watch my love virtually dance across the room, forward and back, left and right, investigating here and there.

Michelle's lavender gown hisses as she crosses the floor. "It's yours, Edmund. Here, you can learn the history of our people and find the evidence you seek. Andrew says that if anyone can find a long-lost Elder, it would be you."

He pauses. "What?"

Michelle moves ever closer. She pushes a few dark curls behind his ear. "You'll find your Elder and become like one of us. Won't you?"

His eyes flit up to me, and oh, there it is again: anger.

Chapter Four

WE MAKE A quick exit, and after a silent carriage ride, we're back at our hotel. Edmund stomps inside our room and removes his jacket a bit more forcefully than I would deem necessary, but—

"How could you not have told me?" he shouts.

"I planned to, but I wanted to give us time to relax. Enjoy." I gesture to the room around us as if the fancy trappings make up for my omission.

He puts his hands on his hips and turns toward the window. "That next adventure you mentioned; this is it. You want me to find an Elder."

I set my hat down and remove my own coat, but I don't step any nearer. "I thought you would want immortality. Imagine all you could do with that much time, all you could discover. I thought—"

"It's not that, Andrew." He rubs his forehead. "Of course, I want immortality. I just wish you would have asked." He turns around, but I still don't approach him. I let Edmund take a few steps toward me instead, and although I can see he's not angry anymore, something does still bother my love.

"What's wrong?"

He closes his eyes and sighs. "Ask me."

Ask him? I try to read some meaning on his face as he nears me and adjusts my waistcoat just a bit. He runs his palms down the material and won't meet my gaze. Face soft but lips pressed together, this must be another new expression. It takes me but a moment to realize this is Edmund vulnerable, which is when I further realize what he means by "Ask me."

I wince at my own idiocy and take one of his hands in mine. "Edmund Baines... I don't know your middle name."

"William."

"It suits you," I whisper.

His cheeks glow red.

"Edmund William Baines, will you spend eternity with me?"

He smiles. "Yes, you utter fool of a man."

I grab his ass, pressing us together. "I didn't know you were a romantic."

"I'm not. Usually." He leans his head back when I start kissing his neck. "But I guess I've never been in love before."

I speak against his skin. "Me neither."

"Well, bugger." He takes a step away from me, which is precisely what I do not want. When I move to crowd him against the nearest wall, he holds his hand up to stop me. He begins to unbutton first his waistcoat and then his shirt. He is pale, lovely skin and lean muscle. He is a strong heartbeat I can hear...and blood.

"Are you teasing me?" I ask.

"No. I don't want to get blood on my new clothes. Hell to wash out. I actually had to throw away one of my favorite shirts after a particularly brutal bar fight on the Amalfi Coast."

"Edmund?"

He drapes his white shirt and red waistcoat over a nearby chair. "At the soiree, I saw the way you watched other vampires feed." He rubs his nose against the side of my jaw.

I rest my hands on his hips. "It made you angry."

"I don't think that's the word." The touch of his tongue on my ear makes me gasp. "Jealous? Definitely. I, too, watched that delicate young thing being bitten—the way it connected him to that black-haired beast. I could see the hunger painted on your face, but that hunger wasn't pointed at me, so I didn't like it. You need to feed." He kisses me. "So feed."

"Edmund—"

"Do you want me to beg?" He rubs his hard length against my thigh. "You love when I beg."

I trace the scar on his back with my fingertips until my hands dip low enough to push beneath the fabric of his trousers. "I can't believe I ever thought you innocent."

He chuckles. "Never make that mistake again."

"No."

He presses our noses together. "Will you?"

I breathe his breath before leaning forward and stealing his lips. By the time we left the island, his mouth was chapped with too much sun and not enough water. Now, his mouth is again plush and soft like rose petals between my fingers. Again, I remember his many contradictions: this creature who has killed men with his bare hands yet has a mouth sweeter than clover honey. Felipe underestimated him immediately. He saw a gentle, pretty thing to be conquered, but it's Edmund who does the conquering. I am certainly his slave.

He walks backward to the bed, tugging me along with him. The dark creature purrs within me. Edmund gave it permission to taste, but I'm the one who must set it free.

We tumble onto the mattress. Edmund seems as starved as me, the way he licks into my mouth and nibbles my lips. He makes the soft groans I adore, hand pawing gently at the front of my pants.

"Please, Andrew." He rolls his hips up to meet mine, and my arms almost go out from under me.

I eye a spot low enough on his neck to be covered by his collar. I tell the dark creature to not take too much and set my fangs free. Edmund doesn't notice, eyes closed and head thrown back as I thumb his nipples.

Then, I bite.

He makes a sound as though he's just emerged from water. He moans a little as his fingers dig into my spine.

Me, I'm floating. Despite the earlier noises from outside—horses, shouts, and an opera singer on the corner—I now only hear Edmund's breath. I only smell Edmund, taste Edmund. It's how it was on our island, back when his heady scent used to distract me from the threat of cannibals. I'm utterly distracted now.

I remove my teeth from his neck and lick the wound before diving in again.

"Fuck," he says. I do know he likes a little pain with his pleasure, so I bite down harder. He gasps, pants, and rides the ache. My sailor does love the deadly.

The dark creature sated, I lean back, still looming over him. Sweat glues his hair to his forehead, so I run my palm over his skin, pushing it back. I kiss his cheeks, his nose, his closed eyelids. "Are you all right?"

His eyelashes flutter. "Mm-hmm."

"My love?"

"Next time we do that, I want you inside me too."

I don't even have the breath to agree.

When he sits up, a drop of blood runs down his collarbone and over his chest. He stands long enough to remove his trousers and white drawers before tumbling back into bed. "Take off your clothes," he commands—albeit weakly.

"We don't need to—"

"*I* need to, you ass." He reaches his arms above his head and points his toes in a full body stretch that's more pornographic than anything I've yet seen tonight. I'm out of my clothes in a rush of immortal flesh. He smiles. "Pin me down. I want to feel how strong you are."

I do as requested, pinning his arms above his head and his body between my legs. He presses up against me, and I marvel at the muscle tension in his arms and chest.

He falls limply back. "Shit. You're made of stone."

I use my tongue to clean up the bit of spilled blood on his chest and neck. "I'm too full to toss you around right now, but believe me, I will."

He laughs silently, just a little tremor of his upper body. "Be a doll and get me off, would you?"

It's reminiscent of our first time—mindless rutting, chasing pleasure. Edmund doesn't seem to mind as I wrap my fist around us both and thrust. He curls one of his legs around my lower back, bringing us ever closer.

"I love you, I love you," I mutter into his open mouth, one of his hands still pinned above us. I intertwine our fingers.

Now familiar with what he likes, I remove my hand from our joined hot flesh and trail my fingers lower. He moans when I press a finger inside of him. My name comes out as a choke as I move my digits in and out. He sobs when he comes, and I follow immediately behind. There's nothing more beautiful than the man's face when he comes—nothing.

I flop down on top of him, again, the way he likes. His arms wrap around me as I bury my face against his neck.

"You're learning my body quite well, aren't you?" he whispers.

"I will always have more to learn."

"True." He sighs. "You haven't even found my ticklish spot yet."

I try to lift my head, but he holds me tight.

"I shall sleep well tonight," he says.

I always sleep well next to Edmund.

Chapter Five

WHEN I WAKE in the morning, the bed is empty and cold—which hasn't been the case since Edmund first washed up on my little island. I sit up and call his name, but I can tell our room is void. I don't sense him nearby, only remnants of him, a spot of blood on the pillowcase. I walk the room naked and find a note on the small table by the door. Heaven knows where he found paper or pen, but the words send a rush of panic through me.

At the library. Love you.

God, he has gone to the coven to begin his research, and this is exactly what I did not want: Edmund alone with other vampires.

I hurry to dress.

I shouldn't be surprised by his immediate ambition to find an Elder. From what I've seen, Edmund is not a patient man. He's a driven, curious man who does everything quickly. Well, except sex. On occasion, the sex between us has gone on for hours. But research, seeking out that which is unknown? Oh, how Edmund loves a puzzle.

I thank the fates that a carriage waits in front of our hotel. The air is already warm and wet as I wave my hand to catch the driver's attention. I give him the address, but for the entirety of our trip, I curse myself for not waking when Edmund left. We always wake together. I blame the blood consumption for my deep sleep. Sated, I drowned in dreamland. I fear even another of Edmund's nightmares wouldn't have woken me.

When the carriage reaches our destination, I throw too much coin at the driver and race into the house. Everything is quiet, most of my vampire kin still asleep, undoubtedly worn out from the night's revelries. I see no one as I hurry toward the library, but as soon as I step into the doorway—as soon as I see *him*—I pause.

He's all right. He's safe. No hungry vampire lingers over his shoulder. He sits at a desk with books spread before him, a teacup near his elbow. He reads with his tongue between his teeth. Despite his age, he might as well be a schoolboy.

"He spent thirty minutes teaching one of the servants how to make tea."

Felipe can be so quiet, like a little mouse in the house. He stands right next to me in one of his patterned waistcoats and lacey shirts. Fashion may have changed over the past hundred years, but Felipe has not.

He looks into the library, looks at Edmund. "He's very particular, isn't he? You can tell by the cut of his suits. The way he smells like a clean shave every day and the way he takes his tea. I'd suspect him of being a spoiled little brat if not for his hands." Felipe points to his own palm. "What kind of spoiled brat has calluses?"

"You've been paying attention."

Felipe crosses his arms and leans against the doorframe. "Of course, I have. You return from exile with a pet that you not only appear to love but also hope to make one of our own. You've never kept pets for long, Andrew, so I intend to find what makes him different."

"Everything is different."

"Yes." He sighs. "Everything has been different since you left. Everything has been boring. Bore-bore-boring."

I smile. "Missed me then?"

"Terribly. No one's up for a good murder anymore, not since your exile. We're all tiptoeing around like ballerinas because heaven forbid anyone upset her royal highness."

I've never heard him talk about Michelle with such disdain. Perhaps things are changing between them.

He elbows me. "How about you? You must miss a good murder."

I consider all the cannibals I slaughtered on the island. "No."

"Oh, it's only your dear Felipe. Be honest."

I glance back at Edmund. "I'm not like that anymore."

Felipe follows my gaze. "All it took was one handsome human, and you've changed completely? Doubtful. I know. We should have one of our contests. See which of us can seduce some pretty thing first and kill it."

I grind my teeth together. "If I get exiled again, you realize Edmund would demand to go with me. You would never have him to yourself."

Felipe laughs, which catches Edmund's attention. His head springs up from where he sits. I lift my hand in a gesture that says wait a moment.

"I don't want your precious human. He seems like too much work. Fucking him must be like trying to fuck a wild horse. I'm saying I just get bored." His lip curls. "We're supposed to be so good. We've forgotten what it is to be bad."

"Maybe that's a decent thing."

He sneers. "Go on. I'm tired of you already."

I chuckle at his obvious disgust, but I do go. I walk into the library and right up to Edmund. I kiss him on the top of the head and rest my hands on his shoulders. "I didn't like waking up without you."

He looks up at me, the crown of his head pressed into my stomach. From where I stand, I can just see down the edge of his collar to my teeth marks, surrounded by bruises from when I bit hard. "I couldn't sleep knowing this was here."

"You won't come here without me."

His forehead wrinkles. "Why not?"

I squeeze his shoulders. He leans his head forward and hums encouragement. "I don't want you alone with other vampires. I don't trust my kind."

"No one's going to hurt me, Andrew. Michelle said so."

I stop squeezing his shoulders. "When did she say so?"

"This morning. She helped me find the books that might be of most interest." He sighs. "Stop worrying. According to Michelle, the entire coven knows who I am, thanks to us being seen together last night. No one's going to fuck with the infamous Andrew's paramour."

I try not to smile.

"Hey." He grabs my hand. "Sit down. Come on."

I droop into a seat.

"I've barely begun to learn vampire history. From what I can tell, many of your stories go back over a thousand years. But..." He grabs for a book, pages thin as a spiderweb. "I think I found *your* Elder. You never told me his name, but—"

"Selwyn."

Edmund grins. "Yes. He sired quite a few vampires in the British Isles before his death. In a way, you're actually English."

Considering I died fighting the bastards, I scoff. "I am in no way English."

Edmund laughs. "You're shtupping an Englishman. Don't sound so affronted."

"Does it say what happened to Selwyn?"

"Yes." He points to the book. "His suicide is actually well documented. He requested a number of his immortal children tear him limb from limb and burn his body." He pauses. "Shit, you weren't there, were you?"

"Uh, no."

He winces. "Horrible mess, I would imagine. As far as other Elders, some have definitely killed themselves. Others have, according to the Latin, 'gone to sleep.'"

"You know Latin?"

"Of course. Don't you?"

I stare at him.

"Heathen," he mutters. "The problem with all these Elders going to sleep is that the books don't say where. I know I'm getting ahead of myself. I've only been here for three hours. There are hundreds of other books to go through, so I can't make an educated conclusion yet, but perhaps an Elder has never been found because no one's ever looked—not really. We have to hope that. Otherwise, you'll have to watch me grow old."

When I notice his knee trembling beneath the table, I put my hand on it. "Are you all right?"

He gazes at the floor. "You said something to me once. You said vampires never mate for life, so how do you know you want that with me? Going to all this trouble to find an Elder... Are you sure you desire this, Andrew?"

I open my mouth to speak, but he cuts me off.

"I'm awful when I want to be. Cruel even. I pout and throw tantrums. I have dark moods. I can never stay still for long. You look favorably upon me now because you haven't seen that side of me yet, but if you're with me for any amount of time, you will. You might not like it."

I take his hand and kiss it. "I'll love every part of you."

He shakes his head. "That's easy to say now."

"Yes. It is."

He smiles. "Fine, you lovesick sod, but I warned you."

"I should warn you: I used to be very fond of killing people."

"Me too," he whispers and says quickly, as if to erase his words, "I think I need more tea."

It's hard to imagine him with blood on his hands, my beautiful sailor, especially looking the way he does here in New Orleans with his clean shave, oiled hair, and tailored suit. He is the very picture of a proper gentleman, but I think I've glimpsed the killer. Once, on the island, he attacked me. He has fists that feel like stone, and when on the defensive, I swear his storm-gray eyes turn the color of moonless midnight. He is a man who would kill to survive, and I know he has. He's told me as much. But I didn't know he enjoyed it.

In a clumsy effort to change the subject, he says, "Michelle suggested we move in here."

"I figured she might."

He stretches his arms above his head and yawns. "She said your old room isn't big enough for the two of us, but there's an empty space on the third floor. What do you think? It would be helpful for me to be closer to the library."

"All right."

He eyes me. "You're not going against me on this? I expected an argument."

I shrug. "It makes sense to be closer, and I'd rather not pay for room and board anymore."

"In my letter to my mother, I asked her to send money."

"Money is no issue. The coven has more than we'll ever spend. It would just be nice to make a home with you."

He leans forward and brushes his nose against mine. He smells of shaving cream and bergamot. "Being near you makes me very happy."

I tangle my fingers in the back of his hair. "I hope to always make you happy."

He tilts his head and kisses me, his face soft against mine. Then, he leans back and stares forlornly at his empty teacup. "All right. Be gone with you. You're a terrible distraction."

I ruffle his hair as I walk past. He squawks and bats at my hands before turning back to his work.

Chapter Six

AFTER DAYS SPENT with Edmund barely speaking, only reading, he demands we go back to Gallatin Street to the famed brothel with the red door. On the walk there, he announces he's going to get drunk, and he does deserve it. He's been working so hard, combing through Michelle's texts. He comes to bed at night exhausted. He's impatient, too, already scared he'll never find what we seek—never find evidence of an Elder. His impatience is that of a child, and even though he's irritable, I find some satisfaction in wrapping my pouting darling in my arms until he smiles.

He smiles now as we walk down stinking side streets and past flickering gas lamps. An over-rouged woman calls to us from the shadows. I tip my hat but keep moving. Down the next alley, we hear the coarse sound of grunting as a man apparently achieves release with a whore.

Edmund sidesteps a pile of horseshit. "I do love your city," he says without a hint of irony.

"I am glad."

Up ahead, the red door beckons us ever closer. I perform the secret knock, and the door opens wide. As soon as we step into the entrance, I hear May's Irish brogue. She shouts at a tall man in a bowler hat—and he shouts back. Something about services not rendered.

"I wouldn't raise your voice to such a fine lady, sir," Edmund says. Even I'm taken aback by the simmering menace in his tone.

The tall man takes in the appearance of my lover—the pretty face and bespoke suit—and apparently finds him lacking. "I won't be taking advice from a limey prick such as you."

Edmund hums, a sound barely heard over the music from the bar. "I'd leave if it were me." He takes his bottom lip between his teeth and chews while staring the man down.

"You heard him," May says.

I swear the room gets colder, due to nothing more than Edmund's glare. He's not a small man when in a good mood, but in this unfamiliar defensive posture, I swear he's grown four inches. It's his calm stillness that rattles my spine. His posture is that of a coiled snake.

Apparently, the tall man isn't fixing for a brawl, or worse, because he waves his hand and stomps out the door. Over his shoulder, he yells, "To hell with you!"

May rests a hand on Edmund's chest. "That was impressive. Need a job?"

He laughs. "I only fight for fun, not money."

"Shame." She extends a gloved hand to me. "Andrew, tell him he should be my bodyguard."

"Absolutely not. Imagine all the trouble he'd get into without me." I smile and shove him toward the bar.

May lingers in the doorway to talk to her doorman—probably forbidding the tall man from reentry. As always, the whites of her eyes seem to glow in contrast to the abundance of kohl. Her skirts are made of layer upon layer of black lace.

I order us a bottle of whiskey at the bar. Patrons of all sexes, ages, and shapes float among us. A half-naked man is being fellated on a dark-red couch. We toast, and whereas I sip mine, Edmund shoots his with a wince.

"You can be terrifying when you want to be."

"Who, me?" His gaze flies around the bar from one decadent thing to another. "I was just playing."

I see Danys before Edmund does. The handsome Haitian holds his finger to his mouth, begging me to stay silent, as he creeps up behind my sailor, puts his arm around his shoulder, and kisses the side of his neck. Edmund freezes for but a moment before recognizing the shaved head and dark skin.

Edmund frowns. "Why are you wearing so many clothes?"

Danys laughs his wide-mouthed guffaw. "I'm not working tonight, *dous mwen*. I came down for a drink, and then, I go to a card game."

"Card game?" He glances at me. "What kind of card game?"

Danys pours himself some of our whiskey and drinks. "Vingt-et-un. You play?"

"Fuck, yes." He grabs onto Danys's jacket and gives him a shake. "Andrew, can we?"

His fervor lights a spark in my chest. "I don't play, but I will gladly watch you."

May is, as expected, disappointed to see us go and spend our money elsewhere, but I promise her we'll be back another time. By the time I say my goodbyes to the madam, Edmund and Danys already walk down the alley. Their conversation is animated and loud. I marvel at their comfortable familiarity and spare a thought for Edmund's lost African lover, Samuel, dead in the shipwreck. Perhaps Danys is a welcome reminder of things gone.

As expected, we do not go to some fancy gaming hall with women in fine dresses and men sipping champagne. If the Gallatin brothel was a bit of dimness, we now wander into full dark. I'm glad Edmund chose to dress down this evening. He left the fancy silk vests at the coven and wore, instead, simple black. He won't stand out—as much—but with his rose petal mouth, he's sure to be labeled a mark.

The bar is long and thin and filled with smoke. Edmund walks on ahead as Danys puts his hand on my shoulder, brown eyes shining in the light of a passing match. We move through a boisterous crowd, singing some song in Italian, and head into a room where everything is quieter but just as smoky.

I spot the round table in the very back where large men, hats down low, watch cards flipped on a beer-soaked tabletop. Edmund is ready to join them, but both Danys and I take hold of his upper arms and tug him back.

"Wait," Danys hisses.

"Why? I came here to play cards."

It's obvious Danys is looking at the card table and trying to appear as though he's not looking at the card table. "That's Jimmy Fitz. Didn't even know he was back in town. You aren't playing against him."

Danys tries to shove Edmund onto a bar stool, but Edmund resists. "And why not?"

"He's a dirty card player. He'll kill you if you win."

"Then, I won't win."

"Edmund," I mutter.

"I'll be nice, I promise." He smiles at me, and his eyes have that bright, burning quality they get when he talks about poisonous tree frogs.

I sigh. "Go ahead."

I can tell he wants to kiss me, but thank Christ he doesn't. In this crowd, we'd be murdered on site. Instead, he punches me lightly in the chest before spinning around and sauntering up to that card table as though he owns it. It takes about ten seconds of small talk before they welcome him to a chair, probably because he resembles an overgrown child with daddy's billfold.

Danys hands me a beer. I try not to consider the mug's filth. We lean against the bar together, arms touching.

"*Li fache*, yeah?"

He's just asked me if Edmund is mad, and although Edmund has deemed himself such, I don't think he's actually out of his mind. "He's wild," I say.

"A wild animal." Danys nods. "And not just between the sheets. Where did you find him?"

"Far away from here."

"You're different, you know, from before you went away." He wipes the back of his mouth with his hand. "*Plis dou*." More gentle. "And your eyes, they don't roam the room like you're searching for something."

That's because I'm well fed and sated on the blood of my lover. I no longer go out every night hunting for fresh meat because I have it at home.

Of course Danys would notice the change. Although I never drank from him, he observed me for years at the brothel before I was sent away.

"Maybe you find what you been looking for," he says. "That wild thing over there." He gestures toward the card players. "You always had something dark about you, Andrew. Visiting your bed was like visiting the legends of my home country." He gazes up at me from below thick lashes. "I think your wild thing needs light, though. Don't smother him in dark."

I swallow around the worried lump in my throat. "That's funny coming from you."

He lowers his brows in confusion.

"You'd love to smother Edmund in your dark."

The loud burst of Danys's laughter almost covers the sound of shouts but not quite. There's a flurry of movement at the card table, so I move. I shove men out of the way as the table is flipped and hats fly, but there's a wall of drunken humanity watching the fight and blocking my way. From where I struggle, I see a man with red hair—I assume Jimmy Fitz—has a knife out. He slashes at Edmund, but Edmund, as always, is grace and speed.

I'm too busy fighting the crowd to watch what's happening, but by the time I finally break through the wall of shouting men, Jimmy no longer holds his knife. Edmund somehow holds his knife, and Jimmy's shirt is stained with blood. I smell iron and rage.

Someone shoves me from behind. It's Danys. He pushes me forward and continues to push. "Get him out of here!" he shouts. "There's a back door. Go!"

I drag Edmund out into a humid night. Together, we run down alleys filled with stinking garbage and eventually find our way back to a main street. Once there, I keep us moving. I don't stop until we're a couple blocks away. Then, I pull Edmund into an alley and hurl him against a wall. The knife in his hand falls silently into a puddle, taking with it the scent of sour blood.

I curl my fists into the front of his coat. "What were you thinking?"

"It's not my fault he was a sore loser."

I smack him hard. So hard that his head spins left.

He opens and closes his jaw. "What the fuck, Andrew?"

"Don't you understand? Now that I've found you, I can't lose you."

He studies me like I'm a puzzle to be solved.

"You are not invincible yet. Someday, you'll be like me, but until that day, you are breakable. You could be killed. A knife could kill you. I realize you've lived a very foolhardy life until now, but for my sake, please, leave that part of you behind until..." I put my hand on his cheek, still warm from the crack of my palm. "I can't be without you."

He wraps me in his arms and begins kissing any skin he can reach. "I'm sorry. I'm sorry. I'll do better."

I hug him and feel his heartbeat against my chest as he continues to whisper apologies into the night.

BACK IN OUR grand, third story room at the coven, Edmund's lovemaking is desperate, as if he proves his dedication to me with his body. I try to comfort him, slow him, but he shoves my hands away. I let him exorcise his demons via the medium of my flesh.

After, he's quiet. We lay side by side, both staring at the thick, red canopy above our bed. We've only lived here for a few days, but I've done my best to make it feel like a sort of home. Our clothes hang in a closet or hide in drawers. Edmund leaves his empty teacups everywhere. The large windows overlook the estate's back garden. From way up here, we can't hear the parties below. I hear only his breath, still labored from the way he rode me until I saw white.

When I reach out to touch him, he sits up suddenly and puts his arms around his knees. I don't move. I simply observe the way his shoulders curl forward. He pushes sweaty, dark hair off his forehead. "I'm sorry."

"You've apologized enough," I say.

He shakes his head. "No. I really haven't." A muscle in the side of his jaw jumps. "I went in there tonight spoiling for a fight. I wanted that rush of blood through my veins. I've always been drawn to it, even as a society boy in London. I've always been smart, but I haven't always been tall. I knew how to spot sore points, so I would pick fights with the biggest boys in school—talk about their mothers or their fathers or their sisters—and see how long I could last."

I sit up but still don't reach to touch him. "Edmund, I've always known you love danger."

"Yes, but I need to grow accustomed to loving you *more*. I've never had someone care enough to worry for me."

"What about your mother?"

He shakes his head again. "No, in that relationship I've always been selfish. She has always worried, and I have never given a damn. Her distaste for my lifestyle has been a wedge between us my entire life."

"And Samuel? Your paramour at sea?"

He wraps his hands around his elbows as if trying to hug himself. "I think he loved me, yes, but many men have loved me. None of them ever made me feel as you do."

"And how do I make you feel?"

"Like I deserve to be loved." A drop of water falls from the edge of his chin, which is when I realize he's crying. I lean farther forward to see his eyes are red.

Now, I touch him. I pull him to me by the shoulders until he melts against me and shoves his face into my chest. His sobs are silent; their only evidence is the occasional tremor that runs down his spine. I wait out this unexpected eruption of pain and know it's about so much more than a knife fight, my earlier anger, even the loss of

Samuel. I suspect Edmund's fit has been waiting to happen for years.

For the first time, I wonder how much of my sailor's confidence is an act. He's spent his entire adult life on grand ships, chasing new discoveries, new species—but what if he has not been the pursuer but the pursued? How many years has he spent running away from himself?

"Edmund?" I push him back just far enough so I can see his eyes, puffy and desperate. I try to think, try to put the proper words together. "I love everything about you. I love that you were the little boy who started fights. I love that you love poisonous dart frogs. I love the way you fuck."

He smiles a little at that.

"But about tonight... You made me angry. You made me afraid. That doesn't mean you lost my love and have to earn it back. I'll never stop loving you, no matter what you do." I take his wet face in my hands. "Do you understand that?"

"No. God, no. Sounds absolutely insane. Or idiotic."

I laugh and try to kiss him.

He turns his face away. "I'm disgusting. Jesus, at least let me wipe my face." He uses the edge of the bedclothes. When he again settles himself in front of me, he stares at his hands. "It's reckless to love me no matter what."

"Well, you are reckless, so maybe you're rubbing off on me."

"God help us."

I lift his chin and make him look at me. "You are not as mad as you think you are."

"I don't know. I am in love with a murdering monster who needs blood to live."

I tilt my head. "When you put it that way."

"I haven't found anything promising in Michelle's books, you know. Not yet anyway."

I tell him, "I know, but you will."

"You realize the list of people who've ever had faith in me is very short. I'm sometimes amazed that you do."

"I have faith in very little, but my faith in you is endless."

He falls onto his back in bed, dark hair spread on the pillow. I rest at his side and tickle the center of his chest with my fingers.

"Not there," he whispers.

I chuckle because he knows me so well. Ever since he told me he had a ticklish spot I've yet to find, I have been seeking it out.

"Andrew, would you…"

I look up at him, and his lips are wet as though he's been biting them.

"What do you need, my love?"

"Your mouth." The shy way he voices his request is so out of character, my eyebrows shoot up. As if I would ever say no.

He is hot and heavy against my tongue. Within minutes, he comes silently on a slight intake of breath with both his hands tangled in my hair. He drags me up and sighs into my mouth as we kiss. I blanket his body under mine and fall asleep.

It's hours before one of his nightmares, and the way he stares at me in the dark—clings to me—forces me to conclude this was not a dream of the sea. This was something about me. I kiss his face until he calms and dozes off, but I don't sleep.

Danys worried about me smothering Edmund in my darkness, but I'm beginning to think my darkness is the lesser of our two.

Chapter Seven

I WAKE UP to something hitting me gently in the face over and over. It's a rhythmic, focused motion, right on the tip of my nose. Eyes still closed, I smell the familiar scent of my darling—and his tea. I grab Edmund's finger before it again taps me on the nose, open my eyes, and find him grinning above me in the morning sun.

He chuckles and lifts a teacup to his lips. He sips and tries to poke me in the nose again, so I hold tighter to his hand. "What's gotten into you?" I ask.

Seated on the edge of our bed in what appears to be nothing but a blue silk dressing gown I bought him, he looks away. "I'm feeling very...needy this morning."

"Needy?"

"The need to be close to you."

I roll onto my back and stretch. "You had one of your dreams last night."

"Sorry."

"You have said 'sorry' more times in the last eight hours than over the duration of our entire relationship."

He clears his throat. "Fine. Not sorry then."

"Tell me you weren't walking around a house full of vampires in nothing but that." I eye the thin fabric that coats his shoulders, chest, and thighs like melting caramel.

"No. Michelle brought it up."

I blink at him and lift onto my elbows. "Michelle now brings you tea in the morning?"

He leans forward and sets what I assume is now an empty teacup on the table by our bed. He runs his hands through his sleep-mussed hair. "No. Well, this morning, yes, but she wanted to invite us to a party tonight. She's having one of her to-dos in the ballroom."

I sit up and brush his wild hair with my fingers. "You can call it what it is."

"Fine. An orgy. It just sounds so *Arabian Nights*." Eyes closed, he teeters into my touch.

"I don't want you in the library today."

"I need to work." He sounds half asleep again.

I move even closer and suck his earlobe into my mouth. His shoulders jump at the unexpected caress. "You need water," I say.

"If you think I'm stepping even one toe into that disgusting excuse you Southern chaps call a harbor, you've lost your damn mind."

"No." I reach beneath the thin fabric that covers his lap. "I have a much better idea."

I TAKE MY sailor to the only public bathhouse in New Orleans, an expensive men-only affair the coven has paid into for years. Much like Edmund, we are a bit of a vain lot.

Earlier, while I spoke to the young man at the front desk, I watched my beloved peer curiously down the white-painted hallway. Then, as soon as he even *sensed* steam, his entire face lit up. As we were led down the hall, he tapped his hand against mine in silent—and socially appropriate—thanks and hasn't stopped smiling since.

I'm sitting on the edge of a steaming tub the size of a large room when he surfaces in front of me, black hair wet and dripping in his eyes.

"I've found fucking heaven," he says.

A threesome of towel-wrapped older gentlemen scoffs at his language, but I smile around my cigar. I haven't smoked a cigar in years.

"This"—he floats up onto his back, naked as the day he was born—"is perfect."

"The heat feels oddly familiar," I say.

He laughs that loud, easy giggle of his. The strange melancholy of last night and this morning is gone. "God, this is just like that bloody island, isn't it? Except no one's trying to kill me." He picks his head up. "It's a bit Grecian, though, isn't it? I thought New Orleans was supposed to be a modern city."

"Perhaps we're showing how modern we are by paying homage to the classics." I blow pungent smoke toward the ceiling and admire the marble columns and frescos of naked cherubs.

He dunks under and up again before asking, "Aren't you going to get in?"

"In time."

He nods to my hand. "I didn't even know you smoked those things."

"I haven't. In a while."

He smiles knowingly before doing an underwater flip and tumble like a rather large, mad fish. Again, he floats on his back, but this time, looks down at himself. "I am getting fat, aren't I?"

"I've never heard something more ridiculous in my whole life." I kick my feet back and forth beneath the warm, clear water.

"Is there boxing in New Orleans?"

"Absolutely not."

His gray eyes shine. "There is. There must be. Modern city and all."

"You are not boxing."

"Come on, Andrew. It's not a bar fight. There are rules. Besides, I'm good."

"I recall." I remember catching his fist in the face on the island once. It felt like a hammer to my skull. Add to that the graceful way he moves and his height, and he would be a boxing phenom exemplar. I'm relieved to have a towel across my waist, because the thought of him beating another man to a pulp is oddly arousing. Damn it, I'm beginning to think Edmund doing just about anything would arouse me.

He swims close, but before daring to touch me in public, reaches for the bar of sandalwood soap at my side. He lathers up his hands before attacking his hair. "Are we attending the party tonight?"

I swallow smoke. "If it pleases you."

"It might indeed." He ducks his head underwater, and I don't worry when he's down there for a while. I know my sailor can hold his breath for some time. From below the surface, he gives my toe a playful pull before standing and shaking his head like a dog.

Once we're both sufficiently clean, I watch him shave in the changing room. Watching the man run a sharp blade up his neck is truly an art form. He's meticulous about it, his daily routine.

Back at the coven, florists and caterers rush in and out. Edmund and I hide in our room. There is no sex between us, as the early afternoon turns to late. We rest together above the sheets, touching, kissing occasionally.

Edmund reads not research but some penny dreadful we picked up from a street vendor on our way home. It doesn't surprise me that Edmund enjoys sensational stories, but it does surprise me that I would be content to merely be near my lover, doing absolutely nothing.

It's true we aren't exactly intimate, and yet, this is the most intimate thing I have ever done. I sit and watch Edmund read. He laughs and recites particularly preposterous scenes until I'm laughing too. For years, I lived on an island, surrounded by solitude, but being with Edmund makes me think I've actually been alone for hundreds of years—surrounded by people but separate, literally immersed in flesh but self-contained.

Now, I am no longer alone. More than that, I no longer seek something bigger, better, *more*. With my head resting on Edmund's stomach, listening to his breath, I am complete.

I tell him I love him.

He tickles my ear with his fingertips. "Love you more."

Chapter Eight

I HEAR THE music before I see a single soul. It wafts up the steps like the buttery scent of cooked crawfish. A skilled violinist plays a shrewd gypsy tune as Edmund and I reach the ballroom. Tall, golden candelabras are strategically placed along walls and in corners where they won't be knocked over. Above us, the large chandelier glows and casts attractive shadows on the bodies below, already writhing in low beds and on silken pillows. Vampires look up when we enter. They pause in their sex and their feeding to inspect Edmund, whose silver vest catches the light and reflects back their lust.

Even my cocky companion ducks under the collective gaze and runs a hand through his oiled black hair. "Jesus," he whispers. "I feel like a prime cut of meat."

I put my hand solidly on his shoulder. "That's because you are."

"Cute."

Michelle waves from her couch at the far end of the room. She smiles with Felipe at her side. I notice his dark eyes never waver from Edmund, so I put my hand on the back of my sailor's neck and squeeze as if to tell the entire room, *Mine.*

Before we even reach them, Edmund grabs a glass of champagne from a passing tray and finishes the entire thing. He reaches for a second as his eyes wander. No longer the target of so many heated gazes, he becomes the observer. He elbows me and points to that lovely young thing from last time—the boy with the red hair—currently being pleasured by two male vampires in the center of a purple satin bed. Edmund tugs at his collar, and the gesture is almost comical. If he wore a cravat, it would have been the ideal moment to remove it and complain of the heat.

Michelle lifts her hand to Edmund when we approach, and he bows to kiss it. "You smell delicious," she says. "Trip to the bathhouse today?"

Felipe glares up at me. "And I wasn't invited?"

It's as if they've stepped out of a French Renaissance painting, covered in cascading fabrics that must weigh a ton. Michelle's emerald corset nearly bares her pale breasts, and I could almost fit one hand around her waist. Felipe wears his characteristic lace cuffs and a high-necked, multicolored coat that probably belonged to a long-dead king. I watch Edmund's eyes take them in, but he doesn't say anything. He doesn't have to for me to know what he's thinking. They look ridiculous to him because he is modern and minimalist. My darling doesn't even wear the traditional breeches or cravat. The dark green suit he now dons is the most color I've ever seen on his body, so I'm sure their old school decadence amuses him.

"Sit with me and tell me all about your day." I'd forgotten how none of her phrases sound like mere suggestions.

Edmund takes his place at Michelle's side, and I watch them chat.

Felipe stands and steps so close our arms touch. "I want to kill him."

I smirk. "No, you don't."

"No, I don't, but he makes me mad with jealousy. She hasn't acted like a tittering school girl in centuries, and then, your pretty Englishman shows up." He waves toward them but eyes the orgy behind us. "Will you fuck him in front of me? I want to see him dumb and melting with pleasure."

"I'm sure you would."

Felipe rolls his eyes. "You are no fun." He spins and lands heavily beside Michelle, surely in an effort to get her attention.

I smile when he fails and sit next to Edmund, whose hand goes to my knee and squeezes. I intertwine our fingers and reach for a passing glass of absinthe just as Edmund says, "It was a pleasure. I haven't been to a proper bathhouse in ages."

"Surprising," Felipe shouts, "considering you obviously come from money."

"Quite a lot of it actually," Edmund says. "Let me guess, you didn't come from money, so you hate me for my privilege."

"Oh, I could never hate you, Edmund."

He chuckles. "I somehow doubt that."

Felipe crosses his legs violently. "What was it, then? Some kind of luxury ship that washed up on Andrew's island?"

Edmund glances at me, amused. "No."

There's a long pause between us, our silence filled with violin, joined by cello.

"Well?" Felipe asks. "Do tell. How on earth did you end up shipwrecked? Ah, it has to do with your calluses, doesn't it?"

Edmund looks down at his hand and up at me. "How did he know I have calluses?"

Michelle takes Edmund's hand I'm not holding and turns it over, running her small fingers over his palms. "You have the hands of a working man. But you certainly don't resemble one."

I sip at the herbaceous bouquet in my hand. "Edmund is a traveling scientist. A naturalist. He has spanned the globe discovering new species."

He nods. "But, to achieve that, I couldn't just sit on my ass. I had to, um, well, do my part on board." He shrugs. "I've spent most of my adult life on ships. God, the last ten years." He squeezes my hand. "That is a long time."

"It won't seem so long when you're one of us," Michelle says.

Felipe snaps at a passing servant and grabs a glass from her tray. "I suppose you must have had a lover on this ship of yours."

Edmund clicks his tongue. "Do you practice saying the rudest things possible?"

I snort into my drink, and even Michelle tries to hide a smile.

Felipe huffs, stands, and walks away with his head held high, which allows me the freedom to break down laughing.

Edmund watches him go. "He's going to murder me, isn't he?"

Michelle reclines into the empty space Felipe left. She carefully pats at her white hair, piled high on her head and decorated with pearls. "He's fond of you, actually."

"My God, why? That man brings out the worst in me."

"I think he likes your worst." I kiss the side of his neck.

"But you did have lovers over the course of your travels, didn't you?"

Edmund's eyes move toward the writhing bodies around us. "Of course."

"Anyone special?"

Based on the downturn of his lips, Edmund doesn't like this question. His eyes flit about the room, and he squeezes my hand tightly. "No one like Andrew."

I catch Michelle's gaze, and she stares at me as though pleased. She enjoys his discomfort, possibly because she's never seen it before. I admit, Edmund uncomfortable is novel, a deviation from the norm when the relentless of day-to-day can be disastrous for an immortal—when boredom can be an ultimate cause of death.

He stands suddenly, our hands still entwined, and pulls me to my feet. He slides his jacket from his shoulders and hands it to Michelle. "Don't spill anything on it, love." He winks at her and again takes my hand, dragging me forward.

"Edmund, what—"

"Finish your drink." He turns to face me, smiling, and walks backward through pillows and beds.

I shoot the last of the absinthe and drop my glass on the floor when his fingers start unbuttoning his vest. I wrap my hand around those fingers and squeeze. "No."

His tongue pokes out to wet his bottom lip. "Yes."

"No. Felipe, in particular, does not deserve to see you."

He shakes his head. "No sex. But you know how I feel about stains."

God, he wants me to feed. In front of so many monsters, he wants me to open his vein. Already, people have paused in their ministrations to watch as Edmund steps back and continues unbuttoning his vest. He turns away and wanders toward an empty bed, and I am quick to follow.

I watch him tug the tails of his white shirt from his trousers as he moves. I can't see his fingers, but they must move quickly, because a moment later, his bare shoulders are revealed, then his muscular back and the scar—that gorgeous scar. Humans and vampires alike sit up straighter to get a look at the thing, and I have never been thankful for the existence of electric eels until now. Edmund's scar adds so much to his allure. He is a pretty thing with an ugly mark that is not ugly thanks to the pride with which he wears it. He once said he has a taste for the unique, but I don't think he's ever realized he is more unusual than most.

He sets his shirt and vest on a bed covered in red fabric and turns to face me, broad chest bared for all to see. He tugs me forward with his hands on my lapels and whispers, "Show them I belong to you."

My knees tremble a bit as I hold his hips in my grip. I see Felipe lingering a few beds over, blood on his chin. The human woman at his side dozes, forgotten, as my old friend has eyes for nobody and nothing but my sailor. Behind me, I can feel Michelle's violet eyes on us. Half the room is waiting to see what I'll do—me, the monster, sent away for murder. It's hard to tell if they're more curious about my beloved or me.

He doesn't wait for my permission before falling back onto the bed, and like that red vest he wears, the bed complements every inch of him, from his black curls to his pale chest to the thin trail of dark hair on his stomach that disappears ever so teasingly down the front of his trousers. He smirks as he backs up and rests, stretched out down the center of silk.

Based on the hunger around us, if I don't crawl on top of him, someone else will—and soon. I cage him in with my knees and elbows, fingertips caressing his face. "You are so beautiful."

He grins, his breath coming faster. "You are a giant beast of a man, and I adore you."

I laugh, my concern over "performing" forgotten. A crowd of people might surround us, but Edmund is all I see, especially when he's like this, cheeks rosy and parted lips so wanting. I lean down and kiss him, and he moans beneath me. I roll one of his nipples between my thumb and forefinger and tug his hair back, licking up his exposed neck. There is a chorus of pleased sounds from beds close by, but I'm not even near finished. Edmund wanted to prove my ownership over him. I'll prove it and then some if it means no bloodsucker will even hazard to come near the wild creature between my legs.

I unbutton the top of his pants, and this simple movement rouses him. He halts my hand. "I thought we said no sex."

I suck his bottom lip into my mouth. "I want to touch you. No one will see."

He lifts an eyebrow.

"No one will see *all* of you." When my fingers tease the tip of his cock, he relinquishes control and melts back onto the pillows.

I reach my hand farther into his trousers and rub my palm up and down his shaft.

He says, "Fuck," on an exhale, and it comes out as three syllables. His hips roll up to meet me as I suck on his neck.

Around us, the room is silent but for music. It seems everyone wants to watch Edmund fall apart. His chest heaves as I increase the pressure and pace. He nuzzles his face against mine, seeking my mouth, so I give it to him. Instead of clutching to the red blankets, his fingers wrap around my head and grip my hair. His tongue explores my mouth, and I'm now somehow palming him and rutting against him at the same time. I'm fairly certain my cock could tear through fabric at this point.

He pushes my face away and stares up at me, mouth wet, and I know what he wants. I nod and kiss behind his ear, across his jaw. My fangs spring free, and I bury my teeth in the soft skin where marks still linger from my last feeding. At the intrusion, Edmund's chest surges up below me, and he makes a sound like a sadist who's been punched. His blood pours down my throat, and it's as I told him once before: feeding from humans is so much better than feeding from animals. I swallow bits of his passion, digest tiny tastes of the bright light inside him. He pants my name and claws at me. I pull back in time to see the round shape of his mouth as he comes. I wipe the blood from my mouth before kissing his trembling lips.

In the moment it takes for Edmund to return to himself, I notice bodies have started moving around us, rutting and fucking now that our show is over. At some point, Michelle joined Felipe on his bed, but they do not move. They cling to each other and look not at me but at Edmund, limp and lovely beneath me, his stomach stained with his own seed. I use my tongue to lick him clean.

When I glance up, he watches me. He pulls me on top of him as though hiding from prying eyes. I drink in the scent of him, the feel of his warm skin.

"Did I do all right?" he mutters.

I lick the wound on his neck. "You're like Helen of Troy. You could start eternal wars over the right to touch your body."

He shakes with silent laughter. "I demand wine and warm, soft, female bodies all over me."

My startled guffaw breaks the tender moment. I lean back and rest my weight on his thighs. "Then, you shall have both."

He remains shirtless—no need to get a drop of blood on his white collar—as I walk the ballroom, seeking out willing young ladies to fulfill Edmund's request. It takes all of thirty seconds. They rush to him and curl themselves around his body, plying him with champagne and shy giggles. I pace in an effort to cool my loins. I'll have him later in our private quarters, but for now, I allow him anything he wants. I feel a new sense of ownership over my sailor, an ownership he bestowed upon me in front of my entire coven. I will cradle my prized possession with a benevolent hand.

Back on her couch, Michelle fondles a buxom beauty in nothing but her undergarments. I feel Felipe's approach, and although I expect some scathing remark, he says, simply, "I've never seen something so fuckable in my entire life," and walks away.

Chapter Nine

I WAKE TO a large child jumping on me. Or, no, it's Edmund, but the way he's carrying on, he might as well be five years old. My head aches with all the booze and blood from the night before, and our bed reeks of sex. I mutter and bat at him. I try to burrow deeper into my pillow, but he pulls on my shoulder.

"Have mercy, man," I growl.

"Wake up!" He shouts but doesn't sound panicked. He's not in danger, so I try to ignore him until he pulls my hair.

Well, that does it. Still high on Edmund's taste, I move faster than human eyes can see and immobilize him.

He freezes. "Are you hard?"

I nestle my nose behind his ear. "I have you pinned beneath me with my arm around your throat. Of course, I'm hard."

"Not now, Andrew!" He tries to push back against me, but it's a losing battle. "You need to come to the library."

"Even God is still sleeping, Edmund. What on earth would get me out of bed at this evil hour?"

"I think I found an Elder, you fucking idiot. Now, let me up!"

He drags me from bed and drapes a dressing gown around my shoulders before latching onto my wrist and tugging me out the door and down the stairs. The house, as expected, is silent but for a few quiet sounds from below in the kitchen. The scent of several sleeping bodies wafts from the ballroom, along with the strong stench of stale alcohol and all manner of bodily fluids. It's almost enough to make me retch.

We make it to the library, and I am flabbergasted to find Michelle and Felipe already waiting, although they seem about as awake as me. They're both in their nightclothes, artful hair askew.

Felipe rubs his eyes. "You should keep him on a leash."

"I'm seriously considering it."

Edmund shoves me into a high-backed chair, ignoring us both, and I finally get a look at him. He's half-dressed in trousers and his crisp, white shirt. His hair is sleep-addled, and there's a mouth-shaped bruise just below his jaw. I notice a smattering of teacups arranged between open books.

"Edmund, how long have you been awake?"

"A few hours." He moves some of his research around, his gestures twitchy, agitated.

I stand and put my hands on his shoulders. "Hey."

He looks up at me, eyes bright.

"I practically broke furniture fucking you last night," I whisper, "and probably drank more of your blood than I should have. You need to be resting."

"I know." He taps the side of his head. "My brain, Andrew." He leans closer in an effort to find a modicum of privacy with Michelle and Felipe staring. "It's stagnating. Hasn't had any proper challenge in weeks. It starts to move too fast, and I can't sleep. Does that make sense?"

I nod. "You're too smart for your own good."

"It's been suggested. Part of my so-called *madness*." He says the word with disgust, and even I wince at the thought of the nasty things they may have said about him in London, back when he was too young to defend himself.

"But, now, you've found something."

He grins and turns away from me. "Yes. Sit."

I do as told.

He stands before us as though giving a performance. "I've read, I don't know, three dozen books, and none of them gave me anything. Nothing made any sense. Then, this." He points to a small, handwritten book on the desk. "It's the journal of a sailor, which seems a bit apropos considering I'm a sailor, as well, or maybe just meant to be, if you believe in that sort of thing."

I love when he gets like this, hyperactively rambling and ridiculous.

"The journal talks about a monster. Michelle, you knew this man wrote of an Elder, which is why this book is part of your library. You recognized what was really occurring in his narrative, but this sailor merely describes a live burial. He calls it barbaric, interring a living man, but he didn't understand the Elder was merely hibernating. 'Going to sleep,' as other books have phrased it."

Felipe yawns loudly. "It's a good thing I like his accent, or I would have knocked him out cold by now."

"Oy, fuck off."

"Fine. Bend over."

Michelle shouts, "Please, gentlemen...if either of you could be considered such this morning."

"I wouldn't suggest it," Edmund replies.

"No," Felipe agrees.

I stifle a giggle and consider whether or not I'm still drunk.

She eyes the heavens for help. "Edmund. Continue."

"The sailor writes that the island where the burial happened is small. Very small. His ship came upon it accidentally on its way to the Gold Coast." He turns around and points at the world map on the wall. "The ship was taking a roundabout way to get there, from Italy..." His finger points. "Around the west coast of Africa. I've done this route. I know this path. Now, the sailor, he mentions strange statues on the island. Tall figures, hewn from black stone. 'Skeleton people,' he calls them, although, um, anatomically correct skeleton people. Seems that the natives were very sensual beings, which was why, seven years ago, when a volcano sunk everything, those who escaped said it was a reckoning of the gods."

I lean forward in my seat. "Seven years ago?"

He grins at me. "I was there, Andrew. I was there, on that bloody island, before its destruction, and I thought back to something you told me once: vampires don't *need* to breathe. This Elder, he sleeps beneath the sea, waiting for us to find him."

I stand and approach the map. My knees feel unsteady, because this is it. Edmund has done what so many others have failed to do, simply because a dead sailor left clues only my dearest love would be able to follow.

"My God," Felipe mutters.

I hear the creak of a chair as Michelle stands. "But how can we find a sunken island?"

"I know the latitude and longitude."

I turn slowly to face him. "You remember such a thing?"

The side of his mouth quirks up. "When I was sixteen, the gardener's son sucked me off in the hedge maze. His birthday was January twelfth. I remember lots of things. That's why my brain gets so loud."

I cup his face in my hands. "I swear you're already a creature of myth."

He chuckles, and his breath smells of black tea. "We need a ship."

"We have one," Michelle says, eyes on the hand-drawn continents behind us as if she might be able to see the Elder from where she stands. "It's the same ship that brought you here, Edmund, but it's not currently in port. I will inquire as to its return."

"Good," Edmund says. "They seemed an efficient crew."

Michelle spares him a look. "How do you know? You were on your back the entire time."

He leans against me. "I didn't know she made jokes."

"I'm coming with you," she says.

Felipe stands. "Me too."

Before Edmund can say anything, I cover his mouth with my hand. "I need a moment alone with Michelle please."

He pulls my hand away gently, eyes darting back and forth between me and the woman who forced a four-year exile on my person. "Felipe, want to watch me eat too many beignets in the kitchen?"

"Very much so."

Edmund presses a single kiss to the corner of my mouth before leaving, a bedraggled Felipe in tow. Michelle won't look at me. She stares at the map as though hungry for it.

"Why would you want to come with us?" I ask. "Felipe, I understand. The man just wants to be near Edmund, but you... You have changed since I went away.

You're different. You and Felipe are different, not as close. Now, you would volunteer for this mad voyage with us—you who has only ever traveled out of necessity. Or to chastise me." I think of her annual trips to the island. "Why do you care if we find an Elder? You do not love Edmund or me that much, to dote over our happiness."

"It's not always about you, Andrew, or your sweet Edmund." She wraps her dressing gown tighter around her waist. "I fell in love while you were away, to a human who got sick and died. Yes, Felipe was furious that I might love someone else—truly love them—and perhaps he has not forgiven me for that. But I loved…" She holds her chin high. "I had to watch him die, and it wasn't the first time. When I was younger, I fell in love with a man who knew what I was, and I watched him grow old and waste away. Our time together was but a blink." Her voice turns icy. "So don't you dare think you are the only one who has sought an Elder. I had given up until Edmund, and now, he has found one."

"We haven't found anything yet."

"Well, I want to be there when you do." She tries to step past me, but I hold tight to her arm. I don't say a word, but she glares up at me, eyes sharp. Any sign of her earlier exhaustion has disappeared. "I know you think me callous," she says, "for what I did to you. For punishing you, making an example of you, but think upon this, dear Andrew: if I had not sent you away, you never would have found him."

She rips her arm from my grasp and leaves the library. I stare at the map, surrounded by the lingering scent of my lover and dry, dusty books.

OF COURSE, HE wants to go out that night. Of course, he does—my brash young love. He wants to see Danys and Gabriel and May to tell them we'll be traveling soon. He wants to say goodbye just in case we leave suddenly—just in case we can't get back to them.

His affection is palpable as we walk into the brothel. He embraces May and moves her in a quick waltz. She laughs at his attentions, revealing a mouth of smoke-stained teeth. Danys is otherwise engaged, but Gabriel, dressed as a woman, accepts Edmund's advances daintily, a fan half covering his painted face.

As Edmund drags Gabriel to the bar, careful not to step on his skirts, May lays her hand on my shoulder. "What's gotten into him? He's bright as a star."

"A bit of good news is all." I lean in and kiss her cheek.

"Would you like a private room this evening?"

I glance at Edmund who is avidly engaged in conversation with half the room. "Not tonight, thank you." I have something particular to show my sailor, and it cannot be found in the back room of a Gallatin Street whorehouse.

While Edmund consumes rum and has a heated discussion with what appears to be a bearded man of the sea, Gabriel pets his hair, his cheek, and his chest like he's a thoroughbred horse. Midsentence, Edmund clasps Gabriel's gloved hand in his and kisses it. His gaze—and probably his mind—bounces about the room. In his current state of excitement, I think he could run for miles and not be spent.

Gabriel steps away from Edmund and wraps me in an embrace when I approach. I kiss behind his ear. His long, blond hair tickles my nose. "Has he told you we're going on a journey?"

The red-stained edges of Gabriel's mouth turn down. "No! You mustn't." He bats me in the shoulder with his fan. The man missed his calling as a stage actor. "You must take up residence in my bed and never leave, the two of you."

I smile and rub my nose up the side of his neck. He smells of flowers and sweat.

"Edmund," Gabriel croons. "Andrew said you are leaving. *Ce n'est pas vrai.*"

My beloved glances at me. "Well, not just yet, but soon—which is why we're here tonight. I couldn't very well set off without seeing you."

Gabriel bats his eyelashes. "*Mon chat noir...*"

It isn't long before Danys joins our petit party, wrapped in nothing but a long piece of dyed silk. He attaches himself to Edmund's back like a very large, affectionate leech and only intensifies the image when his mouth latches onto Edmund's skin.

At the unexpected assault, my beloved's lips part. His eyes slip shut. Danys sucks his earlobe and whispers something that makes Edmund laugh. I'm tempted to ask how Jimmy Fitz fared after Edmund cut him open with his own knife, but I'd rather not remember the night I was so violently reminded of my darling's mortality.

Although Danys begs me to get a private room, I turn him down.

Edmund studies me silently before tilting his head.

"What?" I ask.

"I don't think I want to fuck anyone but you anymore."

The idea of him forsaking all others makes something big and warm blossom in my long-dead chest. I hug him to me and consider the idea of just us...for eternity...

before he pushes me away, smiling, rushing off to find more rum.

It is a peaceful respite, our time in the brothel. I mostly lounge with Gabriel. We talk quietly of New Orleans and share gentle kisses but nothing more. Danys drags Edmund around, introducing him to everyone, telling the story about the card game. Occasionally, Danys and Edmund whisper together. Their body language is less that of lovers and more of friends.

When I announce we must leave, we are showered in hugs and shouts of "Don't go!" Danys does plant a lingering kiss on Edmund's forehead. He holds him close, hand in Edmund's dark curls, and says something that looks serious. Edmund nods in reply before accepting a few caresses from Gabriel.

May waits by the door. "Will I see you again in another four years?"

I kiss her cheek. "Sooner perhaps."

She grabs Edmund by the chin and stares up into his face. "Never change, you beautiful thing."

We step out into a night warm and welcoming. Since it is still early, voices shout from the street. The sound of celebration shudders like a storm up the alley, but before we emerge back into reality, Edmund gives me a single abrupt shove that plants my back against the wall. He kisses me, hot and hard, tongues dueling, breaths panting. I lean down to intensify the kiss. I bite his bottom lip and whisper his name.

"What did Danys say to you back there?" I ask.

He smiles against my mouth. "He told me to take care of you. Where now?"

"Just a short walk."

As two men, we're required to place a respectable distance between us as we rejoin the chaos of humanity. No matter how much I would love to link arms with Edmund, I walk with my hands in my pockets and guide him away from the drunken screams and whistles. As always, his eyes, as though starving, take it all in.

It's not long before we reach our destination, but I pause prior to entering the alley of my memory. I haven't been here since...

"Andrew?"

I had picked up the young whore on a darkened corner, mostly because he was smaller than the others and had a lovely mouth. I hadn't planned on killing him, but I had enjoyed it. I'd loved it, in fact.

"Are you all right?"

I nod and set foot into the scene of my crime. Things are the same but different, foreign but familiar. We are near a street that becomes a market come day. I smell fish and rotten fruit—and Edmund, of course. That night four years ago, I had smelled nothing but my young prostitute and his fear.

"This is where I did it," I whisper.

Edmund steps up to my side. Quarters are close since the darkened alley is lined with barrels. "Where you did what?"

"I killed a young man. His name was Azrael. It was my final sin before being sent away. He was the last corpse I left before Michelle exiled me to that island."

Edmund studies the area. He glances back toward the street. "You enjoyed killing him."

"Oh, yes." I could still hear the panicked little noises he made. "He was a gentle whore, small, much smaller than you. I wanted to taste his soul—the innocence of it. I left his body here, never knowing that one bit of mess would send me away four long years."

Edmund moves so close I have to move back. Still, he keeps moving until the backs of my thighs press against a barrel. Filled with what smells of ale, it does not move beneath my weight.

"My marvelous murderer," he says.

I pull back to understand the expression he wears, but he hides his face against my neck.

"Do you not see? But you must." His nose tickles my cheek. "If you hadn't killed that boy, you wouldn't have been there to save a lost sailor on your island. You wouldn't have me."

"You sound like Michelle."

"We have much to thank her for." He takes my hands and places them on his ass. He grinds against me, cock hard as stone.

"Edmund..."

"Did you fuck that boy before you killed him?"

I nod against his forehead and knead firm muscle.

"Then, you'll fuck me here. Reclaim this place as ours." His tongue touches the side of my jaw, followed soon after by his lips. "An offering to the gods to celebrate your return."

I press my cock firmly against his, and he chokes on a breath. "You would be my sacrificial lamb?"

"Yes. God, yes." He surges forward and attacks my mouth.

Sadly, we must part in order to unhook trousers. The barrel of ale turns out to be the perfect height for Edmund to bend over. He does so willingly and parts his legs for me, as far as he can with his pants around his ankles. I use my fingers to work him open. He is warm and tight as always. The light from the street is just bright enough to cast him in grayish shadow. His fingers curl, and his mouth drops wide in a silent scream as I add more fingers, more pressure.

I tease him a little. He's plenty prepared for me, but I keep going, keep fucking him with nothing but fingers until he gasps and whimpers, "Andrew...for fuck's sake..."

I chuckle before replacing fingers with cock. Edmund's whole body tenses, so I still. I know I can sometimes feel like too much for him, even after all our time together. Of course, it does not help that we have no oil—but neither did we on the island. Edmund is a man who likes his pain with his pleasure.

He reaches blindly back, and we clench fists. I move a little, in and out. He relaxes some and pushes back against me. My sailor is ready now.

It's not frantic or forceful. It's deep and slow and saturated with his sighs. Edmund is no whore. He's not a nameless meal. He is everything I want in the world, and I show him with the movement of my hips.

He is the one who eventually says, "Harder." He plants both his hands on the wall to steady himself before I thrust in earnest, threatening to knock us both to the ground. He can barely contain his moans, and God, I can barely stay on my feet.

Suddenly, he's coming, his fingertips scraping against brick. It's so rare that he comes without me touching him. The shock of his body clenching gives me pause—but merely pause before I drive into him another dozen times. His pale fingertips shudder and shake against the wall until I take pity, accept my own release, and rest my chest against his back.

He's barely coherent on the carriage ride back to the coven, leaning against me. If he were a cat, he would have purred. Sated as he is, I do as instinct bids. I unbutton the top of his shirt and feed, careful not to spill a drop. He accepts my teeth in his neck with a soft hum and holds tight to my shoulders until I've had enough.

In the privacy of our room, we wash and slide beneath the covers. I expect him to cling to me as he so often does after a night of pleasure, but he remains on his back, bright eyes on the ceiling.

"What on earth can you be thinking about right now?"

He smiles without showing his teeth. "Did becoming a vampire change you?"

"Well, I suppose. I never hungered for human blood before my rebirth."

He sighs. "No, I mean the person you were. You were a Viking soldier in life, so killing was part of it, but do you enjoy killing *more* as a vampire?"

I take a few moments to think before replying. "Perhaps becoming a vampire simply amplifies what you already are. As a human, I enjoyed sex and..." I clear my throat. "Carnage. I enjoy both more as an immortal."

"Not carnage anymore, though."

I lean up on my elbow to better see him. "No."

"How did it happen, anyway? How exactly does one become a vampire?"

I run my fingers through the tangled curls at his forehead. "I don't know *exactly*. I was dead when it happened."

He lowers his eyebrows. "I'd forgotten that part. I have to die."

"Yes."

He closes his eyes as I continue petting him. "Will you do it, when the time comes? Will you kill me? I'd rather it not be anyone else."

I think of the way his soul will taste, his blood pulsing down my throat, and immediately agree.

Chapter Ten

ON MANY LEVELS, Edmund and I are similar creatures. In the practice of patience, we are not, although some of that might have to do with our immense difference in age. Whereas I am content to sit and ponder—a practice perfected alone on a tropical island—Edmund is more of a constant wanderer. He needs something to do, which I expect will be something of a challenge once he begins to understand immortality. For now, he leaves me at home with my newspapers or books and walks New Orleans.

Oh, and this morning, he boxes, because he is apparently "getting soft."

I don't only sit on my hide. I do walk the city, too, mostly worrying that Edmund will get in another knife fight, brutal boxing match, carriage accident...the list of my anxieties is endless now that his immortality is in sight. He seems so fragile to me suddenly—although, Lord knows, he is not. So I walk and worry over silly things.

Today, I take my worry to the harbor to check in with the harbormaster. Michelle's vampire crew should return any day. Hopefully. It's been a thick and heavy fortnight since Edmund pinpointed the Elder's location, and every day we wait, he grows more agitated.

Visiting the tailor Peters was a welcome distraction earlier in the week as it allowed Edmund to wrap his great mind around something of personal interest: the art of style. Unlike our first jaunt to the talented old man, though, this was functional. We needed clothes for travel, so instead of delicate silks, Edmund forced us to buy heavy breeches—he claimed trousers were no good on a ship—coats made of leather, and leather gloves. When I asked about shoes, he smiled and said it was better to go barefoot, which explains a lot about Edmund's lack of footwear on the island, but I refuse to go barefoot anywhere but the boudoir.

I have a very distinct memory of peeling several items of soaking wet clothing from his unconscious person back on the island when he first washed to shore. The leather gloves give me an unexpected thrill, although I'm not sure why. I adore the feel of his hands, so why would I want them covered—but maybe that's just it. There's something Puritanical about covering so much flesh, which makes it all the more enjoyable when that flesh is exposed.

There is also the matter of letters. Edmund has been waiting to hear from his trading company—the owners of his sunken ship—as well as from his mother, who I should think would be overjoyed to hear he lives. He's not so sure, considering he's caused her nothing but worry since the day he sprung forth glowing and filled with intention. I don't know why he hopes so heartily for word from the woman who has done nothing but hold his head under metaphorical water for twenty-eight years. But I do not remember my mother, so perhaps that is why I cannot understand his devotion to a woman who resents the very thing he is.

In the matter of the returned ship, I have no news. In the matter of letters, well...

The gym reeks of filthy men, but it doesn't take long for me to scent Edmund among them, especially since his fragrance is now home to me. I walk among them in my fancy suit, and no one pays me any mind, too busy are they grunting and groaning over heavy weights. Two behemoths battle upon a raised square, tossing occasional punches but mostly just tossing salt water. It tumbles down their chiseled faces and flicks from the edges of their hair.

In the far back, I see Edmund's scar. He's shirtless and faced away from me in nothing but breeches, pounding away at a punching bag. I enjoy the waves of tensing, rippling muscle that cascade across his back and shoulders as he throws another punch and another. The entire bag shakes beneath his onslaught as I am reminded, again, that my Edmund may be pretty, but his punches rattle skulls—even immortal ones.

I step up to the side of the bag, and he pauses. "Andrew." His fists are wrapped in some sort of white fabric. I know nothing of modern boxing. In my day, throwing punches was not an art form but a battle tactic. He pushes sweaty hair off his forehead with the back of his hand.

"Are you trying to break it?" I gesture to the bag. It heaves to and fro like the bow of a ship.

He smiles, out of breath, and puts his hands on his hips. Being in public, I try to ignore the sweat that drips down the center of his chest. It would not do to lick it away.

"I have something for you."

"Is it a ship?"

I pull the letters from the pocket of my jacket.

"Oh, thank Christ." He leaps forward and rips the envelopes from my hand. He tucks them under his arm as he unwraps his hands, tossing white fabric to the floor before tearing into the first one, his eyes dancing left to right, left to right. "From my company… An inquiry? What the…?" He wipes a drop of sweat from the tip of his nose. "It's not as if they can blame anyone for what happened. Everyone's dead." He shakes his head. "Fucking bureaucrats. Half the men at this bloody trading company have never been on a ship in their lives, yet they hope to pin the blame on some poor sailor simply because the night was dark. *Dead* sailors, at that." He drops the letter to the floor as though disgusted by it. "I suppose we'll have to pay them a visit once we reach London."

"I hope I never get in an argument with you."

He chuckles and looks at the second letter, but his amusement soon falters, disappears. "This isn't my mother's handwriting." He unfolds the thick paper, and it's like watching a storm come in from the sea. A deep wrinkle appears between his eyes. "She is ill."

"What?" I step up to his side.

"She's not in London. They've moved her to the Baines country estate. They send for me." He chews at his bottom lip. "Andrew, we have to go."

"Michelle's ship is due back any—"

"No, we have to go now. We have to go to England."

"England? But the Elder—"

He puts his hand on my forearm. "Love, I know, but it has to wait."

I stare at him, study the furrow of his brow, the unfamiliar downturn of his eyes. For just a second, I see it. He might normally be a full-grown man, but right now, he is a little boy who needs his mother.

I nod. "All right. You'll go bathe. I will go back to the house and prepare our things."

"What of Felipe and Michelle?"

Yes, they were supposed to travel with us, but... "Let me speak to them. I fear it's too late to book passage for today. We will have to leave tomorrow at the earliest anyway."

He sighs. "I know. You're right. Okay. Jesus, I feel like a fair maiden about to have a fainting fit."

I put my hand on his sweat-soaked shoulder. "Go. Meet me at the house."

He nods and walks away.

God be praised, as soon as I hurry into the foyer of my coven, Michelle awaits with a note in hand. She waves it in the air, announcing the vampire ship has finally returned to harbor. I think she might even dance a merry jig until I tell her we no longer seek the Elder. First, we must go to England.

BY THE TIME we board the ship and find our quarters, Edmund is vibrating with nerves. It's the same room we were given on the trip back from my exile, so it is lush and probably deserving of the ship's captain, but no matter— it's ours, and I'm thankful for the sizable bed. Edmund doesn't seem to notice. He shoves his hands into his hair and struggles to breathe.

"We need to leave," he says. "What's taking so long?"

I grip his forearms and pull his hands away from his head. "You can't be this way. You of all people know travel takes time. We have weeks to spend trapped on this ship, and I forbid you to be agitated for all of it."

He stretches his neck from side to side. "I know." He wraps his arms around me and squeezes me until I feel bruised. "I don't want to be like this, I just... My mother has always seemed... I suppose *permanent* is the word.

And now, she's ill, and I... You know, I think I believed I would die before her."

I pull back enough to look at him and hold his cheeks in my hands. "She's not dead."

"Yet."

I kiss his forehead. "Edmund, you are the most joyful person I know. This is not like you." I notice the way his chest quickly expands and contracts. "Breathe with me. Slowly. In...out." I sigh a breath, and he does the same. "In...out."

We continue breathing in sync until his eyes close and he leans against me. I'm not sure if the scent of salt water is from the open sea or his tears.

He chuckles. "For someone who doesn't need to breathe, you do it very well."

"Well, you seem to have forgotten how today."

He laughs some more before wiping his eyes.

"Let's go on deck and wave goodbye to New Orleans."

He nods, so I take his hand and lead him up into the sunlight of an early afternoon. Immortal sailors hustle around us—many of them barefoot, as Edmund said. They climb rigging and pull ropes. It's all a foreign concept to me, but Edmund watches them with fondness. Michelle and Felipe stand toward the back of the ship, but they pay us no mind.

Our vampire captain looks out over it all in his navy-blue jacket made of velvet. We met fleetingly on the trip from my island, home to New Orleans. I don't know his name because everyone calls him "Captain," but he has short, black hair with streaks of white, a wide jaw, and blue eyes that seem to always be watching.

He watches Edmund and I as we walk across the deck toward the rail. What different creatures we must be to him this voyage. No longer am I a blood-soaked murderer. No longer is Edmund an underfed, filthy, exhausted mess with the beginnings of a beard. We've been reborn.

As our ship leaves the harbor, I stand behind Edmund and wrap him in my embrace—just as I did when we watched our island of exile disappear into the distance.

He leans against me and sighs before pressing his forehead to the side of my chin. "I'm going to teach you how to be a sailor."

"You're going to find that's impossible."

He twists his fingers between mine. "We have plenty of time."

On a cross-continental voyage: yes, don't I know it?

Chapter Eleven

EDMUND IS VERY good at monotony when on a ship, which is contrary to every behavior he has ever exhibited on land. Imagine my surprise. He claims routine keeps him sane on long ocean voyages, so every morning, he wakes early, goes on deck, and does strange stretches that he learned from a Chinese monk. From what I have observed, the crew enjoys this sensual performance almost as much as me—as if they don't have their share of devoted blood slaves below deck.

Some nights, Edmund volunteers to take watch. Other nights, he wrestles me into bed and takes me apart one kiss, nibble, and lick at a time. He never wears shoes. He climbs so high into the rigging that my dead heart skips a beat. Although he gives up on me, he does teach Michelle and Felipe all about life at sea—and they seem legitimately interested, especially Felipe, who sometimes climbs the rigging too. The idiot almost fell off deck one afternoon when a spectacular wave hit. Edmund had to grab onto his lacey frock coat and lurch him backward.

Edmund spends time with the captain often. They talk about places they've been. They discuss our route. Our eventual hunt for an Elder is of particular interest to him.

A human sailor—one of the few on board—tries to teach me something called "fancy work" to dull my ennui. It's an art form what these men can weave with small pieces of string when not working, working. It seems they're always working, while we, the passengers, fester in boredom.

One afternoon, I tumble into the common room where the humans aboard take their meals. Seated at the table, Edmund laughs. "How have you not earned your sea legs yet?"

I huff and watch him use his magic fingers on a deck of cards. He makes them move in waves across the wooden table.

I fall forward when someone runs into me. Felipe groans and shoves me out of the way, followed closely by Michelle. She smiles up at me, luminous as though she's just left her New Orleans washroom, as opposed to having been cooped up for ages on a ship rife with stinking men.

Across from Edmund, Felipe falls into a chair. "Thank Christ. Something to do."

Edmund, in nothing but shirtsleeves and breeches, suddenly looks like a hungry predator. "You play?"

"Anything. Yes." Felipe wears his long hair free around his shoulders but now pulls a band from his coat and ties it back in a bow.

"Poker? I understand it's popular in America, but we'll need more players."

Michelle and I know nothing of the game, so we are tasked with finding additional men to fill chairs. It's an easy business, and soon, four of them await Edmund's deal. The game begins, as does the smoking and drinking. I could almost pretend I'm back in New Orleans, if not for the slight rocking to and fro.

Edmund wins and loses and wins some more. I stand behind him sometimes and watch his hand. I stand across from him sometimes and try to read his tells—but he

Chapter Twelve

FOR WEEKS, WE'VE had nothing but sun, so a small storm comes as a relief—except, based on the captain's worried frown, this storm will not be small. I stand on deck next to Edmund and watch it creep ever closer: a wall of black clouds and bolts of yellow light.

"Jesus," he mutters.

"It doesn't bode well that you're worried."

He glances at me. "No, it... I'm sure we'll be fine, but they'll certainly need my help on deck."

My fingers curl into the fabric at his shoulder. "You will be safely below deck with me for the duration, wrapped in my arms."

"Andrew. I've assisted on deck during storms a million times. Nothing has ever happened, beyond me getting very wet."

Felipe steps up beside us, back in men's clothing, although he did indeed wear Michelle's dress for the agreed upon two days. "I'll help too."

Edmund smacks him on the shoulder. "Good man," he says, and it's true, Felipe might as well be a sailor with all he's learned from my darling over the course of our trip. I think learning from Edmund has been the only thing keeping Felipe sane—that and the occasional human-vampire orgy in the captain's quarters.

"You're both idiots." I glare at the ever-moving black clouds. "I guess that means I'm staying up here too."

Edmund playfully elbows me in the ribs. "Just don't fall overboard. We'll never find you in the storm. You'll end up at the bottom of the sea like our Elder." He looks around, searching the deck for something, and apparently finds it because he starts walking. "Let me get us knives. The last thing we need is a broken sail tearing the mast down."

I watch him go. "What the hell am I supposed to do with a knife?"

Felipe shoves his shoulder against mine. "Nothing. Leave it to the professionals."

"Oh, and are you a professional now?"

"Edmund is a good teacher. I'm sure he's taught you all sorts of things."

I roll my eyes at the innuendo.

Someone puts a hand on my shoulder, and I turn to find Michelle, her slim body wrapped in a long, thin blanket. She speaks to Felipe. "Are you coming below deck? I do believe our devoted humans could use a distraction."

"I'm going to stay up here with Edmund and the crew," he says with the gravitas of an ancient Roman war hero.

"Well, be careful." She walks back to the stairs, fabric dragging silently behind her. I watch her head disappear below deck and wish I could join—wish Edmund would join, too—but, by now, he's gotten Felipe and me knives to attach to our person as the storm hovers ever closer.

When it hits, it's a deluge. At times, I can't tell if I'm above water or below, but I keep my eye on Edmund always. He moves as though he's done it all before, and I suppose he has. He climbs rigging barefooted, no matter the bruising winds. He carries his knife between his teeth like a mad pirate. Felipe tries to follow close behind, but his shoes slip across the deck. For my part, I never let go of something sturdy, and I never stop watching Edmund.

A flash of lightning illuminates the deck and makes the scurrying sailors resemble panicked insects. I almost fall over at the force of the thunder, especially when the ship lurches right, but I catch myself on the railing before knocking myself out cold. The day is black as night.

Then, I hear it: something screams.

A moment later, while my eyes search the deck for a wounded, dying animal, I realize the sound was a sail ripping in two.

The sailors shout. Even the captain, who usually seems content to hide below deck, starts yelling, pointing. I find Edmund, his chin tilted up, lips murmuring what is possibly a prayer. And everyone moves. Sailors hurry up both sides of the rigging, one of them Felipe, whose gritted teeth flash as he climbs.

One of his shoes slips, and... God, my old friend is falling.

I lurch forward, but Edmund is there to save him. He has to reach over the side of the ship to catch one of Felipe's flailing hands. I latch onto Edmund's free arm as Felipe disappears over the rail, hand clenched in Edmund's.

Edmund's body stretches taut between Felipe and I. I feel a violent jarring go through him—probably beneath the full weight of Felipe's body—and Edmund howls. He tears his hand away from me and reaches over the side, both his arms grasping for Felipe. I watch him put one foot on the rail and tug. Felipe flies back on deck, and both men fall to their backs in the rain.

Only then do I smell Edmund's blood.

In a single flash of lightning, I get a glimpse of his right arm. I don't have time to fully understand what I'm seeing, but it's all blood, bone, and twisted skin.

A sail flaps in the wind above us, successfully cut before pulling down the mast and cursing us all. The captain appears at my shoulder, his hair lank and wet around his face. "Get him below deck! For Christ's sake!"

Felipe and I are careful as we lift Edmund and carry him down the steps. He's awake but strangely quiet, his lips pressed together in a thin, white line. He groans when we lay him in the center of the hallway. The boat lurches too much for farther travel.

Flat on his back, he cradles his arm. "Fuck, I don't even want to see."

I wave at Felipe. "Get Michelle." I look at Edmund and think I know what needs to be done—but I cannot do it, not to him—and I don't trust Felipe to be of any worth either. In fact, I want to kill him, because his fall did this. His idiocy cracked Edmund's arm over the railing with enough force for bone to break skin. My sailor's blood drips everywhere, but I am not hungry; I am horrified. "Edmund," I say. "You need to see so you can tell us what to do."

He takes a deep breath and lifts his head to inspect the damage. His skin turns the color of parchment. "Jesus." His head falls against the floor, and he closes his eyes tight. I think he's trying not to be sick. "You have to...shove the bone back in place."

With shaking hands, I wipe the wet hair from his forehead. He feels too cold and too hot all at once. "I can't."

He has enough energy left to laugh. "Well, someone bloody well has to."

"Andrew?" I hear Michelle behind us. She moves quickly but freezes when she sees Edmund coated in his own blood, bone exposed and covered in what looks like strawberry jam. "Edmund!" she shrieks. She falls to her knees beside him but doesn't dare touch.

"Andrew, lift me up."

I wrap my hands under his arms and tug until he's sitting upright in my lap, facing Michelle. I feel Felipe behind us, watching.

"Michelle...look at me." His words explode between panting breaths. "You have to...break it again. Break it back in. Do you understand?"

"Oh, my God." She covers her mouth with her hand. "But can't Andrew—"

"He needs to hold me." Amazing that Edmund is the calmest among us. "Please. Quickly, before I lose too much blood. Just do this, and we'll bandage me up, and I'll be fine."

She nods, and he slumps back against my chest. Thankfully, we vampires are too panicked by the scent of his blood to feel the usual excitement, or Edmund would have made a beautiful meal. Above us, the sound of running feet and shouts echo as the storm continues to wreak unholy havoc.

I can't watch, but I know when it happens—when Michelle fulfills her task—because there's a wet popping noise, and Edmund's whole body tenses. He curls in on himself, me above him. There's a long moment of silence before: "Captain's quarters has bandages," he whispers. He goes limp in my arms. I wish he'd lost consciousness sooner.

I STAND IN the doorway and watch him sleep. He's in our bed, bandaged and resting. I told Michelle to keep Felipe away from me because, at this point, I'm liable to kill him. The storm has passed—on deck. My anger rages below, much darker than any meek thundercloud. I hear scattered voices behind me. Two of the sails tore, so we're merely floating for now as the sailmaker—a tall vampire with freakishly long fangs—does his harried duty.

The captain stomps up to my side, but I don't spare him a look. "Bad luck," he says.

I curl my fists at my sides to keep from throttling him.

"But Edmund is a man of the sea. He'll be fine. Just hope it doesn't get infected." He smacks me on the back and leaves as if he's done some great service.

Fucking sailors.

I close the door behind me and sit on the edge of our bed. After we got his arm bandaged, I stripped him of his wet clothes, so he's wrapped in nothing but sheets and the long blanket Michelle carried around earlier. It smells a little like her. I run my fingers across his collarbone, over the bite mark low on his neck that's becoming practically permanent. God, but it's just like when I found him washed up on the beach.

As if an echo of my former self, I tell him once again, "Don't die."

He mumbles something upon waking. I think it was my name. He opens his eyes and gasps. "Mary, mother of God, I need rum." He grimaces and squeezes his eyes closed as I rush from the room. I come back with two jugs, quickly handing him the first. He takes three long pulls before falling back amidst pillows. "Is Felipe all right?"

"Is Felipe...?" I stand and pace as much as I can in the close quarters. "You should have let him go over."

"No. I was serious when I said we never would have found him again."

"So?"

"Andrew, he was trying to help. Let it go. It doesn't matter now."

"And if the wound gets infected?"

"It won't." He lifts the jug. "I'll drown any illness with rum."

I cover my face with my hands and barely notice I've started crying. I haven't cried in... I don't remember the last time.

"Andrew?" His voice cracks. "Stop, please. Come here."

I rush to him and press my face against his chest. His good hand relinquishes the rum and runs through my hair.

"Love. It's going to be all right."

I chuckle against his skin, although my eyes still burn with salt. "I'm hundreds of years older than you. How do you still manage to make me feel like a child?"

He shushes me and squeezes the back of my neck. Together, we drink rum until Edmund's pain goes away and I have, for the moment, numbed my fear.

Chapter Thirteen

HE SPENDS MOST of his time on deck now, soaking up the sun. I swear he grows more freckles every day. The crew skirts around him, worried over the state of his arm. There's a chance he could even be lame once it heals.

If it heals.

If he lives.

The nights are spent drinking too much rum and making love—gently. I tell him we can rest, just go to sleep, and he refuses, as if his time is running short. He has another of his nightmares, and he wakes with the now familiar look on his face as he clings to me with one hand.

"What is it you dream?" I ask.

"You. Underwater. Dead."

"It's not possible."

"You're slipping away from me," he says and falls back to sleep.

It is only due to our close quarters that I am the first to scent the change in him. Edmund has always smelled sweet to me, but one night, I wake before dawn and he smells sweeter. He smells *wrong*. I hold him tightly, and he mumbles. Only then do I notice the way our sheets are soaked with his sweat.

Before he wakes, I rise and bring water. I wait an hour for his eyes to open, unwilling to hurry his understanding. It is with some peace that I realize there are enough vampires on this blasted ship to tear me to pieces, for if Edmund dies, I'm going with him.

I'm staring when his eyelids flutter, and eyes like the sea stare back. "Andrew?"

"You should drink some water."

He leans up on his good elbow before glaring at his bandage-wrapped arm. "I'm sick, aren't I? You can smell it. Rotting meat." He sighs and bites his bottom lip. "Well. I have no words."

Edmund without words is almost as terrifying as Edmund without his head.

We send for the captain, the only creature on board with any kind of medical training—although he's been nothing but a disappointment so far. As soon as word spreads that he's been beckoned, the area outside our room fills with vampires, Michelle and Felipe shoving to the front.

Felipe claws at me, his long hair a mess, dark circles under his eyes. I don't believe he's slept a peaceful wink since the day of the storm. "What's happened, Andrew? God, tell me he's not dead!"

I shake my head, no, and Michelle speaks with authority. She is, after all, our leader. "Everyone clear the space. Go back to your quarters." She waves her hand as if the immortal crowd is a hungry herd of cats.

The three of us squeeze into the room I share with my darling, where the captain, in his velvet jacket, perches like a gargoyle on the side of the bed. Edmund, his freckled face dripping sweat, nods at him and looks up at me. "Come in and sit."

Michelle and Felipe do not ask if he refers to only me. They accept his invitation and pile nearly on top of each other in the only chair while I sit on the bed and take Edmund's left hand in mine.

"We're not going to England," he says. "We're going to the Elder."

"No. We must get you to a mainland for proper medical care."

His hand squeezes mine. "Andrew. The Elder is closer."

I turn to the captain. "How close?"

"I could get him there in four days," he says.

I close my eyes. *Four days.*

Edmund's fingers find my face. "It's too late for medical care anyway, unless you plan on chopping my arm off—which is not happening. I'll probably just get another infection."

I bring his hand to my mouth and kiss. "But what if you're wrong? What if the Elder isn't where you think he is?"

He shrugs, bare chest glistening as the rising sun peeks through our window. "Then, I'm dead. I've always been a gambling man. Hey, Felipe, what will you do if I win this bet?"

Felipe moves with vampire speed and kneels by the bed. "I will wear a dress for a hundred years."

Edmund laughs and ruffles his hair. His eyes crinkle around the edges. "Why do you look like dog shit?"

I laugh as Felipe turns an amusing shade of red. "Me? You..."

Edmund is smiling that giddy smile of his.

Felipe puts his hand on Edmund's ankle. "You must live. No one else...amuses me as you do. And I would be bored again without Andrew. I will not see him broken."

"Neither me," he says, although it is a promise Edmund cannot possibly make.

FOUR DAYS IS much too long, although the wind assists. I feel as though even the weather knows the direness of our cause as she hurries us ever closer to the proper longitude and latitude off the coast of Africa. Edmund stays mostly in bed, although he makes me guide him upstairs on occasion to stare at the sea. He tries to hide that the fingers on his right hand have turned black, but he hides nothing, not even his fear.

Not fear, perhaps, but a strange melancholy that stoops his shoulders and steals the light from his eyes. He seems so much older.

All night, he shivers and shakes. Fever dreams. Michelle worries for me and makes me rest in her room while she or Felipe keep watch over my darling boy. One night, I find Felipe curled around him like an undead blanket, murmuring sweet words, petting Edmund's head. I have never seen Felipe so kind, and when he notices me watching, he looks up at me, eyes red, and apologizes over and over until I shake him and make him stop.

Each morning, I wake and know Edmund to be alive. I believe I will feel it if he dies. I will feel it and follow him into the abyss.

Edmund must realize my intentions, because on the third night, he holds me close and says, "You mustn't. You will not kill yourself when I've gone. Who will remember me if you're gone?"

I make no promises, and I don't know how much he remembers anyway.

The morning of the fourth day, the captain comes into our room. It stinks of illness, I know, and his face betrays nothing. "We will be there within the hour," he says before turning stiffly and hurrying back on deck.

Edmund blows shallow breaths against my neck before pressing his lips to my jaw. "You know what to do."

I nod and kiss his forehead, his cheek. His face is lined with stubble because he's been too sick to shave every day as per usual. I think of the long-ago night of cannibals and how my beautiful Edmund has stared death in the face too many times.

But he does have a plan for catching our Elder. Of course he does. Edmund always has a plan, even if it's mad. Ever since changing our destination, he's asked that we hold back portions of meat and fish. He's asked that we create a sort of blood stew to draw the Elder up from the depths. The time has come to put his plan into action.

I help him dress: nothing more than breeches and a shirt. He's barefoot, as always. I have to carry him upstairs, and it appears every single passenger has made his or her way on deck. Humans and vampires alike turn to Edmund and try not to stare at how his boisterous, charismatic presence has wasted away to weakness.

I set him in a chair, but he pulls himself up to stand and leans on the rail. He has a few curt words with the captain, and soon, the cook and two sailors come huffing and puffing up the stairs with the Elder's repulsive cocktail.

At Edmund's signal, they pour it into the churning waves. Whitecaps roll red, and now comes the waiting.

We all watch at first, but after several minutes, spectators lose interest—but not Edmund. His eyes never falter.

A dark fin breaks the surface, followed by another, another.

"Oh, my God," he says and smiles. "Sharks, Andrew. My beautiful monsters." He turns and reaches for my hand. "Like you." He laughs, and I'm mystified that he has the energy for amusement. The spark is back in his eyes as he watches the massive, dark shapes dance through our blood bath.

Time passes. Hours. The water below runs clear, the sharks disappear, and Edmund eventually folds back into his seat. I crouch next to him and hold to his left arm, too fearful to even look at his right.

"Behind my knees," he says.

"What?"

"My ticklish spot is behind my knees."

I force a smile. "I would have figured that out eventually."

He shakes his head. "I am going to die at sea."

"No," I say. "No, you're to outlive Armageddon. I told you that."

He turns to me, and he's like a walking corpse with his gaunt face and pale skin. "I'm sorry, Andrew."

"No." I pull him to me and rub my face all over his. "No, you are not going anywhere." I press my face against his neck and try to find his scent, but it's gone. He doesn't smell like himself anymore, which is when I realize... I hold him at arm's length. "Edmund, I've got it."

He blinks at me, waiting.

"The Elder needs *human* blood."

He takes a sharp inhale.

"Human blood, Edmund. It's what we long for—not animal blood. We want the taste of love and hate and passion. We want the taste of a soul. I've told you, haven't I?"

His eyes widen as he reaches for me. "Yes, you have. You're brilliant. Now, how are you at swimming?"

"Swimming? What? I..."

He grins. "I'm the bait." He stands, right arm useless at his side. "Come save me." He leaps over the rail with the grace of a man leaping from a carriage.

I shout his name and try to catch him, but down he falls over the side of the ship and into dark-blue water. All around me, voices scream, but I hear nothing as I follow my beloved into the depths.

The water steals my breath when I hit, but I find Edmund immediately—my strong swimmer. Even with one arm, he floats better than me, keeping his head high as I swallow salt water.

"I'm going to kill you myself!"

"Liar!" he yells over the slopping sound of waves.

I can't hold his body to mine, because we'd both sink, but I do keep a hand on his shoulder as we bob up and down, feet kicking.

"I hope this Elder doesn't mind the blood of a dying man," he says, but I am busy watching the water for sharks. I don't know how long I can keep kicking, swimming, and Edmund is too weak for this. The ship lingers nearby, and someone throws a rope to us, which I hold onto tightly.

"This is madness."

"Perhaps," Edmund says, "but I need you to bite me. Open my skin."

"You have a massive arm wound. Why would I need—"

"Fresh. Not rotten," he shouts. "Here." He lifts his left arm from the water and extends it my way. "Just take a quick bite. Hurry!"

I do as I'm told and take a quick nibble of his wrist. His blood tastes less of him and more of death. He plunges his arm underwater and continues to float.

"Jesus, I hope this Elder is quick at waking."

I cling to the rope and try not to drown.

"Lovely day for a swim," he says. "I do prefer the sea a bit farther north, but—" His head disappears below water, but I'm quick enough to grab his good wrist and tug him back up. He sputters when he breaches the surface and immediately screams a litany of, "Oh my God, oh my God."

"Edmund!"

"Something grabbed my ankle and pulled." He doesn't mean to, but he almost pushes my head under the water when he wraps himself around my chest.

"Christ."

I hold to the rope—and Edmund—as our gazes spin around us, searching for a sign of the hand that just tried to drown my sailor, but the water is too dark and moves too much. I see nothing but the frightened whites of Edmund's eyes, and I assume I look no better. What kind of battle can I be expected to win underwater?

Five feet in front of us, the water breaks. At first, I think it's nothing but seaweed, but the seaweed spreads. It rises. The seaweed is long, tangled hair, painted onto a skeleton with skin. Five feet away, an Elder appears. He is gray, sunken flesh and black eyes. He is open jaw and pointed fangs. He does not come closer or rise above chin level. He floats and watches us.

Edmund turns in my arms to face him. There is a long moment when I truly believe the monstrosity before us will simply disappear back into the black depths. But then, Edmund speaks: "We need your help."

ESCAPING

MORTALITY

Chapter One

EDMUND TRIES DESPERATELY not to shiver, but he forgets himself every minute or so and allows a full body shake that vibrates the wet edges of his hair. We're back on deck after our desperate leap into the ocean, my sailor and I. A half-hysterical Michelle wrapped us both in the heaviest fabric she could find once we were both safely lifted back onboard with our new passenger: the Elder.

He sits across from Edmund at a large table in our ship's common area while I stand and glare. Michelle and Felipe linger silently to my left and right.

This Elder is nothing more than a rotting skeleton, covered in loose, hanging flesh. He smells of dead fish and refuses to take his dark eyes off the man I love.

"You are dying," the creature says, his voice like the swinging of a rusted gate.

Edmund chuckles. "Yes. So you understand why I need your help."

"Why do you want this gift, dead man? Power? Prestige?"

"No."

"Then, why?"

"Love."

The creature's gaze momentarily swings up, and I stand straighter. For the first time since we escaped the rolling waves, the Elder addresses me: "How frustrating for a strong vampire such as yourself that you cannot save the one you adore."

I'm about to respond when Edmund speaks first. "I would prefer to keep this conversation between the two of us, if you don't mind. It is, after all, my life we discuss."

The Elder studies Edmund and says nothing. For a long moment, he merely observes. Although the blanket covers Edmund's black, infected flesh, it's impossible to miss the green pallor of his skin, the purple circles around his eyes, and the color of his lips, now practically white. All signs of the healthy young man I first met are gone.

"You have no fear right now, dead man. Strange for one with so little time left. I tasted it underwater, your fear. Quite a strong bouquet." A tongue like a slippery snail pokes out from the Elder's mouth to lick cracked lips.

"You tried to pull me under."

"You offered yourself."

"I needed to get your attention."

I'm not sure, but I think the Elder smiles. He shows his teeth anyway—long, pointed fangs bigger than any I've seen. "And now, you have it, dead man."

"My name is Edmund. And you?"

Again, those eyes—so dark as to be almost black—glance at me. "Brien." He growls the *R*. "If the world is still how I recall, *Edmund*, nothing is free. You woke me with your dying flesh because you need something." He opens his hands before him, skin wrinkled, sharp fingernails like weapons. "What do I get from you?"

Edmund shivers and groans. When he bends over in pain and rests his forehead on the table, Michelle stops me from rushing forward. "What do you want?" Edmund asks.

As my darling struggles to find the strength to sit, Brien watches with interest—I assume. It's difficult to tell with the sagging, wet flesh. Logic says the Elder should be dry by now, but he continues to drip foul water as though made of the stuff.

"You can have anything," Edmund says.

Brien leans forward and sniffs, seeking Edmund's scent. "I want to kill you."

I step toward them. "No."

The Elder stares at me. "No?"

"Edmund requested I do that." I could say more about how I want to taste his soul, how I want that moment to belong to me and me alone. I want him in my arms the moment he takes his last breath. So many things do I want, and this monster of the sea would steal it all.

"Dead man?" Brien practically purrs.

"Damn it." Edmund closes his eyes. "Fine. My life is yours."

"But—"

"It is better than the alternative, love," Edmund mutters. "Is that all you require?"

"I will travel with you wherever you now go."

"Michelle?" Edmund says her name but doesn't turn. I don't think he's strong enough to move anymore.

My old friend—once enemy, now leader—steps forward in her sweeping skirts. "Of course, Elder Brien. We are at your service."

"You might want to..." Edmund coughs. "Find something to wear. They frown upon naked corpses walking around London."

Felipe laughs—one short burst of amusement.

"Do we have a deal?"

Brien lowers his head. "Yes, Edmund." He looks up and shows his teeth. "Ah, there it is—the smell. Now, you are afraid."

Edmund's eyes are red. I don't know if he cries from pain or from the thought of his own murder at the hands of a hideous monster. Perhaps he found comfort in the thought of me doing it because he knew I wouldn't let him hurt. Brien appears liable to chop off each of Edmund's fingers before letting him die—but I will not let that happen. I will be at his side. I will hold Edmund's hand as his heart stops beating. Thinking of this, my own chest begins to ache.

My God, what if this doesn't work? What if the Elder kills my darling and jumps back overboard? What if these are the last moments I have with the only creature I have ever loved? I lean down quickly and kiss Edmund's forehead.

His hand finds my face. "I'm ready," he whispers. "Are you?" He smiles at me.

I pick him up and carry him to our room. The others follow close behind. In fact, the entire crew stands in the hall, watching us pass. What's about to happen hasn't happened in centuries, and I suppose everyone wants a view.

By the time I rest my shivering love in the center of our bed, someone has given Brien a cloak, although it does little to hide the emaciated ground meat of his face. Michelle comes in but locks everyone else out, for which I am thankful.

I kiss Edmund, and Jesus, he smells almost as bad as the Elder. I kiss his lips softly as he whispers he loves me.

"I love you too. I'll be right here." I squeeze his hand and kneel on the edge of our bed.

From across the room, Brien watches me again with what I suspect is delight. I want to bark at him and ask what on earth could be so funny, but I bite my tongue.

Now is not the time to provoke the only man who can save Edmund. As he leans forward, I lean back, paying the Elder respect.

He looms over Edmund, but strangely, instead of beginning his feast, he rests on his side and touches Edmund's hair with his pointed nails. "I am going to kill you now, but I will give you a new life. One without sickness or death. Do you accept this gift I give?"

Edmund nods.

"As I feed, I want you to think. Picture yourself healthy—the way you were before this. Perhaps, the way you were when you first met your vampire."

"Half drowned on a beach?"

Although I can't help but smile, the Elder seems confused. "Perhaps not. Picture yourself how you want to be, and in a little while, it will be so. Do you understand?"

Edmund nods again and flails for my hand. I entwine our fingers.

"Thank you for your offering," Brien says. He then moves faster than even my eyes can manage to follow.

Edmund whimpers when fangs break flesh. For a second, I think he's going to fight back. His arm tenses as though he might rip his hand free and start punching, but he doesn't. He gasps and sucks more air into his lungs than I would have thought possible. His heels dig into the blankets, and his last moan sounds like my name.

Then, he's gone. I feel it as if I myself have died with him. His body is an empty space in the room, and I want to start screaming, but Brien holds his hand out as though to calm me. Maybe he feels my panic, my pain. God knows what strange powers he might have.

I'm so busy staring at Edmund, gray eyes open and vacant, that I startle when I notice a walking corpse no longer stands among us. Full on Edmund's blood, Brien is now a man with long, black hair and pale skin. He is a man with fingers and a nose, and he climbs on Edmund as if to embark on some sexual act.

"Stay back," he commands. His voice is no longer an aged growl but a bit of sweet smoke in the room. He opens his mouth over Edmund's as one might before a kiss but, instead of kissing, he exhales.

I stumble back, right into Michelle, when a rolling, black cloud tumbles from his lips and right into Edmund's mouth. I, of course, remember none of this from my own turning since I was quite dead at the time. Michelle is probably just as mystified. Her grip feels like sharp metal spikes around my arm.

The black smoke increases. Brien whispers quiet incantations as the smoke he exhaled pools around Edmund's body. They float together in a dark cloud that moves as calm as ocean waves. It's strangely beautiful. How I wish my sailor could see.

Brien leans back. He dances the edges of his fingers through the smoke that still surrounds my darling.

"Is he—?"

"Shh," Michelle hisses. "Look at him, Andrew."

The fog dances and caresses every inch of Edmund's body. Everywhere it touches *...changes*. The blackened, infected rot of his fingers washes to a clean, pale white until I again recognize those hands I love so well. His chest fills out. The strong muscles, weakened by illness, return in shape and size. His ribs are no longer so prevalent. His cheeks are no longer hollows of disease. His eyes are—God, his eyes are moving!

"Edmund!"

"Wait." Brien holds his hand out to stop my approach and stares at my sailor. The Elder resembles a painter admiring his handiwork and rightly so. If I thought Edmund was a beautiful human, immortality has made him a masterpiece.

He sits up suddenly. "Fuck." Tendrils of smoke still curl around his calves.

Brien takes a firm hold on Edmund's chin and turns his face toward him. "Hmm."

"Who the hell are you?" Edmund asks.

"I am well fed."

"Brien?"

"Offering accepted, dead man."

"Oh, shit." Edmund turns his head away. "Andrew?"

"I'm here." I lurch forward and land on the bed before wrapping Edmund in my arms. He presses his face against my chest and clings. I kiss the top of his head, his forehead, the tips of his ears. I hold him at arms' length. "Are you all right?"

He gazes at his hands. "I...don't know. Do I look all right?"

"You've never looked better," Michelle says.

"Andrew?"

"She's right." I hold his face in my hands and nod as if he needs to be convinced. "You're—"

"Perfect," Brien says.

Edmund studies the stranger in our midst—this man with hair the same color as his own and eyes that do not linger so much as devour. "Thank you."

Brien tips his head in recognition and addresses Michelle. "I would bathe."

"Yes, of course."

The Elder gestures to Edmund. "He needs to feed."

"We have humans on board," Michelle says.

I can't consider leaving Edmund to go find him a human, and Michelle seems to know this. She doesn't even wait for my request before saying she will send Felipe on the errand while she tends to the Elder's needs.

Finally, we are alone.

Edmund, once again sheltered in my arms, speaks against my chest. "I didn't enjoy dying."

"Well. You never have to do it again."

"It was too quiet. Dark." His voice shakes. "Lonely."

I loosen my embrace enough to see his face. "It's done. You have come back to me." The curls I push from his forehead are more lustrous than Italian silk. And is it possible his eyes are even brighter? Brien has indeed worked some kind of magic.

A loud voice from behind us interrupts. "Where is he? Where is the mad fool?"

I turn to see Felipe in the doorway, hair and eyes equally wild. I lean back in time for Felipe to leap forward and tackle Edmund on the bed. My old friend rubs his face on Edmund's chest like a cat and claws at him just the same.

"You..." Felipe mutters. "You stink! Get this off!" He tears Edmund's shirt, stained with the reek of illness, and throws it across the room. "Let me see you!"

By now, Edmund is laughing under the force of Felipe's attention.

Felipe grabs his face and stares. "For fuck's sake, you're even more beautiful now than you were before!"

"Can you stop screaming at me, please?"

Felipe sighs and melts. He presses his face to the place where neck meets shoulder and hugs Edmund tight.

Edmund hugs back, eyes on me. "I'm all right, Felipe."

Felipe sniffs and pulls away. He wipes his face with the back of his shirtsleeve. "I haven't cried in a hundred years, and here I am, wasting my tears on the pathetic likes of you!"

Edmund falls back on the bed, smiling, still being straddled by the vampire who almost caused his death.

Felipe puts one hand on the center of Edmund's bare chest as if checking for a heartbeat—which, I realize with a start, is no longer there—but he glances at me. "That Elder is a bit different after a meal, hmm? Could be Edmund's older brother."

It's true their hair color is similar, although the Elder's is much longer. Their eyes are nothing alike, however. Yes, both blue, but Brien's are a dark navy while Edmund's are the gray-blue of a sunny sea.

Even though Edmund's heartbeat no longer echoes around our room, another one does. I finally notice the living, breathing creature in our midst. Wearing little more than a long shirt, he stands in the doorway: the beautiful redheaded youth I have so admired at coven orgies. I didn't even realize he was on board with us, but my ignorance makes sense—I have fed from no one but Edmund in months.

That will have to change, won't it? I'll never feed from my beloved again. Damn Brien for robbing that right. A dark cloud arrives but quickly passes over me when the redhead walks farther into the room and Edmund, for the first time, notices his scent.

My sailor sits up straight and almost knocks Felipe from his lap.

"Oh, yes, I was sent to bring you dinner," Felipe says mockingly as he slides from the edge of the bed and stands, adjusting, as always, his heavy lace cuffs.

The redhead stares at Edmund and does not conceal his wonderment and lust. Hours before, my darling was a pale-green weakling. Now, he's back to his usual splendor—and then some.

Edmund extends his hand forward, and the redhead comes closer.

"Felipe, get out," I command.

"No!" He pouts. "I want to watch."

"Out, Felipe," Edmund whispers, gaze never leaving his prey.

Felipe rolls his eyes but leaves, slamming the door behind him.

I sit beside my sailor and run my fingers up his spine as he beckons the beautiful blood slave ever nearer. Without preface, the youth climbs onto the bed and right into Edmund's lap. Edmund's hands wrap around his slim sides, and from this vantage, the redhead appears taller.

"I've admired you from afar." Edmund noses at his neck, smelling.

The blood slave's eyes slide shut, hands on Edmund's shoulders. "I am yours, sir."

"What's your name?"

The redhead giggles when Edmund playfully nibbles his ear. "Flynn. And you are Edmund and Andrew. You fell in love on an island far away."

Edmund smiles at me, arms still wrapped around Flynn. "Yes, we did." He looks back at Flynn, back at me, and the smile is replaced by something akin to fear.

I put my hand in Edmund's hair and furrow my brow in question.

"I don't really know what to do."

"Oh." And I've never had to teach before. "Can you feel your fangs?"

"Right now?"

I shrug. "They are now a part of you."

Flynn shifts on Edmund's lap as though seeking friction. "Lick here." He tips his head to the side. "I'm told I taste of vanilla."

No wonder this slave is so popular.

Smiling, Edmund does as instructed, and Flynn gasps at the flick of tongue. Edmund closes his eyes and opens them, and I can see the pointed tips of fangs between his parted lips. "Jesus, I feel like a twelve-year-old boy with an untrained prick."

I snort, and Flynn pulls him closer. "Feed, sir."

He blows out a breath as though to calm himself, and although he now doesn't need to breathe, it will take time for the lifelong habit to die. He leans forward and tilts Flynn back, the boy pliant in his arms.

"To us?" Edmund asks.

I nod and rest my hand in the center of his back.

He bites into the side of Flynn's pale neck—a neck decorated in old scars from years of living in Michelle's New Orleans coven. Flynn croons at the sensation. For his part, Edmund groans and leans forward on his knees, resting Flynn on the bed beneath him. I watch and listen for when he has had enough, and when the moment is right, I tell him so.

He pulls back, but Flynn still clings to his hair as if he wants more. "Make love to me, sir."

Edmund licks a spot of blood from his top lip. "I cannot. I have only one beloved now."

My dead heart soars at the very idea.

"But I believe you would be so gentle..." Flynn rolls onto his side and begins to doze.

Edmund admires him for a moment before gazing at me. "Gentle is not something I want to be right now."

I hurriedly carry Flynn from our room. In the hallway, I hand him to Felipe—who was apparently listening at the door—and tell him to fuck off. I have very important things to do. Well, one thing in particular.

When I turn around, Edmund has shed his breeches and wears nothing but muscle and skin. "Jesus." I sigh and put my hand to my chest.

"You're too far away for what I intend."

"I can't believe you're mine."

He smiles, revealing his white, pointed fangs. "Come on, then."

I try to tackle him onto the bed, but he moves too quickly—and he's much stronger now than he used to be, especially since... "No fair. You've just eaten." He has me pinned, straddling my hips with his hands holding mine to the bed. I know I could buck him off if I chose—I am hundreds of years older—but I choose not to, allowing him his current study of my face.

He lets go of my left hand and touches my lips. "I can really see you now. You're different."

"Am I?" I run my free hand up the outside of his bare thigh. "Better or worse?"

"Neither. No, it's..." He gets that look of his, the curious one he assumes when he's figuring something out. I think back to our time on the island when my beloved naturalist wanted to know about my "species." I wonder what experiments Edmund might soon run on himself— and the Elder. Good God, I hope Brien is prepared for a battery of questions.

"Edmund?"

"I can see into you—see the very love on your face." He relinquishes control of my right hand too. His fingers tickle down my chest.

"I do love you. More than anything." I squeeze his ass and press my clothed cock against his bare skin.

He gasps at the contact, tears my shirt open, and tongues my nipple. I actually wince when one of his fangs makes contact. I wrap his hair around my fingers and pull until I can see his face—and his fangs.

"You need to put those things away."

He blinks. "Right. Hmm. Well."

"Think about them. They're like any other part of your body."

"Other parts of my body are quite easily excited."

I chuckle. "And thank God for that, but..." I tilt my head.

He closes his eyes and takes a deep breath. He takes another. I've seen him breathe this way, deeply and slowly, when he does his morning stretches on deck. I wonder if it's his way of quieting his ever-racing mind. When he opens his eyes, he shows me his teeth, and they are white and straight and human again.

"You're going to be brilliant at this." I pull him to me and suck his bottom lip between my own. With our mouths still connected, he leans up higher on his knees and taps my hip. I understand the silent entreaty and raise my bottom half off the bed long enough for him to divest me of my breeches. Finally, we are skin to skin.

When our cocks touch, he lets out an inhuman moan. I shush him and put my hand over his mouth. "The whole ship will hear."

"Let them." He moves his hips in circles above me until my head falls back on the bed and I lose the ability to speak. I grip his hips and move my own body in small waves that meet his gentle whirlpool. "Fuck." His hands clutch to my chest.

I open my eyes and want to sob at his beauty. "Are you all right?"

"Yes. It just feels...*more*." His mouth drops open as he presses down roughly against me. "I didn't know anything could feel this good."

I caress his lower back before moving my fingers lower. One teases against his entrance, and the shock of sensation makes him shout. I push the fingers of my other hand into his mouth to stifle him. His hips lose their careful rhythm as he ruts against me.

With him so distracted and despite his newfound vampire strength, it's easy to flip him onto his back. He makes a quick noise of protest before I lift one of his long legs over my shoulder and push two fingers into his hole. Holy Lord, the expression on his face is almost enough to make me come. He clutches to the headboard above him and absolutely keens. His whole upper body arches off the bed.

"So beautiful," I manage, although I'm surprised I can string words together.

When I enter him, we're both beyond incoherent. We mumble endearments into each other's hair. Now unafraid of hurting him, I unleash some of my immortal strength until his entire body shifts up the bed with every thrust. Soon, he's half sitting with me riding him. He clutches to my shoulders, and I hold tight to his hips.

For a moment, I slow and kiss at his neck. I lick glittering sweat from the side of his face, and he stares at me like he wants to speak but cannot.

I continue my pounding pace and wrap my hand around his straining member. The back of his head makes a rather alarming sound against the headboard, but he doesn't seem to notice as he comes with a howl that I swallow with a kiss.

I usually pride myself on tormenting my sailor by withholding my own orgasm, fucking him until the pleasure-pain becomes too much and he begs for mercy, but I can do no such thing. No, as soon as I feel his muscles clenching around me, I let go and melt against him. We are a tangle of tingling limbs and heaving chests when I return to my surroundings. His fingers dig into my scalp so much it hurts as I pant against the side of his neck.

"We will fuck every day, you hear me?" he says.

I huff out a laugh and thrust my softening member into him once more. The pleasure of even that makes my toes curl before I slip out. I realize I have him trapped, and the way his legs are angled—well. I run the tip of my finger over the soft skin behind his knee, and he jerks beneath me.

"Andrew, don't you dare."

I repeat the movement, and he giggles. He tries to shove me away, but he's curled up in a way that hinders his strength. He is completely at my mercy, so I test pressures and motions on his only ticklish spot until he's writhing with laughter beneath me.

"Please, stop!"

"Did you think I had forgotten?"

He teased me for ages about the ticklish spot I had yet to find. He ultimately disclosed its location only when he thought he might die. I assume it was his parting gift to me, his little secret. Now that he will live with me forever, I plan to utilize my priceless knowledge in abundance.

"Yes. No. I..." He goes limp beneath me. "I admit defeat."

I stop tickling. "And what do I get as your forfeit?"

He looks up at me, eyes aglow with pleasure and glee. "I'm pretty sure you have everything you need."

I lower his legs from my shoulders, use his hips to shift him down the bed, and spread out on top of him the way he enjoys. I don't need to say anything. Edmund is asleep in mere moments anyway.

Chapter Two

IN THE MORNING, I'm not surprised to find him gone—but I am annoyed. I have grown accustomed to Edmund rising before me, especially during those days when he lost himself in the library in New Orleans. I had thought maybe he would wait for me on this, our first day together as immortals, but I shouldn't be shocked. I really shouldn't.

I dress quickly and set off to find my sailor. I wander the hall, wiping sleep from my eyes, then finger brush my blond hair. It must be very early indeed because the ship is quiet and I come upon no one as I approach the common area, where Edmund occasionally takes his tea.

Took his tea. He won't drink tea anymore. I wonder if he'll miss it.

I push the door open, walk inside, and find not Edmund but Brien. His dark eyes lift when I enter. He is nothing like he was yesterday as he is now a man, not a monster. I was thirty when turned and Edmund, twenty-eight. Brien must have been older—I would guess upper thirties, which had probably been considered ancient in his time. Even I, a Viking soldier living to see thirty, had been miraculous.

"Good morning," I mutter. I should bow at his feet for what he's done for me, but I still resent him for swallowing Edmund's soul.

He tilts his head forward just a bit. His long, black hair is now clean and pulled behind his head. He wears a simple shirt and coat.

"Have you seen Edmund?" I ask.

"Not yet."

I turn to continue my search, but Brien's voice, smoky and deep, stops me.

"Why did you try to subdue him last night?"

I freeze.

He takes a long, slow breath. "It seems a waste. He makes such...decadent noises."

I mimic his long breath to keep myself from jumping the table and clawing his throat.

"My apologies for hearing, but it is a very small ship."

The ship is huge.

"You should be careful. He might eventually tire of your jealousy."

I'm about to retort, but the door opens and I smell Edmund and the sea. He smells different, of course, now that he's dead—but he still smells sweet to me and like the bright, sunshine scent of open air.

"Hey! Morning." He pulls me to him and kisses me. "I didn't want to wake you. You looked so satisfied." He grins. "Brien. Morning. Did you sleep well?"

A long fingernail taps the table. "The noise will take some getting used to."

I try not to glare by focusing on Edmund, who no longer dresses as a sailor but as a society man in the green suit we bought, along with a matching waistcoat and no cravat, as usual. "You're gorgeous," I say.

He rests his hands momentarily on my hips. "Well, I spent the past week dying. I felt the need to be fancy."

"Is this how men dress now?"

I turn to see Brien gesturing to Edmund's tailored coat and long pants.

"Only the stylish ones." He smiles and pulls out a chair across from the Elder before sitting with a satisfied sigh. "I have so many questions for you, I don't know where to start."

"Questions?"

I put my hands on Edmund's shoulders. "He's a scientist. His curiosity never ends."

"How'd you end up sleeping on that sunken island, anyway?" Edmund asks. "I'd been there before, you know, before it went under. Seven years ago. Hell of a party."

The chair creaks when Brien leans forward. "I thought you smelled familiar."

Edmund chuckles. "I don't know whether you're being truthful or not."

"I might be a very good liar."

"You can't lie when I ask you questions. That's cheating."

Brien leans closer. "Cheating?"

"I mean not fair."

"What is fair?" Brien asks.

When I look at Edmund, he's not smiling anymore. He stares at Brien the way he once stared at me: like a puzzle that needs solving. Only there are more crinkles around Edmund's eyes. I'm not sure, but I think he might be scared.

He blinks and rests one of his hands on mine. "Let's go on deck. It's a beautiful day."

The chair creaks again when Brien leans back, and Edmund stands.

I run my thumb over his cheek and up into his hair. "Will you miss tea?"

"What's tea?" He winks.

HE'S SLICED INTO his palm so many times I've lost count. He doesn't even wince when he does it—just presses the knife against his pale skin and pushes. I suppose Edmund is good at pain. He's never complained about it, at least. I sit across from him at the common room table reading a book while he does his experiments.

"Holy Christ, my calluses are gone."

I glance up from my book. "You only now noticed?"

He glares at me as though I've done something wrong. "When did you?"

"The first time you touched me."

Most of his scars are gone, too, except the long one on his back. That one remains, thanks to an angry electric eel. When the Elder told him to "picture himself healthy," apparently Edmund believed that lovely scar was important enough to retain. I wholly agree.

He stares at his hand. "And now, the cut's already healed." He sighs, picks up his knife, and makes another deep cut.

I wince.

Silently, he counts. "Five seconds." He writes this number on a piece of paper and scrawls additional notes while muttering, "Amazing. Bloody amazing."

"Yes, you are."

He smiles at his notes.

The door swings open. "Edmund!" Flynn ever so dramatically makes his entrance and rests his slight weight across Edmund's shoulders. "Darling, I'm so full of blood! Won't you take some?"

Edmund chuckles as Flynn rubs against him. "I cannot. I have eaten more than enough."

He does not exaggerate. Over the past two days, humans have offered their throats to him in every dark nook and cranny of this ship. He is a novelty, this new vampire, and he is Edmund, charming and handsome as ever—perhaps more so with the loss of his mortality.

"Andrew," Flynn whines.

I set the book down. "Come on then."

Our little redhead hurries to my lap and curls himself within my grasp. I nibble at a fresh wound on his neck and drink until he moans. Lucky for me, I have regained my hunger for humans other than my sailor, although I will always carry the ghost of him on my tongue. No one will ever taste as good as Edmund once did.

When I pull back, Flynn hums and pets my chest. He leans his head on my shoulder and makes no move to stand.

Across the table, Edmund licks a drop of his own blood from the blade and frowns. "Well, that's disgusting."

I laugh at my scientist.

"Have you ever cut off a finger before?"

"Don't even think about it."

Edmund pouts adorably. "Poor sport." He sets down his knife and writes, writes some more. I have no idea what he's writing, what could be of such interest, but I'm not as smart as he is.

Flynn nuzzles ever closer as if to remind me he's there on my lap—and wanting. Every time Edmund drinks from the diminutive young man, he requests they make love, and Edmund always turns him down. It's sort of a shame that Edmund refuses all sexual advances but mine, considering mixing blood and sex is quite a high. But Edmund is resolute. He's done with everyone else. It's a heady, delicious burden I bear.

"I see you're still breathing," I say.

"Haven't forgotten how yet." He lifts his hand to reach for his knife.

I wouldn't have noticed if I hadn't been paying attention, but when he raises his fingers, the knife *moves*. It shivers as though cold. Edmund curls his fingers into a fist. His light blue eyes are huge in his face.

"Andrew. Did you..."

I shift Flynn on my lap and lean forward. "I..."

No, Edmund hasn't forgotten how to breathe. He's breathing quite quickly now, in fact. He opens his fist toward the knife, and instead of shivering, it scoots across the table right toward him.

Edmund draws back as though burned. "Oh, my God."

"It's magic," Flynn gasps.

Lips parted, Edmund gazes at me. "Brien," he says, and we both shoot to our feet.

Ever since that first morning, Brien has spent all his time alone in his room. He does not feed or socialize, much to Michelle's chagrin. She had hoped to spend a plentitude of time with our newly discovered Elder, and maybe she will eventually. Maybe he simply needs to adjust to a world that will only get louder once we reach London. Based on the way my beloved stomps down the hall, it's going to get louder sooner rather than later.

When we reach Brien's door, I push Edmund behind me before barreling inside. Despite his immortal status, I still feel the need to protect. Brien barely glances up from his seat against the wall.

"What have you done?" I shout.

Brien blinks at us from below dark brows. "I do not understand."

Edmund places his hand on my shoulder. "Andrew."

I shift out of his way but stand at the ready to attack.

My sailor doesn't speak as he glances around the room. Eventually, his gaze settles on a pointed cloak pin. He lifts his right hand and spreads his fingers wide. It takes a few silent moments, but then, the cloak pin flies at us. Shocked, even our immortal speed can't catch it before it lodges in the wall.

Edmund cusses, and Brien stands.

"So it did work."

"What did?" Edmund asks.

I take a threatening step forward. "What did you do?"

He wastes no attention on me, only Edmund. "Nothing awful, as your tone would suggest. I merely shared with him some of my abilities. I did not think it had worked, but apparently, it did."

He reaches his hand as if to caress my darling, but I catch his fingers in my fist and squeeze.

Brien slowly, calmly shows me his teeth. "He is my creation. I have as much right to him as you."

I open my mouth to speak as Edmund says, "What the bloody fuck?" He shoves us apart, and both Brien and I have to stutter-step to keep from falling. "Excuse me, but I'm not a possession. I don't belong to either of you."

I start to say his name, and he points at me.

"Shut it, Andrew." He stands tall between us. "Now, listen, both of you. I will not stand for your petty jealousies. I think we are all a bit old for that." He chuckles and turns to Brien. "Christ, you were probably helping the Egyptians build the pyramids, and here you are, acting like a jilted eighteen-year-old lover."

Brien lowers his chin.

"For the time being, we need to live in some sort of harmony. Brien, when we reach London—which will be very soon—you can do whatever you please."

"It would please me to stay with you."

"Fine, but...you and Andrew have to be friends."

I scoff.

Edmund grabs my arm. "Can't you do this for me?"

"Why?"

He steps closer, so close I can almost taste his lips. "I need him," he whispers. "I need to understand the full extent of what he's done to me."

"It's called *influence*, Edmund." Of course, the Elder would hear every word.

"Influence?" He turns his back on me, and God, I want to wrap him in my arms.

"It will start with objects. Perhaps, in time, you will be able to influence people, as well."

Edmund runs his hands through his black hair. "Any other surprises I should know about?"

Brien steps closer, and I have to tense the muscles in my legs to keep from stepping between them. "The only limitation to your abilities is you. I will help you hone your skills, one day at a time." He smiles and is almost handsome. "Now, would you give me a moment alone with your beloved?"

Edmund nods and squeezes my hand as he leaves the Elder's room. Now, I am alone with Brien, and it occurs to me that this ancient monster could probably tear me limb from limb singlehandedly. This Elder could kill me if he wanted and have Edmund to himself. Perhaps my animosity has been a rather idiotic emotion. I wait, watching for some violent move, but instead, Brien puts his hand on my shoulder. He is not quite as tall as me, but he still looms large.

"Your love for him is impressive. I see it in every gesture, every look. I was wrong to claim ownership. Forgive me."

I search for the lie on his face but do not find it. "You will help him?"

"As long as he needs."

"And then you will leave."

"If Edmund requests it." He drops his hand from my shoulder, and I swear I smell the wet, rotting scent of the sea. "He is extraordinary, I think. I had believed him beautiful—and he is, as are you—but it is more than that. *He* is more."

"Yes."

Brien wanders toward the wall and puts his hand on it as though he can see outside. "You loved him quite easily, did you not?"

"I did."

"Then, I shall be of help to both of you."

"Thank you." The words curdle in my mouth.

"My utmost pleasure." He laughs once at something I cannot see, so I leave the room. In the hallway, I find Edmund and drag him to our room and pleasure him until he makes loud gasping, begging sounds I am sure the Elder can hear.

Chapter Three

THIS IS NOT the time to laugh at Edmund, but his childish annoyance is almost as amusing as it is adorable. We've been on the sunny deck for hours—all of us. Most of the humans, as well as our vampire crew, refuse to go below because the Elder is helping Edmund master his abilities and they're desperate for entertainment. It's not going well, however. I should have expected as much. Edmund's mind has always been all over the place; why would it be any different now?

He buries his head in his hands and groans.

"Edmund. Try again." Brien is the picture of patience. His face shows not a wrinkle of irritation as he stands ten feet in front of my sailor with a hand extended, pointed toward a heavy metal ladle from the galley. "Focus."

"Focus. Fucking focus," Edmund mutters to himself. Standing behind him, I can't see his face, but I watch him lift his hand toward the ladle. It vibrates and moves. Suddenly, it flies toward us, completely off course. I twist around in time to see it make contact with Felipe's face with a comical *thunk.*

Felipe howls while Michelle laughs.

"Shit, Felipe, I'm sorry, mate." Edmund sighs toward his feet. "Damn it."

Felipe, for his histrionics, picks up the ladle and extends it to my love. "Your weapon, sir."

Edmund chuckles, but I can tell he's not amused. His forehead is wrinkled, and he chews on the inside of his lip.

"Again!" Brien demands.

Edmund closes his eyes and takes a deep breath.

"You can take a break," I say.

"No." He shakes his head before tossing the ladle back to Brien who catches it easily. Edmund removes his jacket, and Flynn rushes forward to take it. My darling unbuttons his cuffs and rolls up his white sleeves as if about to wash dishes.

"Might help if you take it all off," Felipe shouts.

Half the ship crows their approval.

I don't even think he hears them. He steps up to his place across from Brien—across from the dreaded ladle—but before lifting his hand, he glances back at me. "Andrew?"

I linger at his side.

"Put your arms around me."

"Hmm?"

"I always feel stronger in your arms. Come on."

I step up behind him and wrap him in an embrace. I kiss the side of his neck. "You know your mind races too quickly," I whisper. "Think of your morning stretches. The way you breathe. Can you use that here?"

He leans back against me. "Maybe."

Brien watches us. He waits.

"You can do this. You can do anything."

"Liar," he mutters, but he lifts his hand. I feel his chest expand on a long inhale. When he exhales, the ladle vibrates and moves. He doesn't breathe—he doesn't have to—as the ladle lifts and floats toward us. It lands silently in Edmund's outstretched hand, but the silence doesn't last. The deck erupts in cheers as Edmund drops his chin to his chest and curls his fingers between mine.

"You all right?"

He nods. "It's...odd, but yes. I feel as though we're characters in some fantastical penny dreadful. Monsters on the high sea." He lifts the ladle in his hand. "Mystics. Does that make sense?"

"Can't it be a love story instead?"

"Oh, you romantic fool." He leans farther into my embrace, and I kiss any skin I can reach.

When I open my eyes, Brien stands directly in front of us. He taps a long fingernail against the big spoon. "Again."

"Let us take but a moment to celebrate." Personally, I'd enjoy a few private moments to ravage my sailor, but Brien shakes his head. His long black hair blows free in the sea breeze.

"Land is already in sight." He gestures toward the far, faraway coast we spotted yesterday. "On the captain's word, we will see the coast of Great Britain any minute now. His abilities must be honed before London. It would not do to have an *accident*," he hisses, "in public."

Edmund pets the hand I have wrapped around his stomach. "He's right. Thank you, Brien."

"Anything for you," the Elder murmurs and bows his head.

Edmund inches farther toward me, back into my embrace, and again, I get the feeling he might be just a little bit afraid of Brien. I cannot see why. Brien has been nothing but adoring of Edmund since his rebirth. Brien would never hurt him.

When Brien walks away, Edmund relaxes and spins out of my arms. He shouts, "If we're going to be stuck up here all day, we should at least be drinking rum!"

The sailors laugh and erupt in a chorus of, "Here, here!"

Soon, we do have rum and chairs and cards—all on deck. I allow myself the pleasure of a few sips and even a cigar while I spend equal amounts of time watching Edmund and watching the sea. Despite my time trapped on this infernal vessel, I have learned to appreciate the ever-moving waves and the tall expanse of blue, blue sky: a blue that, when bright, reminds me of Edmund's eyes. It will be strange to be on dry land again. And what awaits our arrival?

I will not mourn the woman, but for Edmund's sake, I hope his mother is not dead. Her illness was never specified in the letter, so there's no way to guess what state she will be in. Then, there's the issue of business. Edmund must meet with his trading company and do his best to explain why their ship wrecked off the coast of South America. But business must wait.

We have discussed his plans already. Depending on the hour of our ship's arrival, we will either rush to his family's country estate, where his mother awaits us, or remain in London for a single night before hiring a carriage and making the trek. As far as I can tell, Michelle, Felipe, and Brien plan to accompany us wherever we go— for the time being. Flynn keeps trying to make his case, and although Edmund initially said no, I believe Flynn's constant arguments are beginning to wear through my sailor's resolve. Flynn adores us both, and it would be convenient to have a hot meal readily available. Especially since Edmund is still but a child in this and needs to feed often. A hungry young vampire is a dangerous vampire indeed.

By the time I've finished my second mug of rum, the ladle flies effortlessly into Edmund's hand. He takes a startled step backward when the ladle flies back to Brien, and Brien smiles that wicked, wide-toothed smile of his.

Of course, Brien would have the ability to move things with his mind; he gifted it to Edmund, after all.

The gray cravat around my throat slithers like a snake. I drop my rum and grab at the material, but it flies free, dances through the air, and wraps itself around Edmund's throat, tying in a perfect knot.

The side of his mouth quirks up. "I don't wear them."

"You should." Brien points the ladle at my darling. "The temptation of your skin is liable to cause others to sin. In their minds, at least."

"Sounds like a challenge." Edmund winks, and dear God, I think Brien actually blushes? He looks away at least.

Edmund unties the cravat and walks toward me. He tucks it back around my neck and ties it before running his hands down my chest as if adjusting my waistcoat. My waistcoat is perfect, so I assume he just wanted an excuse to touch—which is always welcome. He stares at me with shining eyes but is soon distracted by something over my shoulder. His small smile blossoms into a grin, so I turn around.

I see land ahead, different than the land we saw before. I see land and know, based on Edmund's expression alone, this must be England.

Somewhere, someone screams, "Land, ho!"

I sling my arm around his waist. "When was the last time you set foot on home soil?"

He takes a breath that raises not only his shoulders but his eyebrows too. "Seven years, and it was for but a moment: business and lunch with my mother and one of her friends, Lady Patricia. An awful bitch of a woman. Here's hoping she's dead."

"Tell me how you really feel."

"Flocks of devils would probably welcome her to hell, and Satan himself would cheer, 'Well done, good and faithful servant.'"

I laugh, half bent with amusement, and stand to find Edmund watching me with unbridled glee. I grab him by the back of the neck and kiss him. "I adore you."

"For my sacrilege or my exposed throat?"

"Both. Yes. All of it." I kiss him again. "Are you ready to return home?"

His expression darkens. He ducks his head and fingers the buttons on my shirt. "No. I keep thinking she might be gone already, and I never got to say I was sorry."

"What on earth do you have to be sorry for?"

He shrugs. "For not being who she wanted."

I take hold of his shoulders and give him a little shake. "You can't be sorry about that. Right now, this minute, you are surrounded by a ship full of people who love you just the way you are."

"But she's my mother, Andrew, and I destroyed her."

"Then, she will not be dead."

He rests his forehead against my chin. "How do you know?"

"Because she's still waiting for your apology."

He chuckles a little at that and leans into my chest. I hold him and run fingers through his hair.

"Whatever we face, we'll face it together."

He nods against me and holds tight.

Chapter Four

WE RUSH TO pack our things, and by the time we've tucked everything back into trunks, our ship already floats quickly up the Thames. The waterway is crowded, although ours is one of the more impressive vessels making its way toward London. The port is different than New Orleans—dirtier, more people, louder—but I see the city when we disembark, and I am excited to explore this unfamiliar country. Even if it does appear covered in smoke.

On the dock, I glance at brown-black water as Edmund speaks to a man about a carriage. "And you said *my* harbor was disgusting," I mutter. The world tilts below me, so accustomed am I to the sea. I plant my feet and focus on standing straight. I will not take a tumble into that water.

It has been agreed: the crew will remain in London for a time while we travel to the country to check the state of Edmund's mother. We'll eventually return to take care of his business dealings in the city. Michelle, Felipe, and Brien will be our companions, as will young Flynn, whose sweetness finally won Edmund over.

As the crew unloads our belongings, Edmund takes hold of my arm. "I've hired a carriage. I have a few errands to run, but you go to the hotel." He pauses as if he has more to say as he gazes over the water.

"Are you well?"

He nods. "I'll be back within the hour. Tomorrow morning, we ride for Heavenhill."

"Heavenhill?"

"My family's country estate." He buttons his coat. It's colder here, wetter. "It's a half day's ride north."

"Doesn't your family own property in London?"

He hesitates. "Yes."

"Yet, we stay in a hotel?"

He scratches his neck and finds sudden interest in the ground. "I don't know where I'm going to be welcomed, Andrew. At least I know my mother's doctor will let me in, considering he wrote the letter asking me to come. Our family servants might not be so..." He winces.

"Okay." I stop him from having to say more. "Is it a nice hotel, at least?"

He smiles. "The best."

Edmund directs me to our waiting carriage and, with a wave of his hand, disappears into the harbor mob. Luckily, the driver knows where to go, as I am lost in this massive city. The ride is bumpy, loud, and reeks of horse dung, but we eventually arrive at a place Edmund called Brown's.

Felipe steps out first and cusses immediately. "Oh, for fuck's sake."

I glance out. He's ankle-deep in what appears to be shit.

"Welcome to London."

"Shut up, Andrew."

With the help of Felipe and the driver, the rest of us avoid the worst of the muck and are welcomed into a lobby with a high, white ceiling and walls covered in dark wood. We're lucky our clothes are so expensive because we surely look disastrous, fresh from the boat. Then again,

Edmund walked into our New Orleans hotel barefoot, so I suppose we're not so bad.

Michelle pays for our lodgings. We end up with a suite—a group of interconnected bedrooms with a common area in the center. Everything is simpler, less gaudy than New Orleans. As opposed to gold, the rooms drip with luscious dark wood, silk pillows, and wooden floors that creak in places. I stand by a tall, thin window, admire the wrought iron balcony outside, and try to ignore the hubbub of the street, crowded by carriages.

The hubbub in our rooms is almost as bad, as Felipe demands a bath, as do Michelle and Flynn. Frankly, we all need baths, but we'll have to take our turns in the grand porcelain tub wedged in the washroom.

As hotel staff runs in and out with hot water, soap, and copious towels, Brien sits quietly by the door.

"We'll need to get you to a tailor," I say.

He nods but doesn't respond. He seems to be listening for something. Perhaps, as I expected, the noise of a modern city is too much for him. We exist together over the sound of splashing water for some time. I think it must have been an hour at least when Brien suddenly sits up straight mere moments before Edmund comes through the door.

He walks in as though his feet are heavy, and something in his gait, the look of his eyes, makes me run to him.

Brien stands too. "Dead man?" he asks.

Edmund chuckles a bit at the Elder's nickname but stares up at me. "I went to see my family solicitor." He pauses. "She's alive. My mother's still alive."

I put my hands on either side of his face. "That's what was worrying you on the dock."

"Well, it was a long journey. I didn't know…"

"But she is still alive?"

"Yes. Unless she died an hour ago. He wouldn't tell me anything more. I know Lady Patricia is indeed with her, but I know nothing of Mother's condition."

"We'll know by tomorrow night."

He leans forward and gives me a quick kiss. "I miss New Orleans already." He steps past me as Brien returns to his chair by the door like some sort of watchful gargoyle. Edmund pulls a paper-wrapped parcel from the inside of his suit coat and tosses it on a marble-top table.

"Currency?" I ask.

"I'm tired of Michelle paying for everything. It's not as though I'm lacking." He takes off his jacket and begins unbuttoning his waistcoat. "I don't care who's in that bath, I'm getting in with them."

"Flynn will be thrilled."

"At least we'll both fit. Which room is ours, love?"

I point. "Second from the right."

"Ta." He disappears inside but reappears in nothing but a blanket. "I'm tired of clothes," he says, but he does carry some breeches and a shirt under his arm. He sweeps across the common area and disappears into the washroom. I hear Flynn make a delighted squeak and pour myself a drink.

I drink and doze a bit. Brien sits still as a statue, but his presence is no longer threatening to me. Surreal as everything feels back on dry land, he might as well be a room decoration.

It's not long before Edmund emerges from the washroom with wet hair, wearing loose-fitting clothes. I grunt as he sprawls across my lap, smelling of sandalwood. He steals my drink and takes a long, healthy sip of scotch.

"Flynn refuses to get out of the tub until you join him."

I chuckle. "Ah, but we will *not* both fit." Edmund is thinner than me and shorter. Despite being an imposing figure, he can seem quite small when he wants to.

Edmund takes my glass and stands. He refills it with a bottle that had been already waiting in our room. His hair is beginning to dry. As it does, the shaggy, black locks curl into tendrils above his ears and forehead.

"How does it feel to be back?"

"More dream than reality." He remains standing by the window, staring out. His bare toes tap the floor. "It's bigger than it used to be."

"Things change."

"Not us," Brien says.

We're interrupted when Felipe and Michelle come prancing from their room, fully dressed in their bright colors and lace. I admit my interest is piqued.

Edmund gawks at them. "What on earth are you up to?"

Felipe crosses his arms. "We demand to see the city. You will take us to a party."

"No. Absolutely fucking not. We leave first thing in the morning."

"And it is not yet nightfall," Michelle says. She floats toward my beloved and rests her small hands on his chest. "We have been on a ship for ages. Tomorrow, we go to the country. We require entertainment prior to our next journey—specifically, sustenance. There must be someplace we can go with you as our guide."

"Well, he is a duke," I whisper.

Felipe gawks. "A duke? You must be joking!"

Edmund glares at me. "Now, you've done it."

Michelle coos. "Then, we shall go to a nice London society party."

"No." Edmund shakes his head.

"Oh, let's."

"Traitor!" he shouts at me.

"But, Edmund—"

He holds his hand up in my direction. "Don't you dare."

"Hmm, the young *duke* is quite amusing when he's angry." Felipe drinks right from the scotch bottle.

"I will kick your scrawny ass."

"But please do."

Edmund leaps at Felipe, and they're soon a twisting whirlwind of legs, arms, and Felipe's lace. Flynn comes traipsing from the washroom in nothing but his skin. "Why is everyone yelling?" He notices Edmund with his arm around Felipe's throat, Felipe's dark eyes threatening to bug out of his head. "Edmund, stop!"

He does, and Felipe chokes, his hair a mess. Between sputters, he says, "So that's what sex is like with you."

Edmund flops onto his back laughing.

Michelle, in wide, purple skirts, bends down beside him. "Please, darling, let us have some fun."

He sighs and stares at the ceiling. "Give me half an hour."

AFTER I BATHE, I go to the bedroom I share with Edmund and find him buttoning his silver waistcoat in front of the mirror. He wears his bespoke black suit. Although as a vampire he no longer needs to shave—he admits to missing the habit—his curls are oiled and shining.

His reflection glances at me, and my expression must speak volumes. "Oh, do I look that good?" he asks.

I drop my towel from my waist and walk up behind him. I press my naked front against his back and reach immediately for his clothed cock.

He chokes on an exhale, and his mouth drops open. "Fuck, Andrew."

I run my palm up and down his growing length, trapped in his pants. "You're going to seduce the whole party with your appearance alone. Every one of those posh society brats is going to want to fuck you...or be fucked by you."

His head rolls back onto my shoulder. "They never did before."

"They were blind."

"No," he huffs. "I was a bit different when I was eighteen, darling." He rests his hand on mine over his cock. "You'd better stop that. I'd rather not ruin these trousers just yet."

I suck his earlobe and taste the usual sweetness of his skin. "Fair enough." I step away after planting a last kiss to the side of his neck. "You are beautiful, though."

"Thank you." He sighs. "I haven't been to a society party in a million years."

Earlier, he sent out notes of inquiry, announcing his return to London but also asking about any society soirees. The response was almost immediate. *The seventh Duke of Wilshire back in London? Yes, please, join us!* Three invitations had vied for his attention, but he'd chosen what he called the "best party"—in other words, the one most likely to include passionate trysts in corners and opportunities for feeding. Still, it would be "formal and boring and uptight and so very *British*." He said the last word with such disdain, you'd think he wasn't an Englishman—although he never had spoken of his country with too much pride. He obviously did not love it the way I loved New Orleans.

I pull my suit from the wardrobe. "Do you remember how to behave?"

"No. God, no. I never behaved in the first place. That's why I didn't fit in and had no friends."

"You with no friends?" I shrug into my shirt. "I can't picture that."

"Well, I..." He slumps onto the edge of our bed. "I didn't care really. I despised them. Their forced frivolity and manners. It was all a load of horse shit."

"And you're too honest for that."

"I can play a part. I just didn't want to play that one. They probably won't even recognize me anyway."

I turn to face him as I pull on my pants. "You've changed that much?"

He smiles. "Andrew, you would have considered me feminine back then. I was so much thinner, weaker. Smaller. Men loved throwing me around." He looks at his hands, no longer covered in calluses but large and strong nonetheless. "Wouldn't be so easy anymore."

"I still can."

"Because I let you."

I scoff. "I'll always be stronger than you."

He grins. "Don't bet on it."

I reach for my waistcoat. "You'll be escorting Michelle. Just so you know. I can't very well show up on your arm."

"Fuck, I hadn't even thought of that."

"I assume 'fuck' is frowned upon at these things."

"Oh, everything is frowned upon at *these things*." He stands and dons his beautifully tailored black coat. "I'll have to sneak you away somewhere private and suck your dick."

I almost fall over, reaching for my shoes. "Good God." One of my shoes, though, flies from my grasp, and Edmund catches it midair.

"Hmm. Wonder how much trouble I could cause with that trick tonight."

"Absolutely not." I grab my shoe from him. "You will not use your abilities in public, particularly not in front of humans. Brien told you. We're not to draw attention." I appraise him up and down. "Well, we are not to draw attention to our immortality. Looking the way you do this evening, you'll be the talk of the town."

"It'll have little to do with how I look. As soon as I'm announced as the Duke of Wilshire..." He closes his eyes. "This is going to be a massive cock-up."

Chapter Five

WE MEANDER THROUGH the stinking streets of London in a carriage. It's just the four of us: Edmund, Felipe, Michelle, and myself. Brien showed no interest in attending, and although Flynn wanted to join us, he has no proper clothes for such a soiree. Edmund begrudgingly agreed to visit a clothier first thing in the morning to buy things for both Flynn and Brien. Although they won't be bespoke, they'll have to do, as we leave for Heavenhill straightaway.

My love is pretty much begrudging about everything right now. I watch him watch the city pass by, and unlike the overwhelming enthusiasm he held for New Orleans, he seems downright depressed here.

I put my hand on his knee and squeeze. "Edmund."

"Hmm."

"Look at me."

He does.

"I love you."

He smiles immediately. "Is my misery that apparent?"

"Yes," Felipe announces.

Edmund glances back at the window. "I never missed this place."

I take his hand in mine. He wears his black leather gloves, which send a pang of lust through me every time he dons them. "We won't be here long, and I say we enjoy ourselves while we're here."

"You haven't met these people."

"But I know you, and we always enjoy ourselves, don't we?"

He smirks before leaning forward and kissing my cheek. "Fuck them and their quiet, little minds. And I could go for a bit of strange meat."

"Oh, yes, please," Felipe agrees.

Michelle and I share a smile.

Minutes later, the inside of the carriage glows orange with lamplight as we pull up to a massive, three-story home wedged into what I presume to be the center of London. I actually have no clue, but it feels crowded here as if we step out into the city's beating heart. I pull my collar up against the cold and damp as Edmund helps Michelle from the carriage. He is, after all, her escort. I admire the gray brick façade and Doric columns. Candles flicker in each and every window.

Michelle curls her arm around Edmund's as they step up to my side. Her white hair turns gold in the nearby flames—torches set high and bright on either side of the house's grand entrance. "Shall we?"

"If we must," Edmund says, and onward they march.

A doorman welcomes us, and a servant silently takes our hats, gloves, and overcoats. Unlike our coven parties, I do not smell decadent foods. I barely hear music, just a bit of strings, over the quiet sound of muffled voices. Gaudy, white flower bouquets are everywhere as if we've interrupted a wedding.

A man ahead stands stiffly, waiting. Beyond him, I see women in fancy dress, men in high-collared suits, and more flowers. The people stand with champagne in their gloved hands, chattering quietly, laughing. Once we reach the stiff man, Edmund leans close and whispers his name and title. There's really no turning back now.

With a volume I wouldn't have expected, the stiff man shouts, "Madame Michelle and the seventh Duke of Wilshire, Edmund Baines."

It's like someone sliced all their pretty throats.

Edmund mutters, "Fucking hell," as the polite chatter disappears, replaced by a silence like water. It's impossible to take a breath, which makes me glad I don't need to. Glares, gazes, and curious quirked eyebrows akin to physical touch strip our skin.

Michelle, bless her, is lady enough to digest their attentions and walk farther into the room, smiling, dragging Edmund along by his arm. Felipe and I are quick to follow.

Conversations slowly start up, even quieter than before, but I hear Edmund's name whispered, whispered. They're talking about him.

Felipe whispers too. "That was..." He tugs on his collar. "Well. It's no wonder he doesn't want to be here."

A few steps ahead, Michelle pets Edmund's arm and presses her lips practically against his ear to speak. Whatever she says makes him smile, at least.

When a servant passes with a tray of champagne, we're all quick to grab. We stand in a little circle, the four of us, and I try not to stare—but there's so much to see. It's much like New Orleans but then, not. The fashion is similar, although several men still wear breeches, unlike Edmund's trousers that go all the way to the floor. Michelle fits in well, as there are exuberant frills everywhere and hair stacked high. Yet, the women stand taller, their corsets perhaps tighter. Due to my previous experiences with the British, I recall them being morally upstanding. All right, *uptight* is the word, until I met Edmund, of course: my foul-mouthed sailor. These people seem uptight, but then again, I am accustomed to orgies.

Michelle finishes her first glass of bubbly. "Edmund, dance with me."

"I don't dance."

"What?" This seems odd, even to me.

"I never learned so I wouldn't have to."

I nod. "Sort of brilliant really."

"Felipe."

"At your service." He takes her hand, and they walk toward the back of this grand ballroom toward the dance floor near the string quartet. The ballroom is set up like an outside courtyard in New Orleans with balconies on the second story that allows people to observe from above and, I assume, judge.

Edmund relinquishes his empty glass and grabs another. The maneuver is a dance in its own right. "There isn't enough champagne in the world."

I lean a bit close but not too close. "You're the most handsome man here."

"That was never much of a challenge." He downs his second glass. "The aristocracy does love its inbreeding."

I guffaw into my glass.

"Edmund Baines." A light female voice invades our revelry.

Edmund's eyes slide shut. His shoulders creep ever closer to his ears, but he quickly opens his eyes and plasters on a grin even a blind man wouldn't believe. "Veronica." He turns and takes the extended hand of a tall blonde with brown eyes and a deep-green gown.

"You look different," she says.

"As do you." He kisses the back of her hand, covered in black silk.

"I wouldn't have recognized you if not for your hair." She smiles something strange and small. "All of us girls envied your hair, but of course, you were such a pretty child." She says it with such veiled vehemence, you'd think she'd accused him of sucking a priest's cock.

His Adam's apple bounces, but he keeps smiling.

"I believe you know my husband." She looks back over her shoulder. "Thomas."

Edmund laughs once, quickly, and I try to remember why that name sounds so familiar. Oh, yes. Thomas was Edmund's first kiss. Happened in a broom closet, if I recall, when Edmund was fourteen. Thomas busted my darling's lip in his haste to touch and taste, but who can blame him?

And isn't Thomas a delight? He turns at the sound of his wife's voice, giving me a perfect view of his chestnut-gold hair and full lips. He chokes on his champagne when he sees Edmund, however. "My goodness, Baines, but you look..."

Edmund flutters his eyelashes, waiting.

Thomas clears his throat and steps from right foot to left. "Apparently becoming a mad seaman has been good for you."

Now, my Edmund is truly smiling. No need to fake amusement anymore. "And you married Veronica. How lucky for you."

Veronica taps her gloved fingertips on the side of her glass. "I saw you arrive with a stunning beauty. Madam Michelle, was it?"

"Is she your wife?" Thomas asks.

"Oh, we both know I'm not the marrying type, Thomas."

The man turns red.

"You never did seem the sort to settle down." Veronica's eyes immediately dart in my direction. "Your friend, is he a sailor, as well?"

Edmund clasps me on the shoulder. "Andrew? God, no. He's from New Orleans. Andrew, meet Veronica and Thomas. Old *friends*."

I kiss Veronica's hand and nod at her husband. The poor bastard can't take his eyes off Edmund. He goes so far as to lick his lips while taking in every inch of Edmund's impressive physique. "A pleasure to meet you both."

"American." She smiles that little smile of hers. "How novel. How did you two meet?"

Edmund and I glance at each other.

"Uh…" he starts. "It's kind of a long story, that. There was a shipwreck. And cannibals." He scratches the back of his head. "A good bit of carnage, really."

"Oh." They both stare at us, eyes wide. "Well. At least you found time to see a good tailor. Your suit is exquisite."

I don't mean to, but I laugh. It's so ridiculously polite.

She touches his arm. "My mother mentioned your mother is ill?"

"Indeed, it's the reason I'm home. My friends and I travel to Heavenhill tomorrow."

"Well." She spares one last glance at me, and it's as though her eyes say, *I know you're fucking him.* "Our prayers go with you. It was wonderful to see you, Edmund."

As they back away, we share little smiles, and that's when I realize why Veronica's grin struck me as so strange. A smile is supposed to be an indicator of happiness, but hers is nothing more than a trained expression. There is no joy behind it. It's almost like having the ability to walk but never knowing where to go.

"You don't talk as they do. Your accent sounds different. I never noticed before."

"Well, I assume they've never left England." He winks when Thomas takes one last look back and almost trips over his wife's dress. "I've been around the world. It was bound to change me, whereas they are exactly the same."

"You think he's still kissing boys in broom closets?"

He smiles and shrugs. "Perhaps. Or perhaps he gave that up years ago. Doesn't mean he still doesn't want it. If I truly set my intention, I could seduce half the men in this room. Hypocritical cowards." He reaches for a passing tray of champagne, but before he can touch a glass, the glass leaps from the tray and, unbalanced, into his hand. He spills some on the floor and glances at me, eyes wide.

"Careful," I mouth.

I have a feeling Edmund's abilities are directly affected by his emotions. When he's happy, with my arms around him, he's better at control. That was how he was able to control the ladle on the ship, after all. When he's stressed, objects fly every which way. I don't want to see what anger might do.

"Right." He makes a clicking sound with his tongue. "Michelle and Felipe are..."

"Still dancing."

"Think they'll be all right on their own?"

"You want to leave already? Not that I blame you, but—"

"No. You see that staircase?" He nods toward a candlelit stack of marble in the back corner of the ballroom.

"Yes."

"I'm going to go up there, you're going to follow me in a few minutes, and I'm going to do unspeakable things to you at a London society party before we do indeed exit to go find dinner. Savvy?"

Now, like poor Thomas, I'm the one staring as I nod. "Good." He walks away with his champagne.

I try to stand around with a disinterested expression, but I'm practically bouncing on my toes by the time I finally decide to move. I'm already half hard in my pants as I climb the steps—but no one waits at the precipice. I think to whisper his name but instead wander farther down a dark hallway, not intended for party guests apparently as it is lit by nothing but a few flickering flames. The music echoes up here as though heard underwater, and polite laughter whispers as the breath of ghosts.

Just when I think Edmund has played some awful joke, a hand grabs me in the dark and pulls me through an open door. I'm shoved against the wall as Edmund presses his chest to mine, hands on the back of my head, and kisses me. Oh, his mouth is a marvel. He has the soft, full lips of a woman but the strength and hunger of a starving man. His tongue touches my lips until I open my mouth and moan around the invasion. I move my hands to his ass and squeeze, rolling our hips together.

Edmund drops to his knees. He mouths at my clothed cock, and my head tilts back against the closed door. Only then do I realize we're in a small bedroom—hopefully abandoned. When he unbuttons my trousers and exposes my dick, I'm too gone to care. He takes the entirety of me into his mouth, and I hold tight to his hair. For a dead man, his tongue is certainly hot. I don't even worry about his fangs.

Chasing release, I thrust gently down his throat. I know he can handle me. Jesus, I've literally fucked his throat before until he choked. He got off in the midst of it, untouched.

As I consider reenacting that exact thing, Edmund's lips release me and he stands. He squeezes my cock in his hand but doesn't move.

"And what if I left you this way?" he whispers, mouth against my ear. "What if I made you go back out to the party, rock-hard and wanting?"

I latch onto the lapels of his coat. "Wouldn't happen. I'd bend you over that bed and fuck you first."

He hums. "I'd let you."

I nibble at the side of his neck until he tilts his head. "Get on your knees."

At my command, he drops and gazes up at me, waiting.

"Hands behind your back."

Even in the dimness, I see one of his dark eyebrows raise. He does as told, though, folding those long fingers at the base of his spine. He licks his lips until they shine.

I take full control of that sinful, brilliant mouth of his. I'd like to say I make him work for it, but honestly, I'm coming two minutes later. Anticipation can make the finale sweet, but soon. Of course, he dutifully swallows my dead seed and doesn't stand until I give him a nod of permission.

I taste myself on his tongue. "You'll fuck me later, won't you?"

I run my nose across his cheek. "Quietly, yes. Brien hears everything, you know."

He freezes in the midst of a delicate caress. "God, does he?"

"Perhaps he will be asleep."

He sighs. "We're going to have to be quiet for a long time, love. We are headed to the country. Sounds echo through old country estates."

"*You're* the loud one."

He grunts and rests his forehead on my shoulder.

"Hungry?"

"I just ate," he mutters.

I laugh into his hair.

"Let's go find some stumbling drunk. I do prefer a little wine with dinner."

Chapter Six

MY LOVE IS impatient and has every damn right to be. Michelle and Felipe are late, still shopping. Edmund took Brien and Flynn early this morning to a London tailor and bought them every bit of clothing they desired. Flynn wanted suits that fit Edmund's style—complete with colorful, silk waistcoats—but Brien resembles a Puritan in his all-black, high-collared affairs. Now, with two carriages waiting downstairs, Edmund paces and tugs on his hair until it looks tangled.

I grab him by the elbows and make him stop. I even brush his hair with my fingers and kiss his forehead while Flynn primps in his bedroom and Brien probably stares at the walls of his own. I've noticed the Elder values his alone time greatly. The only creature he lingers over is my sailor.

We freeze at the sound of an abrupt knock on the door. It echoes through the large room like thunder.

Edmund frowns. "Now, who the bloody hell is that?"

"Maybe the carriage drivers are getting impatient."

"God, why? I paid them enough to wait."

I kiss him on the nose and go to answer. As soon as I turn the knob, the door is forced open. A middle-aged man with a sizeable gut and a silver cane rushes inside. "Where is he?" I'm about to step forward and inform the man he has the wrong room, but he shouts when he sees Edmund. "Baines! Alive!"

"Conroy, I—" He coughs at the force of the fat man's sudden embrace.

"You just won me fifty pounds! They said you were dead, and I said, 'Baines! Never! That foolhardy idiot will outlive us all! If anyone could conquer death, it'd be Edmund.'"

My darling sort of chuckles.

"Everyone else dead?"

Edmund's eyes go to the floor. "Yes."

"Awful business." The man, Conroy, clears his throat and taps his cane on the floor. "It's all over the city that you're back." He digs around in his breeches and pulls out a paper. "See! You made the society column. Seventh Duke of Wilshire. A reprobate like you, a duke? Laughable!" And so he laughs. "But you must come straightaway to the trading company. We have serious business to discuss." He latches onto Edmund's arm and starts pulling.

Edmund plants his feet to stop the fat man's tugging. "Conroy, I cannot."

"You must. There is an inquiry, and you know we must close the case on this unfortunate event. You must tell us everything."

"I will, but later. I must leave straightaway to see my mother. She's ill."

Conroy hasn't asked for an introduction—or even shown knowledge of my presence—until he turns and glares at me. "Tell this rascal that business must be attended to."

I don't bother responding.

Edmund finally shakes his arm free. "Conroy, when I return, I—"

"No, my boy!" he shouts. "This is a matter of the utmost importance. We've lost an entire ship and crew to, what, a storm? Fine, fine, but it must not happen again. Now, come to the offices and sign a few things. Your mother can wait."

Edmund takes a slow breath in through his nose and appears to grow—as he always does when he's spoiling for a fight. "You will wait until I return from Heavenhill."

"No, I shall—"

"Conroy. You will wait until I return from Heavenhill."

The fat man, for all his earlier boisterousness, stands perfectly still, staring at Edmund. I watch him blink. His fingertips tap the top of his cane.

"Do you understand?" Edmund asks.

"I will wait until you return from Heavenhill."

"Thank you, Conroy. Now, please, depart."

Conroy turns and leaves the room, shutting the door gently behind him.

Edmund crumbles to one knee, one hand on the floor. He groans, and I run to him. "Edmund?"

He weaves and appears to faint dead away, limp on his back on the hardwood.

"Brien!" I scream.

The Elder is at my side before I even hear his bedroom door open. The sound lingers behind us like an echo in a cave. He sits on the floor and scoops Edmund into his arms. "What happened?"

"He...influenced a man, I think."

Brien grins, not even bothering to hide his fangs. Then, he turns his attention back to Edmund. He speaks with his lips against my love's forehead and rocks him back and forth. "Edmund...Edmund. Wake up."

"Mm." He curls into Brien's embrace.

"You need to drink from me."

Edmund doesn't open his eyes. "But you're dead."

"Not to you."

My gaze certainly asks a question, but Brien only has eyes for Edmund.

"Have you not noticed I smell different?" His long, pointed fingernails caress the side of Edmund's neck.

"I just thought you needed a bath."

Brien chuckles and, without letting go of Edmund, manages to roll up his black coat and undo the row of buttons at his cuff. He holds his wrist to Edmund's mouth. "Drink."

Insatiable as always, my darling doesn't hesitate. His fangs flash in the late morning light before disappearing into Brien's pale flesh. The Elder makes a deep, pleased sound that makes me want to claw his throat out. I curl my hands into fists on my folded knees to keep from attacking.

It's barely a minute before Brien pulls his hand away. Edmund leans up to take more, but Brien holds him back with a hand in his hair. "That is enough. I would not want you to have too much." He hides his wrist but not before I see two black holes.

I'm sure Edmund has questions—hell, I've got about fifty—but instead of asking, as I might expect, he smiles and melts back to the floor where Brien leaves him and stands. I stand too. Between our feet, Edmund stretches and smiles. "Shit, this is better than rum."

Brien grins down at him. His long, black hair obstructs half his face.

"What happened?" I ask.

"Influencing requires strength. He requires me to recuperate, or the ability could kill him."

"He never fainted from moving ladles."

"Moving the human mind takes a bit more."

Still on the floor, Edmund hums to himself, completely lost in sensation.

"But what did you feed him? You have no blood."

Brien's dark eyes run over the length of Edmund's body. "No, I do not. I cannot be certain, but I believe it was part of his soul. When I killed him, I took that. I feel it inside me sometimes, the taste of it—his passion, his fortitude."

I clench my fists.

"I know you wanted to swallow those things. I am sorry I took them from you, but this is the reason I did." He stares at me now, gaze firm. "An Elder and offspring have a certain connection that others do not. When I created Edmund, I gave him *more*. But to be more, he needs the gift I give—the breaking of my skin and the consumption of what I have."

"His own life."

Brien shrugs. "It is the only conclusion I've been able to draw."

"So you've done this before, made someone like Edmund?"

Before we get any further, Felipe and Michelle come tumbling inside, followed by several hotel staff carrying bags and boxes.

Felipe hoots when he sees Edmund on the floor. "Drunk already?"

"Not exactly," Edmund replies. He sits up and stands, one hand on my shoulder and the other on Brien's. "Jesus, did you buy out Savile Row? You're late. Get your things."

My old friends tut and apologize and wander toward their bedroom as servants set their new purchases here and there.

Edmund speaks quietly. "Let's keep what just happened between the three of us?"

"Of course, Edmund," Brien says.

I nod. Due to our audience, I do not pull him to me in an embrace, but I want to. It never occurred to me that Edmund could be weakened in his immortal state or that Brien could conceivably become an eternal necessity in our lives. I never felt much of a connection to my Elder, but oh, then, I remember: my soul was gone when my Elder found me. He may have given me life, but he never took or cherished mine.

I'VE NEVER SEEN Edmund quite this moody, but I don't blame him. I can't even consider the thoughts raging through his rather gargantuan brain. I know his mind rushes, but I've never had to watch it circle and circle and circle itself like this. I have no choice, trapped in our gently rocking carriage with Brien and Flynn. Michelle and Felipe follow close behind—the two of them and our belongings, which have recently doubled thanks to their morning shopping spree.

Beyond the window, the English countryside passes green and lush beneath a gray sky that makes the colors all the more vibrant by comparison. Inside, Brien sits silently at my side. Across from me, Flynn lounges against Edmund's shoulder and reads. Based on a single comment I made during our sea voyage, Flynn knew to buy Edmund a penny dreadful. Flynn seems to remember everything I have ever said about Edmund.

I think Flynn is in love, desperately, fruitlessly. The young man fixates. Today, he bought clothes Edmund would wear. He bought a book Edmund would enjoy. He leans on Edmund as though begging for attention, and he gets it in small bursts. As he reads the tall tale of some horse-riding bandit, Edmund does sometimes run his fingers through Flynn's bright-red hair.

Eventually, Flynn pouts midsentence. "Take off those gloves. I don't like when you touch me in gloves."

Edmund shoots me an amused glare but does as instructed and removes the black leather gloves I find so damned attractive. He lays them across his thigh and again plays with Flynn's hair. Flynn sighs and leans harder against Edmund's body. Although nineteen, his immaturity is proof of his privileged life inside the coven. It can be an annoyance, but his childish behavior is welcome right now as a distraction from my love's troubled thoughts.

I'm sure Edmund expects the worst. His mother has been sick for months at least—maybe longer—and he knows not with what. Perhaps she's wasted away by now to nothing but bones and skin. Perhaps she's confined to bed. Perhaps, perhaps. There are so many maybes. I practically smell the fearful uncertainty that rises like steam from Edmund's skin.

As Flynn reads, Edmund's eyes, bright in contrast to his simple black suit, dart from outside to across the carriage at me. Occasionally, he closes them altogether and rests his nose and mouth in Flynn's hair. It's an endless, ever-moving visual cycle, and I wish he would just sleep, if only to pass the time.

The penny dreadful ends with a massive climax of blood and screams—and a big, romantic kiss, of course. Flynn closes the little book. "Did you enjoy it, Edmund?"

"Hmm?" He sighs. "Yes, thank you."

Flynn yawns and reclines across Edmund's lap. He's such a small thing. It's not long before he sleeps.

Edmund's voice interrupts the sound of horse hooves on gravel. "How old are you, Brien?"

Brien startles at the sound of his name as though he too, were dozing, although I have yet to see the Elder sleep. "What does it matter?"

"Curiosity is my habit."

"Or curse," I mutter.

"*Your* curse," Edmund agrees. "A lover that never shuts up."

"I would have it no other way." I wink.

"Come on, Brien. The book is finished. Indulge me." What a cad. The way Edmund smiles up from below his dark lashes, no one could refuse him.

"I do not know my exact age. Only the things I have seen."

"What have you seen?"

I turn to watch Brien as he considers. He looks to the floor and folds his hands. "All aspects of humanity. Love and hate, war and peace."

When he says nothing more, Edmund asks, "Did you travel?"

"Some."

"Why did you bury yourself anyway? Why would you want to, with the power you have?"

Brien remains silent, but he gazes right at Edmund. After a pause bordering on awkward, he says, "I lost someone. I didn't want to miss him anymore."

"Then, why didn't you have yourself killed?"

The Elder shrugs. "One never knows when an Edmund might show up."

My beloved laughs, but I'm not amused. Brien says so little about himself, which makes it the more apparent to me that he has secrets he does not wish to reveal.

Edmund wipes at his eyes. "You speak in riddles, Brien. Tell a story. Just one."

"You are the one who tells stories, dead man."

"Everyone tells stories. Some are simply better than others."

Brien leans forward as the carriage sways. "Will you tell me another story?"

"About what?"

"Why does coming home make you sad?"

Edmund laughs again, but it sounds like he's been punched. I want to leap across the carriage and hold him, but the sudden rocking keeps me planted. We've apparently turned off the main street and now head even farther into the country.

My darling stares resolutely outside. "You see more than you let on."

"I see you," Brien murmurs.

"Let's not talk anymore."

"I only—"

"Leave it, Brien."

The Elder looks at me. I give a single shake of my head and twist my fingers together in lieu of touching Edmund, who seems as though he might bite. His whole demeanor has shifted—again. The entertainment of Flynn's reading added some levity to his expression, but his frown is back, as are the lines on his forehead. He embodies the clouds that threaten outside.

His right finger taps against his thigh near Flynn's head. *Tap-tap-tap.* It takes me a moment to realize it's not his finger making that noise but the discarded penny dreadful, opening and slamming shut on the seat without being touched.

"Edmund?"

"What?" he snaps at me—and wakes Flynn.

The youth bolts upright at Edmund's harsh tone. "Are we there?"

"Flynn, come sit with Brien please."

It takes some maneuvering in the ever-moving carriage for us to switch places, but as soon as I come to rest at Edmund's side, he hurls himself into my arms. A pointless breath whooshes from my chest. It's a strange dichotomy: the lean strength of his physicality contrasted with the fragility of his mental state. He is muscle and expensive fabric to the touch but tortured to the eyes and ears.

"I've got you," I whisper.

Flynn's small voice: "Edmund?"

"I'm all right, Flynn," he mutters against my coat. The lie is so practiced—perfected over twenty-eight years—that it almost sounds true.

Chapter Seven

AN HOUR LATER, when the carriage man yells, "About there, sirs," Edmund sits bolt upright and stares out the window. Before the carriage takes a slow right turn, I get a glimpse of it: Heavenhill. Christ Almighty, my sailor is rich. Flynn climbs onto my lap to get a better view as we pass lush bushes reshaped into careful spheres. The hedges are trimmed in a similarly geometric fashion, square on the sides. Finally, we see the house up ahead, and Flynn gasps.

I remember Edmund having a shocked response to the coven manse in New Orleans. He had asked if God lived there. It's a wonder he would find our Southern architecture so divine when he grew up surrounded by this. The three-story mansion—or would this be a castle?—is made of light-red brick. Its front façade faces the road, surrounded by forward-facing wings on either side as if the house itself hopes to hug us. Several chimneys line the roof, and windows... there are so many windows.

"Sixty-four."

"Hmm?" I ask.

"Windows. And I have stared longingly out all of them."

The carriages pull to a stop, and I have to latch onto Edmund's arm to stop him from barreling vampire speed into his family's country estate. "Easy," I command.

He nods in understanding.

I follow him out into the early evening gray. He doesn't bother to button his coat as we approach the front door, already opening for us. A servant in a simple black suit stands by the door. He lowers his white-haired head at Edmund. "Your Grace."

By the time we step into the massive foyer—Jesus, the entire house is made of marble and fine art—our group is reunited. We crowd around Edmund as a protective shield: Michelle, Felipe, Brien, Flynn, and myself.

High-pitched voices echo from what appears to be the parlor. A large black piano sits in the corner. Its polished veneer sparkles like diamonds. When I hear running feet, I want to shield my darling. I take a step closer to him and rest my hand on his lower back.

No panicked doctor appears. No jilted ex-lover who might mean Edmund harm. No, a tall woman with wild gray-brown hair rounds the corner in nothing but bedclothes and slippers. I recognize those blue-gray eyes immediately.

A young servant girl in a bonnet is close on her heels but freezes when she sees our troupe. "Madam, please, we have guests," she begs.

"Oh." The older lady smiles and appraises us. "Look at all the handsome men!"

"Mum?" Edmund's voice shakes.

"Mum?" the woman repeats. She takes small, shuffling steps toward Edmund and stares up into his face. I watch the haze of confusion shift and move until she reaches out one lace-gloved hand to touch his cheek. "My boy?"

"Yes." He takes her hand and kisses her palm. "Mum, what's wrong?"

She shakes her head and pulls her hand away. "No. It can't be. No, my boy is dead. They told me."

"Wh-who told you?"

"Everyone." She smiles, eyes wide and darting. "But you are welcome to stay as a ghost. I do enjoy the company." She holds her skirts and swishes them around in grotesque parody of a little girl showing off her new gown. "My dear Edmund is quite dead, but I had thought his ghost might visit, so welcome, at last. Now, I must check on my tea. Someone has been drinking all the tea, and I am so thirsty." She laughs loudly and takes off running back in the direction she came. The poor servant girl struggles to keep up.

Edmund's breath shakes on an inhale, and he makes a sound I've never heard: something between a mumble and a sob. His shoulders lurch forward as he drops his chin to his chest. I don't know what to say, what to do.

My uncertainty is cut short by the sound of a harsh female voice with a posh British accent. She sounds as though she speaks from above when she says, "So the devil returns."

Edmund doesn't bother wiping the tears from his face as he turns around. Halfway up the wide marble staircase stands a woman in a layered black gown as if in mourning. Her long hair, up in a bun, is a watered-down version of Flynn's cherry red. Everything about her is pointed, from her nose to her chin to the long fingers that tap the dark wood banister.

He inclines his head to her. "Lady Patricia."

"Your *Grace*."

"You have no need to call me that."

"I only do so in jest. With your return, you are now a duke, after all." She takes a few steps down but remains even a head higher than me. "You've seen your mother."

"What's happened to her?"

"She's gone mad." The pointed woman smiles. "We are hiding her here in an effort to avoid the society papers. Madness is so unpopular. You would know."

Before I can step forward to murder this creature, Edmund latches onto the back of my coat.

"Did you think she was sick? Dying?" Patricia folds her hands in front of her. "Apologies that you cannot yet profit from her death."

"Christ, Patricia, I've had my own accounts since I was eighteen. I don't need her money."

She finally ignores Edmund and stares at the rest of us. "How nice for you, but what of your friends? Without a mansion at your disposal, I suppose they'll leave you now."

Michelle's voice is strong and loud. "We are not with Edmund for his money. We are here because we love him."

"Has he charmed you the way he charmed my husband?" She glares at Edmund. Her stare moves slowly from his legs up to his chest. I would say it was a look of lust if not for the disgust on her face. "It's hard to imagine now. You were so much more delicate then. Easier for men to believe that sinful mouth belonged to a lovely lady."

"I don't want you in this house," Edmund says.

"It is not your decision, *child*. I am your mother's caretaker now. I never would have written to you, but that doctor felt it was his right to keep you informed. You will stay in the guest wing—you and your friends—and you will not stay long."

I see Edmund's silence not as agreement but as recognition of futility. There is no talking to this beast.

Before she disappears in the direction of Edmund's mad mother, she pauses in front of us. She leans close to Edmund and whispers, "I pray every day that your soul will burn in hell."

I'm so shocked by her vehemence, I don't move. She leaves us, blessedly, and Edmund wipes his hand over his face. "Fucking welcome home."

I clear my throat to quell the strange nausea Patricia's mere presence inspired in me. "Could you give us a moment?" I speak to everyone but Edmund.

"Why don't you sit in the parlor?" he offers our friends. "I'll have someone get a fire started momentarily."

I lean down and speak quietly. "Her husband?"

He rolls his eyes. "He was a baron I sucked off at a society party. Maybe I've mentioned him before. I was only seventeen, but he became obsessed. Our families were so close that Patricia found out, of course."

I sort of want to shake him. "Damn it, Edmund, you could have been hung for buggery."

"And incriminate her husband too? Strip his title, her title? Ruin their reputations? No, she wouldn't dare." He watches our friends poke and prod around his home. "I've always thought her continued relationship with my mother is her way of punishing me."

"What happened to her husband?"

"He caught ill and died a year ago. Maybe two. I don't remember. Mother wrote me with the news. Patricia probably said it was God's judgment. Irony is she thinks she's the most pious woman in Britain, and I've never met anyone less Christ-like."

"I'm sorry you've had to deal with her."

He squeezes my hand. "Getting a clear image of my life here yet?" I think he tries to jest, but there's no humor in it. "I'm going for a quick ride." He nods toward the parlor. "Would you give them my apologies?"

I wish he would come away somewhere private where I could just hold him and kiss him for a while, but—

"Edmund?"

His head shoots up, and he squints at a little wisp of a woman in a bonnet and simple brown dress. "It can't be. Hallie? You've grown up!"

"So have you." She smiles, and although she isn't overly pretty, she seems gentle, sweet. "What on earth have you done to yourself?"

"Uh..."

She laughs and extends her hand. "Come here." Despite her small stature, she wraps her arms around his neck and pulls him into a hug. It's not awkward or strained. It's a comfortable hug between old friends, and Edmund sinks into her embrace with his eyes closed.

"I didn't even know you were still working for my family."

She pulls back but keeps her hands on his shoulders. "Well, my mother died a few years back, so I took over."

"Sorry."

"It's all right. Head of the household now." She reaches up and pulls one of his black curls. "Remember when we were kids, and I tried to braid your hair?"

"Yes, you tied it in knots. Your mother was furious."

Hallie laughs quietly—the perpetual politeness of a lifelong servant. Then, she faces me. "Who is this, then?"

"Andrew." Edmund grabs my hand and pulls me forward. "My beloved."

I almost swallow my tongue.

Meanwhile, Hallie's whole face lights up. "You've found someone? Oh, how wonderful, Edmund. I'm so happy for you." She takes my free hand and shakes it. "Welcome, sir." She turns back to Edmund. "I trust you'll be needing only one bedroom then, you bad boy. I'll set you up in the far room of the guest wing. Patricia won't even notice, the cow."

Edmund snorts and laughs.

"I'm very glad you're back." She bows her head to me. "And you, Andrew. I hope to hear of your adventures."

Edmund leans down and kisses her cheek before she walks away, presumably to prepare our quarters.

I watch her diminutive form climb the steps. "She knows about you?"

"Yes. Always has." He puts his hand on my shoulder. "I need to go to the stables. I'll be but an hour."

He doesn't wait for my blessing. I amble into the parlor where another servant does indeed prepare a fire. The house is cold, but it has little to do with temperature. Soon after I sit, Michelle beckons me to the window. A heavy fog has descended, but I still make out a black horse and tall rider who race over the darkening green hills as though being chased.

IT'S HOURS BEFORE he comes back. Everyone else has already gone to bed, and I stand in one of Heavenhill's sixty-four windows and stare into the black. In the reflection, our room is simple and cozy behind me. There's a large bed and a number of blankets to protect against Britain's damp cold. There are heavy pieces of furniture and golden candelabras. A servant brought a warm water basin earlier. I rinsed my face but did not further prepare for bed. I wait for Edmund.

I don't turn when the bedroom door opens, but I smell whiskey.

"You're still awake," he says.

"Where have you been?"

He stumbles into the room and closes the door. "The village."

"Why?"

I hear him wrestling with his coat. "Needed to get away."

Now, I turn to face him. His hair is windblown, his eyes unfocused. "You're drunk."

"A bit." He sits on the edge of the bed and tugs at his shoes.

When I step forward to help, I also smell blood and freeze. "You fed."

"Just a friendly nibble." He frowns. "Am I supposed to ask your permission first?"

"Don't be an ass."

He chuckles. "I get tired of it, you know—you treating me as your precious little pup."

"I do no such thing."

He laughs now. "God, you don't even see it, do you? You treat me like a child when you're not balls deep." His shoes fall loudly to the floor.

"Well, when you behave like one..."

He shakily unbuttons his waistcoat. "I did fine without you."

"Yes, because you ran away from your problems, as you did tonight. Your mother screamed when they put her to bed."

"Fuck off."

"She called for you."

He pauses in his movement. "Why would she? I'm dead."

I step forward and point at him. "Go ahead, feel bad for yourself. But you are the man of this house now. Start acting like it."

"I thought you might prefer the position." He sneers. "Seeing as how you own me."

I turn away. "I won't talk to you in this state."

"No?" I hear him move, and despite his inebriation, he easily grabs my arm and spins me around. "You love that I won't fuck anyone else. You love having me all to yourself, controlling me. You always have. *Everyone* always has. Why is that? What is it about me that begs for claiming?"

"Edmund—"

"Is it your own insecurity? You spent centuries alone until me. Why?" He latches onto the front of my shirt. "Was I an easy target? A weak, pretty thing on that bloody island. If I had run from you, would you have let me?"

I open my mouth to speak, but something... something is shifting within me. Something bad.

"You would have taken advantage, like so many others." He moves so close, spit hits my face. "You are just like them, the cowards who shoved me over couches and took and took. You are not special. You were merely stronger than them. That's why you have me—because I couldn't get away."

The dark creature, silent for so long, purrs. *And I will never let you leave. If you tried to run, I would chase you to the ends of the earth. I would tie you up and keep you forever...forever.*

"There it is," he says. "Haven't seen that look in ages." He shoves me hard in the chest—so hard I take three steps back. "Come on." He shoves me again. "Show yourself."

"You don't want to play this game," I growl.

"Fuck off, old man." He heaves another shove into my chest. "Scared now that I can fight back? I thought you enjoyed feeling me struggle."

God, I do: struggling and whimpering and begging. I wonder if I can make him cry.

He throws the first punch. I shouldn't be surprised when I see stars. I know he can punch; I've borne the brunt of it before. I punch him back, right in the stomach, and he curls over my fist in pain before stomping his heel right into the side of my knee. I just barely stay standing as the dark creature roars and takes control.

My face must change because his eyes widen in fear as I tackle him onto the bed. I tear his clothes. He tries to fight back, stop me, but I pin his wrists above his head with one hand. I bite at his neck. I don't break skin, but he cries out. Some part of me recognizes it is not a good sound, but the dark creature...

I smack Edmund across the face when he says no. I smack him again on the other cheek. I don't remember tearing his trousers open or shoving my hand inside. His dick is not even half hard. I think he asks me to stop, but...

I barely hear the small sound of his voice as my hungry gaze swallows every inch of his pale chest and abdomen. His whole body shakes with the force of unnecessary breath—quick, panting, terrified breath.

Stop. Stop. Please.

The dark creature flips Edmund onto his stomach and shoves his pants down his thighs. It prepares to fuck him roughly, no mercy, until a heavy candelabra flies across the room and slams into my head.

I tumble back onto the floor, away from him, and wonder who the hell is in the room with us. Oh. No one. Edmund did that. Panicked as he was, he still had the presence of mind to fight back in whatever way he could, even if through supernatural means.

The dark creature disappears back from wherever it came, and only then do I come back to myself and realize it had not been imagination: through it all, Edmund had, in fact, been begging me to stop.

"Jesus," I whisper. I sit up and reach for him, curled on the floor at the foot of the bed.

"Don't," he says. He stands and pulls his trousers back up, buttons torn in the front. He doesn't look at me as he takes a blanket from the bed and wraps it around his shoulders. He walks unsteadily to the chaise by the window and lies down on his side, faced away from me.

I crawl toward him and come to rest on the ground below. He shifts to pull the blanket tighter around himself. I touch the leg of furniture as though touching Edmund.

Still a monster then.

Chapter Eight

OF COURSE, I wake alone. I'm frankly surprised I don't wake on the front lawn. I deserve nothing better. Instead, I'm still on the floor by the now empty chaise. The blanket Edmund wore to bed is draped over me. Did my beloved do that? Why would he show me a bit of kindness after the things I did, the things he said...?

I must find him.

Clothes wrinkled and askew, I rush from our room and into the long hallway, lit by gray morning light. Although connected, the guest wing is a bit of a walk from the main area of the house. I would know as I wandered the property last night while waiting for Edmund. I know my way around, so I consider the places he might be. True, he could be on a morning ride, but hopefully not. With any luck, I can find him and kneel at his feet.

I decide to check the library first. The door is open when I stick my head inside, but Edmund is not there. However, the library is not empty. Brien sits on a couch, an aged book on his lap. When he sees me, he glares and says nothing. The tips of his massive fangs hang over his bottom lip. He glares and glares and—

For God's sake. He heard us. He heard Edmund pleading for mercy.

I back away and run toward the kitchen, dining room, ballroom...anywhere but the library. I almost sob with relief when I hear Edmund's voice. I skid to a halt outside the parlor, and he looks up. There is little resemblance to the man I saw last night. He is Edmund again—*my* Edmund—clear-eyed, washed, in his green suit.

He smiles softly. "Andrew, please join us."

We are not alone. An elderly man with bushy white eyebrows stands with my arrival.

Edmund nods to him. "This is Dr. Watt. Dr. Watt, my friend Andrew."

I shake the old man's hand, skin thin as crepe paper. He is polite enough to not comment on my ruffled appearance.

"We were discussing my mother," Edmund says just as I hear quiet feet behind me.

Hallie enters in her bonnet and bland servant's attire bearing a large plate of steaming scones. She sets them on the table in front of Dr. Watt and smiles at me. "Rough night?"

"Hallie," Edmund says warningly.

She smirks at him. "My mum's recipe. I know they used to be your favorite." She turns to leave just as Edmund's wide eyes find mine, a blatant "uh-oh" expression on his face. Yes, we would have to figure out a way to explain our distaste for human food. Could be a problem.

"As I was saying, Your Grace..." The doctor's voice is warm and musical. "Your mother fell ill with a serious fever last winter in London. Once she was well enough to travel, she came here to Heavenhill to rest, accompanied by myself. And Lady Patricia, of course. Despite your differences, she has been a blessing to your mother during your extended absence."

One of Edmund's eyebrows lifts to a point.

Dr. Watt shoves a scone into his mouth and talks between chews. "I'm afraid we started seeing symptoms soon after. She was forgetful, easily confused. She would have moments of hysterical levity, followed by episodes of severe sadness and weeping. The delirium has only increased. She is practically childlike now."

"And you have no idea what caused it?"

"No, but based on the expression on your face, rest assured it had nothing to do with the news of your apparent death."

Edmund crosses his arms. "I'm that transparent, doctor?"

It hadn't even occurred to me that Edmund might blame his mother's madness on himself. No wonder he's been such a mess since we arrived.

"She was ill long before you died. Or. Well." He throws another scone in his mouth and sips from a small, nearby teacup.

Edmund glances at me before continuing his inquiry. "How have you been treating her?"

"Rest and relaxation. We're hoping the country might do her some good. Proper nutrition. Fresh air."

"But?"

Dr. Watt brushes his crumb-covered hand across his leg. "She's only getting worse, Your Grace. I am sorry."

Edmund closes his eyes tight. "What should I do?"

"Be kind. Enjoy your time with her as she is. Love her as her son." He stands, knees popping as he does. "May I speak freely?" Momentarily, his gaze lands on me.

"Andrew and I have no secrets."

He nods. "Edmund, unmarried as I am, you and I are of a similar ilk."

Edmund inclines his head. "I always thought we might be."

"I've watched you grow up. I know you and your mother... You have not always been close. You fled around the world to escape her expectations, which is why I wrote you. No matter your differences, you mean everything to her. I believe you would have lived to regret not giving her another chance. So do your best."

"Thank you."

"I am spending tonight in the village but return to London tomorrow. Lady Patricia has my address if you should need me."

Edmund shakes the old man's hand before he leaves. Finally, once we are alone, silence reigns. I start to say his name, but he says, "No." I assume he's about to throw me out of his home, so I stand and await my sentence.

He says, "I didn't mean anything I said last night. I wish I'd been too drunk to remember it."

"I do not deserve that mercy."

"Andrew, I made you do what you did. It might not have been influencing, but..." He shakes his head. "I didn't give you a choice. For all your sweet devotion, you're still the murdering beast I fell in love with, and I used that knowledge last night to..." He still won't make eye contact. "I wanted you to hurt me."

I think of the flying candelabra. "But you changed your mind."

"I don't know what happened. I...I suppose I realized I was using you for my gain. So many men have been rough with me. Half the time, I manipulated them into it. I turn men into villains as it has always made me feel better about my own dark inclinations. I could not do that to you." Finally, he makes eye contact. "I am sorry. You are not a villain. You are a better man than I."

"No. No, I am not." I take hold of his hand and pull him out of view of the doorway. We hide in the corner, out of sight, and I kiss him once as though he might break. "You were right. I am overprotective of you, but I don't own you. I'm sorry I ever made you feel that way. Next time I'm acting overly possessive, just tell me to step back."

"That'll go over well."

I put my hands on the sides of his neck. "I will not push you away with my own bullheadedness. Promise you'll tell me."

He chews his bottom lip. "Promise."

I pull him to me, and he welcomes my embrace, resting almost his entire body weight against me. I kiss the side of his forehead and up into his hair. "Last night, you asked why I'd spent centuries alone. It was because I had not met you."

He holds me tighter.

"I love you. I'll always love you."

He chuckles against my shoulder. "I told you I throw tantrums. I'm a disaster, Andrew."

"You're *my* disaster. I would kill every man who's ever hurt you."

He pulls back enough to wipe at his wet eyes. "Me too." He leans up for a kiss more ardent than I was expecting. I moan against his mouth, and he pulls away. His eyes search my face. "You're everything I want. Everything I've always been searching for." He laughs a little. "God, you've made me so disgustingly sentimental."

I smile and wipe tears from his cheeks. "We're all right?"

He nods and leans his face into my touch.

"We'll need to tell Brien as much."

"Hmm?"

"I'm pretty sure he heard what happened last night."

His forehead crinkles. "It's off-putting, that."

"Yes, but I'd rather not have him murder me."

His hands try to straighten the mess of my clothes. "We need to go see Mum. You were never properly introduced."

"Is she awake?"

He nods. "Hallie already took her tea."

I eye Edmund's impeccable suit. "Should I dress first?"

"Sadly, I don't even think she'll notice. One more." He leans up and kisses me, sweetly, softly. He takes my hand as we walk but drops it when we reach the stairs. "I keep forgetting," he says. "Our love is not safe here."

I know he means because of society's rules, but I wonder if he realizes how dangerous it can feel to love him. Despite our shared immortality, there is nothing safe about the way he makes my chest ache. There is nothing safe in loving him this hard, knowing he could leave me.

I follow him up the wide corridors of the second floor, past gilded mirrors, silver knights of armor, and grand paintings that must be relatives. I drag him to a stop in front of one such piece of art and gesture wildly.

"Oh." He winces. "Yes, that's me."

It is and it isn't. Impossible to miss those lips, those eyes, the unruly black hair—but, in the painting, he's so much smaller. He must be forty pounds lighter and shorter too. His face is that of a Botticelli angel.

"Jesus, how old were you?"

"I don't know. Just sixteen, I think?"

"No wonder that icy bitch Veronica was jealous."

He chuckles.

"This is what you looked like at all those society parties?"

"Luckily, my voice had already dropped or I would have been mistaken for a girl."

I give his hand a quick squeeze. "You were beautiful. Still are."

He drags me onward.

Edmund's mother's accommodations take up an enormous amount of space. She has a sitting room, a small, private library, and what I assume is a bedroom and washroom through a closed door. Similar to the rest of the house, the décor is simple. Accustomed as I've grown to the decadence of New Orleans, it's not enough color for me, but at least it's tidy.

The lady of the house reclines on a dark-red chaise lounge, similar to the one in our room. She wears a high-necked dress under a huge, heavy robe of light-blue velvet. When she sees Edmund, she claps her hands and spills her tea. He rushes to help, but she doesn't seem to notice the spreading stain.

"Oh, the ghosts are back!" She stands and dances unsteadily around Edmund before he can touch her. "I know my dead son, but who are you?" She points at me, her eyes so dilated, they're almost black. "Oh, I know. You are a giant. You eat little children for breakfast." She laughs, and that easy smile is so familiar, I gasp.

"Mum, why don't we sit?"

She rushes back to the tea-soaked chaise, and Edmund sits at her side. She grins at him, her dark brown hair ratty and stuck up in points. "Will you tell me how you died, Edmund? I've wondered."

"I'm not dead, Mum. I'm here. I'm home."

She reaches out to touch his face but stops. "I bet you drowned. I always dream about you underwater. Yes," she whispers. "That's it. You're at the bottom of the sea."

Which is exactly how my darling looks, honestly. I have to do something. I hurry and sit at her other side. "My name is Andrew. What's yours?"

She turns toward me and bats her eyelashes as though I'm a suitor. "Evelyn. Did you know my boy?"

"I did. He was wonderful."

"Yes, he was lovely. So smart. And...he had the most wonderful laugh. He was troubled, though." She takes my hand in hers. God, she's warm. "You know, I think I made him quite sad. I think I made him go away. I did not mean to, but he was sick." She stares at me, imploring. "I just wanted to make him better because I loved him so much. He was my boy."

Lord help me, her face goes hazy as my eyes fill. What is this? I don't fucking cry. For his part, Edmund is curled over, a lump of grief, head buried in his hands.

I blink away the salt and hold both her hands in mine. "Well, lucky for you, his ghost is here. You can talk to him as much as you want. You can even hold him. See?" I take one of her hands and press it to Edmund's shoulder.

She giggles.

"He could read you a book. Or—or—" I stammer. "Cards. Do you play cards, Evelyn?"

She smiles, but the smile soon fades. She tilts her head and asks, "Who's Evelyn?"

In the hallway, Edmund leans against the closed door. "All my life, I have feared the loss of my mind. I know I have been considered mad, but..." He glances back at the door. "Not like that." He stares up at me. "If I get like that, you'll kill me. You'll find a way to end it."

Hallie approaches quietly from down the hall, and Edmund stands up straight, brushing hair away from his forehead. "Could you bring more tea? She spilled it."

"Of course." She disappears into Evelyn's room.

I stand, frozen, listening to the retreating sound of his steps.

Chapter Nine

DRESSED IN A perfectly tailored cream-colored suit and coat, Flynn clings to Edmund's left arm, and I meander to their right. We wander into the depths of the Heavenhill hedge maze at the back of the house. Edmund leans close to Flynn and whispers, "I used to have secret trysts back here."

Flynn giggles and holds tighter to Edmund's arm. I run my fingers through the back of his dark hair, and he glances at me, smiling. He's much better than he was earlier. I know he went for a ride after seeing his mother. When he returned, some of the darkness had left his eyes. He kissed me and suggested we go to the village for "dinner" tonight—the better to keep Hallie from noticing we never eat.

But first, we walk through the maze beneath sky the color of a rain puddle.

Michelle and Felipe, in their fancy regalia, walk close behind. "Did you grow up here, Edmund?" she asks.

He tries to hide his yawn. "Not exactly." I don't know how much he actually slept last night, and he probably has a roaring headache. "I spent summers here when I was a small child. Then, boarding schools. Then, London. My mother spent more time here than I. But I did manage to have quite a bit of fun with stable boys and gardeners." He winks at Flynn, and the young man turns the shade of a ripe peach. "The hedge maze was very good for privacy."

As if to prove the point, Felipe scoops a laughing Flynn up into his arms and presses him against the artfully shaped foliage. They kiss, Flynn's legs around his waist until Felipe pulls back and gives Flynn's nose a playful bite. "I need to fuck. Want to skip dinner?"

Flynn purrs. "Mm, yes, please. Edmund and Andrew are dull."

"I do not remotely resemble that remark," Edmund scoffs.

I wrap my arms around his shoulders and kiss the side of his neck. I kiss his forehead and feel the shape of his smile against my cheek.

"Good. Let us escape this dull expanse of greenery!" Felipe puts Flynn down but grabs his hand and tugs him back in the direction from whence we came. "Michelle?"

"I will attend dinner with the stodgy gentlemen, thank you."

"Stodgy? Since fucking when?"

Michelle laughs at Edmund's indignation and rests her hand on his chest. "You, dear, are neither dull nor stodgy. You merely break sweet Flynn's heart."

Edmund ducks his head. "I know," he whispers as he watches Felipe and Flynn race back to the house. "He'll find someone else to love."

Her eyes twinkle. "I doubt you're so easy to forget. Now, come, show me this village of yours. *Your Grace.*"

He rolls his eyes. "Don't you start."

We take a carriage into town, as opposed to riding horseback. Michelle's bright blue gown, covered in frills, wouldn't hold up well to a gallop, I imagine. Furthermore, I haven't ridden in years. I was never very good at it anyway. Not like Edmund. Both of the times I've witnessed him racing away from Heavenhill, he and the horse resemble one quick-moving entity. I know he used to race them in his youth, before he grew too tall, and it shows.

We pass a few small farmhouses, dimly lit in the early night. As the houses get closer and closer together, I conclude we must be nearing the village. Then, through the window of our carriage, I see it.

Edmund calls this a village? It's a few pubs, a ramshackle inn—where Dr. Watt spends the night—and little more. I didn't even see a sign when we entered. Does this place have a name? Perhaps Michelle should have rethought her sumptuous attire.

Unaffected by the coarse environment, Edmund exits the carriage and offers his hand to her. He ignores me but for a waggle of his eyebrows, but it is what it is: necessary in a close-minded environment such as this. Edmund entering the pub has little effect, but Michelle's entrance has men turning to stare. They stare at me too. Perhaps, due to my great height, they wonder how well I'd do in a fight. I glare back.

Despite the low ceiling and rows of rickety, wooden tables, there is a respectable bar on which Edmund rests his elbows. The bartender gives him a massive mug of ale without asking, surely remembering Edmund from last night. I assume this is to where my love disappeared prior to our altercation. Michelle—a lady mostly, but not always—orders two more: one for her and one for me. I think to snarl when the bartender stares at her a bit too long, but she puts her hand on my arm and squeezes. We have nothing to fear here. We could kill them all if we wanted.

She studies the rough men in their stained clothes with hands like mallets. "So this is an English country bar."

"I suppose it's representative," Edmund says. "Unlike the drinking establishments of the wild world, we're simple here. Damp darkness, whiskey, and strong ale."

I take a sip. This is not alcohol; this is a meal.

Michelle consumes hers without a wince. "In your travels, Edmund, where have you had the best drink?"

"Oh." He smiles. His eyes wrinkle around the edges. "That's difficult, um…" He runs his thumb over his bottom lip. "Well. I have had many drinks in many places. There was this artist in Paris who wanted to paint me."

"And did he?"

"There was indeed paint all over me when we were finished."

I guffaw and draw unwanted attention from the muttering men nearby.

"But he had champagne he mixed with absinthe and strawberry juice. I wanted to float away on it, and I did soon after. Headed to port two days later. But that wasn't the best drink."

I smile, waiting. God, it's been forever since he's told one of his stories.

"When I was in Africa, we came upon a native tribe. They would have killed us, but my sweet Samuel was there." His face grows soft, fond. "He said something. I still don't know what, but it saved our lives. Next thing I knew, we were dancing around a bonfire like madmen. The medicine man was singing and passing around a goblet. I took a drink."

"Of course you did." I chuckle.

He nods. "Of course I did. I started seeing things about ten minutes later. Faces in the dark. Strange animals. A native woman dragged me away, and we made love. Her skin was so beautiful in the firelight. She called me…" He looks toward the sagging ceiling as if the words are written there. "*Nyeupe roho.* Samuel said it meant 'white ghost.' I don't know why she called me that. Perhaps, because she knew I'd be gone in the morning. But it turned out I'd been drinking spiced milk. And cow's blood."

Both Michelle and I erupt in laughter. The bar quiets at our outburst, but I'm too busy choking on amusement to care.

"It was supposed to inspire strength and virility." Suddenly, his eyes widen. "My God, I might have a child in Africa."

This only makes us laugh more, and soon, Edmund joins in too.

"But," he says. "But. The best drink I ever had was a bottle of shitty rum on a small island, sitting beside a mysterious man who wanted to kill me."

Because I can't touch Edmund, I rest my hand on Michelle's lower back. "I wouldn't have killed you."

"No, but you thought about it."

"Maybe, but that was before you opened your eyes. Before you made me laugh."

He inclines his head to me, and the affection in his eyes is almost enough to make my dead heart explode.

Of course, the levity can't last.

"Which one uh you is the fancy new duke?"

Edmund's face falls as he glances over his shoulder. I follow his gaze. A bearded brute, built like a brick shithouse, stands a couple feet away. Men of similar size and shape, hands forever stained from farming, flank him on either side.

Edmund winces before turning to face them. "That would be me." Never a small man—not since I've known him, at least—his height, pale skin, and black hair give him the resemblance of an avenging angel.

A goon to the right speaks up. "Another Duke of Wilshire ain't never good news."

Their ringleader, the guy in the middle with the beard and sharp eyes, glares. "Oh, I remember you as a boy. Prissy little thing."

The men rumble with laughter.

"Used to chase butterflies through the woods." He spits on the ground.

Edmund smiles.

"Somethin' funny?"

"Your misplaced animosity, perhaps. I've done nothing to you—unless I stole one of your butterflies?"

The men laugh again, and I realize they're drunk. They don't care who's making the jokes, as long as the jokes are forthcoming. I wonder if Edmund knows this. He's good at picking fights, enjoys it even, but these country folk are harmless...except for maybe the big guy in the middle.

His nostrils flare. "I hear your mum's gone bonkers. That's why you're back, ain't it?"

Edmund's smile slips a little.

"You know what I think?" The brute takes a step closer, lowers his voice. "I think she's been without a man too long. What she needs is a good fuckin'."

Michelle, bless her, speaks up. "And I suppose you're the man for the job? You might want to bathe first. You smell comparable to the ass end of a horse."

There are catcalls all around, and for a second, I think the fiend might grab for Michelle's throat. Instead, he says, "I don't listen to whores," and turns his attention back to Edmund. His voice goes even lower. "Rumor has it that's what you need, too: a good buggerin'. I'd make you cry like a little girl."

I begin to lurch forward, but Edmund's voice freezes me in place. "Leave it, Andrew."

I wonder if he's just thrown a bit of influence my way, because my legs turn to lead.

"We don't want any trouble," Edmund says.

The big man sneers. "Then, don't come into the pub. You fuckin' fairy." Show over, he ambles back to his friends, who nod and smack him on the back. He walks beyond them, to the back of the pub, and out the back door to what I assume is the privy.

Edmund finishes his beer and wipes his hand over his mouth. "Let me have some fun," he says quietly, barely moving his lips.

"Let me watch," Michelle says.

My mouth hangs open in shock, but I blindly follow them out onto the street. Instead of walking toward our carriage, Edmund turns left at the edge of the building. Michelle's teeth flash at me as she glances back, perhaps making sure I'm still there. I don't smile back, but then, I know the dark deeds my beloved sailor is capable of doing.

Michelle and I linger in the darkness of an overhang as Edmund steps into the silver glow of the moon. The privy door bangs open, and the man from inside stumbles out, still buttoning his pants.

He stops when he sees Edmund. "What the fuck uh you doin' out here?"

"I thought you wanted to make me cry."

The man scoffs. "Oh, I'll make yuh *bleed*."

He's bigger than Edmund, practically my size. He wraps his meaty fingers around Edmund's neck and squeezes until my darling chokes. He slams him against a wall, and it's harder to see what's happening without the moon to light them, but I can still see the way Edmund claws at the man's hand. He loosens his grip, and Edmund takes a huge, desperate breath before he whimpers. I assume the brute cut off his air again, but here's the thing about vampires...

"Call yourself a filthy sodomite, and I'll let you breathe."

Edmund gasps again but is almost immediately strangled. He puts up a struggle, his shoes slipping in the damp dirt. I nearly believe his panic is real.

"Say it," the man commands.

It starts softly at first, Edmund's laughter. Then, it gets louder.

"What in the—"

"Hate to tell you, mate, but I don't need to breathe."

The man, for all his great size and strength, flies backward. Michelle chuckles in front of me, but I know to keep an eye on Edmund. He's angry, and I can't let things go too far. He moves quickly, punch after punch, as the brute tries to fight back, but Edmund is not only a vampire but a boxer too. He doesn't lose fights—unless, I suppose, they're with me.

"What should I tell your friends inside?" Edmund ducks an unsteady punch, and the man lurches forward. "Should I tell them the prissy boy beat you to shit in the alley?"

Still trying to regain his bearings, the man catches Edmund's elbow in the back of his neck. He groans and falls to his hands and knees. Edmund circles before kicking the man in the stomach, sending him sprawling onto his back. The big beast groans and rolls around like a turtle on its shell.

"Please," he mutters.

"Please?" Edmund laughs, but it does not resemble the warm, giddy laugh I'm used to. "Please, what? Please, stop? Would you have given me the same mercy?" He straddles his victim, and I think I should say something. I should end this, but I can't stop watching. I love watching him feed. He tears the man's shirt open before leaning down and running his nose up the man's neck. "You shouldn't have said that about my mother."

There is but one small choked sound from the man as Edmund breaks his skin. He shoves at Edmund's shoulders, but I know my darling's teeth are stronger than any vice. He drinks and drinks until I can practically taste the blood on his lips.

Then, suddenly, Michelle emerges from the shadows. "Edmund, stop!"

He doesn't.

"Edmund, stop this now!"

He still doesn't. Michelle has to latch onto his hair and pull to get him to listen. Even then, he stares up at her, moonlight reflecting off his furrowed brow. Blood drips from his parted lips.

"You'll kill him," she says.

"So?" he asks.

She lets go of him and takes a step back. "We don't kill humans, Edmund."

"Why shouldn't we? They are merely food."

Michelle's hand flails toward me. "Andrew?" Her voice shakes.

"He doesn't mean it. Edmund, you don't mean it. You're only angry. My love?"

He glares at me, eyes wide and shining.

"We should go home."

He gestures to the semi-conscious man between his legs. His voice is calm, collected, no longer tinged with blood. "He'll remember what I did. Shit, he'll tell everyone."

Yes, Felipe and I used to have just such a problem, back in the old days when we fed freely and kidnapped humans to become blood slaves. God, it seems like a million years ago.

Edmund gently smacks the man on the ground until he mumbles. Eventually, his eyes open. He shrieks in terror.

"Shh," Edmund whispers. "You're safe now. When you came out to the privy, you were beaten and robbed. There were three of them. You don't remember what they looked like, and you're embarrassed to tell your mates, so you'll make excuses about your injuries. You won't even notice the wound on your neck." Edmund stands and extends his hand to the man on the ground, who takes it willingly, a blank expression on his face. "You're going straight home now, and you will never say a bad thing about my family again."

"Yes," he says. I watch the stranger wander toward the street but am distracted when I hear Edmund's body hit the ground.

Chapter Ten

AFTER A CARRIAGE ride in which I did my best to explain Edmund's growing influencing ability to a panicked Michelle, we carry Edmund into the front hall of Heavenhill. Before I even have to yell for Brien, he is there, flying down the steps like a huge crow. We lay Edmund on a couch in the parlor, and Brien looms over him, hands on my darling's pale face.

I'm about to explain what happened when Brien shakes his head. "I know everything. His mind called to me from outside."

"His wh—" It scares me how connected they are—but not as much as Edmund's bleary consciousness.

His eyes crack open as he reaches for his maker. "I'm sorry."

"Nothing to be sorry about." Brien's thumb caresses Edmund's cheek. "I gave you your abilities to use."

As much as I want to be between them, shoving them apart, I hope the Elder gets on with it. He needs to let Edmund feed.

I hear her before I see her: the sound of high-heeled boots stomping toward us. "Devils!" Patricia screams. "I will not have naked men wandering my house."

I want to tell her it's not her house, but I'm distracted by the naked men comment. Ah, shit. Felipe and Flynn had come back earlier from the maze for intercourse. Jesus.

"And you!" She walks farther into the room and flings her arms out toward Edmund. Despite the late hour, she's still fully dressed in another boring black gown. Some of her light-red hair has fallen from its bun, surely thanks to shouting at our friends earlier. "Drunk! Filthy drunk!"

Edmund stirs at the sound of her voice but doesn't sit up.

"I should have you thrown out of here, the lot of you!"

I hear the musical sound of trembling glass and notice one of the decanters on the drink tray has started to shake. "Lady Patricia," I whisper, "now is not the time."

"You were a prideful, self-indulgent child, and you've grown into the worst kind of man!"

A second decanter shakes, as does a nearby snifter.

"My lady." I step between Edmund and her. "Please, may we discuss this in the morning? We will be more stable-minded then."

"That boy has never had a stable mind! He has been sick since birth. A whore for men and women. Decadent and disgusting." She tries to reach around me to point at him, but I bar passage. "You will burn in hell, Edmund Baines!"

A decanter actually explodes, which makes us all jump.

Patricia gasps and crosses herself.

I take her by the shoulders and try pushing her toward the door, but she smacks my hands away. Before leaving, she spits into my face, lifts her skirts, and tromps off to what I assume is a bedroom covered in crosses and, well, misery.

I wipe saliva from my cheek and turn to see Edmund trying to curl himself into a ball. His face is nothing but wrinkles.

"Edmund, feed. Now." Brien extends his wrist, and Edmund bites down. He doesn't make a noise. He doesn't even look as though he enjoys it, not like he does with humans. He drinks until Brien pulls his arm away and crushes Edmund in an embrace.

I move forward to comfort, but Brien holds him tighter. He turns his body away, moving Edmund farther from me. "No," the Elder says. "You hurt him last night. Did you hope I did not hear?"

"I know you heard. It was a mistake."

"Andrew?" Michelle asks quietly.

I shake my head in refusal.

Brien growls. "Precious things should not be hurt. They should be treasured."

"Give him to me."

"No."

When I take a step forward, the broken decanter glass from the floor rises and flies between us, creating a sharp, shimmering wall.

"Try to walk through, villain. It will not kill you, but the sensation will not be pleasant. I will see to that."

I look to Michelle for help, but her eyes dart between us as though not sure what to do. The Elder is a creature she does not know, does not understand. She just heard that I harmed something she adores, but that very something scared her earlier with his talk of humans being nothing but food.

God, we're all monsters.

"Brien, stop." Edmund's voice is muffled, face pressed to Brien's shoulder. "Last night, it...it wasn't... I am just as at fault as he."

Brien scoffs and curls his fingers in Edmund's hair—as if the more twisted together they are, the less likely Edmund is to leave.

"Brien, please, I...I need Andrew right now."

The Elder only holds tighter. "You need me."

Edmund, bless him, finds the energy to laugh. "I know, but this is different. Right now, I need my beloved."

"He hurt you."

"I hurt him first." Edmund begins to pull back, and Brien's grip loosens. Edmund watches me through the wall of shattered glass. Unlike the quivering mess of flesh he'd been in the carriage, he is rosy-cheeked, glowing. "Let's go to bed." He stands and, using his own gift, sends the shards of glass flying, floating into a decorative vase in the corner. He thanks Brien.

"You should be worshipped," he says.

Edmund kisses the Elder on the forehead. "I am." He takes my hand. Together, we leave the room, but before reaching the steps, Michelle speaks.

"Edmund?"

"Hmm?"

"We will talk in the morning, you and I. Is that understood?"

He nods. "Yes. In the morning. Everything is brighter in the morning." He pulls me up the steps, and we make the long, slow walk to our bedroom in silence.

WITH HIS ELBOWS on the chaise, his spread knees on a pile of pillows and blankets, I'm not sure how much more he can take. His entire back shines with sweat. The nubs of his spine struggle up beneath his skin, back arched, head buried in the furniture. He quietly whimpers as my two fingers move in and out of him, slowly, slowly... It's been almost an hour since I started, but something about the deliberate way we undressed, the careful kisses—I know he needs this. He needs to be overtaken by my touch until nothing but the two of us remain.

I run my other hand up Edmund's back. I add a third finger and thrust. He sobs once, and his fingers curl up by his head. I find the place within him that will make him see stars and push.

"Oh God, oh God... Andrew, I need..."

"Not yet."

"Fuck." He buries his hands in his hair and pulls.

The backs of his thighs tremble. I take hold of his hip and scissor my fingers as I twist in and out. After less than a minute of this, his whole body shakes. I stop thrusting but keep my fingers inside as I lean forward and kiss across his back. "I love when you beg."

"Please, I need you."

I move my fingers a little. It's not enough to achieve any sort of completion, but the movement does force a grunt from his lips. He reaches back for me as though I am ballast in a roaring sea.

I kiss his hand. "I want to see you."

I remove my fingers, and he melts onto his side amidst the bedding we've strewn about the floor. I roll him onto his back, and his chest is as sweat-soaked as the rest of him. Unnecessary breaths pump rapidly in and out of his chest. I kneel between his legs. I push soaked hair from his forehead and kiss his neck. I kiss across nipples, down his stomach. I run my tongue up the side of his cock, and he startles, putting one hand in my hair.

"Don't make me wait anymore." The words are desperate, shaking.

I sit up and lift one of his legs over my shoulder. Edmund reaches his long arms up and drags me into a wet, warm kiss. Mouths still touching, I press into him.

His head falls back on a gasp, and I tongue across his collarbone.

I try to go slow. Every thrust brings another quiet moan to his lips. I move gentle and deep. When fully surrounded by his heat, I even pause and spend several moments just kissing him, caressing his skin. His fingers claw at me and then relax. I whisper words like spells: *beautiful...perfect...always... I'm sorry...love...love...*

Mouth wide, he comes with a cry. I fuck him through an orgasm that makes his muscles tense. Then, I let myself go.

Blind with pleasure, I shrug his leg off my shoulder before my arms go out from under me. I rest my full weight on him and rub my face in his hair.

With his arms around me, he is silent.

"What is it, Edmund?"

It takes him so long to respond, I almost wonder if he's asleep. "I'm scared of what he's done to me."

I don't have to ask, so I wait.

"It's as though I can hear him in my head sometimes. Feel him there. Things get hazy. In the alley tonight, I felt as though I was half there and half not."

I lean up on my elbow and roll onto my side. "You're still you."

"Am I?" He sighs. "Does he have power over me, do you think?"

"From what I've observed, it seems to be the other way around."

"But what does he want, Andrew? He could be anywhere in the world right now, and yet, he lingers."

I frown. "He's the only one who can heal you."

"Then, I won't influence people anymore. I will not be dependent on him." He rolls toward me and pushes his forehead against my chest. "He wants something."

"You."

"No." He shakes his head. "It's more than that. He's up to something."

"What makes you say that?"

"A feeling." His fingers tickle my stomach. "A feeling that he wants...more. He's biding his time to take...something." He yawns. "I'm knackered."

"Let's get you to bed then."

It's a relief that I'm still strong enough to carry him, considering he's basically unconscious by the time I get him beneath the sheets. I sit on the edge and watch him snore, wondering how much Brien just heard. Surely, he heard the sex, but did he hear our whispered conversation? If Edmund is right, well...

I put my hand on Edmund's shoulder. Brien will take nothing from me.

Chapter Eleven

IT'S BEEN AGES since he's had a nightmare, but he has one that night. As usual, he doesn't tell me what it's about. Maybe he doesn't even remember, but he does wake up screaming, reaching for me. I hold him until he stops shaking and eventually goes back to sleep, but I don't— sleep, that is.

For several long minutes, I reacquaint myself with the feel of his sleeping body in my arms, something so easily overlooked in the chaos of day to day. I try to remember the novelty of sleeping beside him, such a blessed thrill on my island of exile months ago. It's still novel now, this being in love, so much so that my chest feels too small and my cock fills up.

He wakes with his member in my mouth, my name on his lips. He comes quickly and rests his hands in my hair. "What was that for?"

I kiss up his inner thigh. "I need a reason?"

"No." He chuckles. "Feel free anytime. Do you need—"

"Go back to sleep."

He lifts his head, but I can't see his expression in the dark. "Are you well?"

"Yes." I run my hands up over his hips. "Just love you is all."

"Love you too." And back to sleep he goes.

EDMUND AND MICHELLE have been locked away in the Heavenhill library for almost an hour, and I can't stop pacing. What is it she wanted to talk to him about anyway, and why couldn't I be present? I already spent a bit of time with Hallie, inquiring into Evelyn's condition. I had to pretend to eat a biscuit. Poor woman probably thinks she's a terrible cook, the way we avoid her food.

I haven't seen Patricia, although there was a dour priest in the foyer, sprinkling holy water. I wonder if he was trying to exorcise us.

I cuss when Felipe appears beside me, sneaky ass. He yawns and ties his hair behind his head with a red ribbon. "You look like a gargoyle in need of a perch."

I ignore him.

"I hear things got a bit wild last night."

I open and close my fists. "It was nothing."

"Nothing?" He clicks his tongue. "Our dear Edmund nearly killed a man. Wish I could have watched." He pauses. "Did it make you hard?"

"No."

He presses indecently against the front of his breeches. "I imagine I would have been hard as rock, seeing those pretty fists doling out moral retribution. Did you know his calluses are gone?"

"Of course I know." I turn to stare into his dark eyes, twinkling with amusement. "Jesus, Felipe, why are you baiting me into an argument?"

"Because I'm bored." He groans. "We traveled across a fucking ocean, had one night in the city, and have been trapped in this gloomy countryside ever since. Granted, Flynn and I were quite acrobatic last night."

"You can't walk around the house nude."

Felipe snorts. "God, that blonde bitch. I thought she was going to just die. Wouldn't have minded. Put her out of her misery."

For a moment, my mind leaves the library. "You think her miserable?"

"People that unpleasant always are. They're disappointed by life, so they act cruel in order to make other people miserable too. The last thing they want is to be surrounded by happiness, or God forbid, *fun*." He glances left and right, the shadows painting his cheekbones into cliffs. "But really, why are you standing out here? It's an odd place to stand."

I roll my eyes. "I thought you would know. Michelle wanted a word alone with Edmund."

He howls like a ghost before laughing. "Oh, is the sweet sailor in trouble? I wonder what his punishment will be? I'd be happy to give him a spanking."

I clear my throat.

"Relax, you fool. She adores him almost as much as you do. Meanwhile, here I am getting nothing but scraps while Edmund has all the fun."

"He's not having fun here, Felipe."

"Yes, poor mummy dearest." He tugs at his lace cuffs. "Do you suppose she and the blonde woman are sapphists?"

I almost laugh at the absurdity of that statement, but the library door opens and Edmund hasn't been destroyed. He seems relieved, actually, with his arm around Michelle's small shoulders. He smiles and kisses her forehead before noticing us.

"Eavesdropping?" He winks.

I sigh out a breath.

Michelle's forehead wrinkles. "God, Andrew, what did you think I would do to him?"

I lower my brows, and her eyes light with understanding. Right, that whole exile thing.

"Oh," she says. "Well." She pats Edmund's arm. "He said we could go riding, Felipe. Shall we?"

"Just what I need. Another wicked creature between my legs. Speaking of, I quite imagine Flynn will sleep the day away."

Michelle takes Felipe's outstretched hand, and they walk together down the hall, painted grey by another day of clouds.

I put my hand on Edmund's shoulder. Before I can utter a word, he says, "I'm fine."

"What did you speak about?"

"Everything. Nothing. I think she wanted to check in."

"Edmund?"

His fingers reach out and play with a button on my coat. "She...wanted to make sure I was okay."

Then, it hits me. I close my eyes and remember Brien's wrath from the night before. "She wanted to make sure I wasn't hurting you."

He chews his bottom lip. "I promised her you weren't."

I pull him to me, my nose in his hair. "And here I thought *you* were in trouble."

He laughs against my shoulder. "Well. She knows how newborn vampires can be, so she understood last night's behavior—with a caveat. It's not to happen again."

"Which part?"

"I am not to feed in anger. We all know I have a bit of a temper."

I run my hands up and down his back. "I think that's fair."

"Mm."

"Now." I pull back and tug playfully at a curl that falls down the center of his forehead. "What do you want to do today?"

"I need to spend some time with Brien."

I'm about to argue, but Edmund shakes his head.

"Andrew. I told you, something is going on. You know how much I ask questions, and he's somehow avoided mine. He said he went to sleep years ago because he lost someone, but who was that someone? Did they have a relationship like you and me? If so..." He glances down the hall. "I know that if anything ever happened to me, you would find a way to..."

"Yes. I wouldn't merely sleep. I would join you in death."

"So why didn't Brien? And what the fuck do I mean to him? Why did he give me the power I have before he even knew me? Why share his power at all? He could rule the entire world with his abilities, and yet, he created his only adversary in me."

"You aren't his enemy."

"I could be." He stares at his hands. "God, you should feel it, Andrew. I swear sometimes my fingers burn with potential. It's beautiful and terrifying and—"

"Did you tell Michelle?"

Edmund shakes his head. "I didn't want to scare her."

"So we talk to Brien."

He nods. "It's time he started answering my questions."

I'm about to suggest we set off to find the Elder, but a scream cuts through the silence. Edmund and I take off running and find Hallie in the middle of the grand front staircase. She shouts and shouts for help, but I can barely make out her frantic cries. When Edmund nears her, she grabs his hand and drags him after her.

We rush toward Evelyn's chambers, the door already open. Patricia is there, as is the unfamiliar priest, and Edmund's mother thrashes on the floor between them in a pool of spilled tea.

"Move," Edmund commands, and Patricia stands with her hand to her chest, mouth pressed into a firm line. Edmund lifts his mother into his arms and tries to hold her as she convulses against his chest. Her eyes have rolled back in her head, only whites showing. She grimaces, teeth bared, and Edmund calls out to her: "Mother...mother, please."

There's no time to find a doctor. Hallie sobs at my side, and we watch, helpless, as Edmund uses all his strength to stop Evelyn's shaking.

After a few minutes that feel like hours, the violent seizing stops, replaced by gentle trembles and quiet groans. Edmund lifts his mother from the floor and rests her body across the nearby chaise. He sits on the edge and takes her hand as she mutters to herself. Then, he looks up at me, terrified.

"You're making her worse," Patricia says. "Your mere presence. You have brought sin into this house."

"Why are you still here?" he asks.

"To protect her from you."

"And not to terrorize me?"

Patricia's smile is a cruel, twisted thing. "You deserve everything you get."

Evelyn mutters Edmund's name but does not wake.

Patricia swishes past me in her black skirts. "Now, get out of the way so the father can bless her."

I swear Edmund's glare makes the room go cold. "I'm not going anywhere, you hateful bitch."

The priest crosses himself.

"You would do kindly to get the fuck out of my house," Edmund tells him. To Patricia: "I'll deal with you later."

I try to shake off the terror that shivers up my spine.

"We will *deal* with each other," Patricia says as she leaves the room. The priest runs after her.

Hallie's quiet voice: "Edmund?"

"I apologize for my language."

The servant girl puts a hand on his shoulder, and the menace melts away. "Shall I bring her some water?"

"Yes. Thank you. Scotch for me?"

She nods. "Scotch for breakfast it is."

I belatedly realize my knees are shaking as I crumble into the nearest chair. I watch Edmund watching Evelyn. My dearest darling can be the scariest thing in the world.

Chapter Twelve

ALL DAY, HE doesn't leave her side. His mother tumbles in and out of consciousness. Any thought of talking to Brien today, confronting him, has apparently been forgotten. I sit nearby and read books about insects, lizards, monsters of Africa... They are strewn about Evelyn's room, although I assume they once belonged to Edmund. The seeds of naturalism were perhaps sewn here. He did once say she was to blame for his adventurous nature.

As the sun begins to sink, he notices I'm here. He stands and stumbles toward me as though drunk. He isn't. He only had that one scotch that Hallie handed to me, silently, before she disappeared back to the kitchen. Another servant did bring up a tray of food, but at least now we have an excuse for not eating: emotional distress.

He leans over and kisses the top of my head. "Let's go find Hallie. Have her bring up some tea for Mum."

I nod and follow him away from the room that is beginning to smell like sweat-slick human skin and sour breath.

Michelle and Felipe returned from their earlier ride and left again soon after to seek entertainment in the village. As Felipe mentioned, Flynn still enjoys a lazy day in bed. We don't pass Brien or Patricia on our way to the kitchen, but Hallie stands up straight and ducks her head when we enter.

Edmund puts his hands in his pants pockets. "I'm sorry about this morning. I should not have behaved that way in front of a lady such as you."

She flashes a little smile. "It's fine, Edmund."

"It really isn't."

She shrugs. "You've always spoken your mind."

They hug, her face against his chest. Her small hands squeeze the back of his dark red waistcoat tight. "When you yelled at Patricia, the look on her face..." Hallie giggles, and Edmund immediately joins in.

"Yes, well. I shouldn't have lost my temper."

Hallie pulls away and grins at me. "We don't care what she thinks, do we, Andrew?"

I shake my head. "Not a bit."

"You must be starving." She grabs Edmund's hand as a young girl would. "I haven't seen you eat a thing since you've been here. What might I prepare for the two worldly gentlemen?"

"Actually, would you make tea for my mother? I can take it up. I'd rather not be away from her just yet."

She pushes a brown curl up into her bonnet. "Edmund, you must eat."

"Later."

She peers over his shoulder at me. "If I send you up with toast, will you make sure he eats some?"

"I will do my best."

"Your best must be pretty good if you won his heart." She kisses the back of Edmund's hand before turning toward the fire.

We stand together in the large room crowded with utensils, pots, and pans while Hallie goes to work. While waiting for the water to heat, she reaches for a ceramic container filled with what I presume to be tea. As soon as she opens the lid, though, I smell something like tobacco and, perhaps, very strong alcohol. It's a bitter mix.

"What is that?" Edmund asks.

"Oh, it's a medicinal soother for your mother. Some sort of magic from London." She wrinkles her nose. "The leaves reek much worse than the tea."

"Dr. Watt suggested it?"

"No." She scoops leaves into a kettle. "Lady Patricia brought it back. Said it would help with ailments of the brain. She probably had it blessed by a priest or some such nonsense."

I think nothing of it, but the way Edmund's eyes crinkle, his lips part...

"What's wrong?" I ask.

He doesn't look at me. He reaches instead for the ceramic container. "Let me see."

"Suit yourself." She hands it to him. "Told you, it smells awful."

He takes a whiff. The reaction is instantaneous. He drops the container, and it shatters on the floor. He reaches for Hallie's wrist and tugs her away from the teakettle. "Do not touch those leaves."

Hallie begins to protest. "But I need to—"

"No." Edmund squeezes his eyes shut. When they open, they're filled with tears. "Where is she?"

Hallie and I speak at the same time.

"Who?"

"Edmund?"

"Patricia. Where is she?" he asks.

Hallie's voice comes out high-pitched and breathless. "She was in the library. What's the matter, Edmund?"

He takes hold of both her upper arms and pulls her close until she balances on her toes. "Are there any other servants in the house?"

"Not this late. They live in the village."

He nods. "Do not leave this kitchen." He rushes to leave, and she moves to follow, but I intercept.

"Hallie. Do not leave the kitchen. Promise."

She nods shakily. "All right."

I race after my sailor, my darling, my Edmund. I find him already standing in the library doorway. He stares at the woman in black, and she stares back.

"How did you know about Devil's-eye?"

Patricia closes her book. Its gilded cover shines in the firelight. "I do not know what you are talking about."

"The tea."

She runs her gloved hand over the huge Bible in her lap. "You used to love tea, Edmund. My husband would buy you the most expensive, exotic leaves. Strange you do not drink it anymore. It would have been so much easier if you had."

"Could someone explain what the hell is going on?" Although Edmund might be smarter than me, I am tired of being left behind.

She sneers and stands, Bible forgotten beside her. "Is your lover as dumb as he appears? Devil's-eye, also known as henbane. Quite poisonous. I read about it in one of dear Edmund's childhood science books while staying at Heavenhill during Evelyn's fever. Oh, the beautiful irony that I would use your own youthful curiosity against you."

"In small doses, it can be an aphrodisiac," he whispers. "I had it in Venice, which is why I recognized the smell. In large doses, it causes hallucinations, convulsions, loss of memory—"

"Madness," Patricia hisses. "I knew your dear mother would beckon you back here, and how I have wallowed in your pain. Then, I thought to serve you the tea, as well."

She crouches as though she might leap at us. "But you don't drink tea anymore, *Edmund*."

I inch forward so I'm in front of him, at least. Physically, he doesn't need my protection, but I fear what more Patricia might say, especially when Edmund asks, "Why would you do this?"

"My husband was never the same after you." She balls her trembling hands into the front of her dress. "I think he loved me once, but after he tasted your wares..." She looks him up and down. "What did you do to him? You ruined him. He never looked at me the same again. You were all he saw—beautiful *Edmund*. I was an ogre by comparison. He used to dream of you, would whisper your name in the night. And then, he died. Died from missing you."

Edmund shakes his head. "No."

"Yes." She takes an ominous step forward. "You took him from me, so now, I take dear Mummy from you. Almost killed her today. I think the dose was a bit high, but what does it really matter? Her mind is so far gone. She might as well be dead."

I'm surprised windows don't shatter. Books don't fly from their shelves. Edmund doesn't even speak. He just stares at her. He's forgotten the human habit of breath.

"This is the cost for your sin," she says. The fire crackles and glows behind her, painting the edges of her hair in flame.

"You know nothing of my sin," he murmurs.

I am torn between telling Patricia to run and forcing her to stay. She deserves punishment in a court of law, but Edmund's simmering wrath is much more clear and present.

He lunges but doesn't attack. He presses a hand to the small of her back, the other on the side of her neck. She gasps and tries to pull away, but Edmund holds her steady.

"Shh," he whispers, running his thumb across her cheek. "You've always called me a devil." He kisses her ear. "Now, I really am one."

He is too quick for me to stop. His fangs dig into the front of her throat and tear. Patricia screams as blood spurts up and out, painting Edmund red. He leans forward to drink as she thrashes. The crackle of fire is gone beneath the sound of her wet, gurgling cries. He drops her body to the floor, but she's still alive. She tries to cover the wound, but there's no flesh left—just the warm slime of her open throat.

Edmund crouches next to her and touches her chin. She moves her lips as though to speak, but no sound comes out as a puddle of blood pools beneath her.

"Patricia," he says. "You are the one going to hell."

Blood drips from her wide-open mouth, and when she tries to suck air, there is nothing but wet choking. Her eyes find the ceiling as she drowns on her own blood, and, then, she's gone. Barely a minute has passed.

"Jesus Christ." I rest my hand on the arm of a chair. "Edmund."

He stands and stares at his blood-soaked hands. He says, "Something's wrong."

"No shit."

He shakes his head and closes his eyes. The fireplace roars as the flames fly high. Every candle in the room suddenly lights. It is bright as day, making it all the more evident that Edmund is painted red—much as I was after murdering so many cannibals to save his life. This feels so much worse.

One should never feed in anger.

Chapter Thirteen

MOMENTS LATER, I smell familiar blood and turn to find Brien in the doorway. His chin is coated in red, and he carries Flynn's limp body over his shoulder. He tosses the youth onto the floor, and Flynn doesn't move. He doesn't make a sound.

"It feels good, does it not? Stealing a soul? You will grow more powerful with every life you take."

"Flynn?" Edmund asks.

I scoop the young man into my arms and lay him on the couch. "He's alive."

"You can feel it right now, can't you?" Brien asks. "How much stronger you are. Think if you killed ten, twenty. You would be unstoppable."

I have to know, damn the consequences. "What happened to the man you loved? Why did you really go to sleep?"

Brien grins, fangs bared. "I made him like Edmund. I gave him everything in the world—some would say I gave him too much. They did not understand that we were to be kings, so my brethren destroyed him, and I hid until you came along."

"You wanted to rule over vampires?"

"We will, Edmund, you and I. We will rule vampires, and the entire human race will be our slaves."

Edmund glances at me. "I told you at the start I didn't want power."

"Yes. You do what you do out of love, and you do love Andrew. You love him very much, which is why you would not want him to die. Agree to be my beloved king, and I will leave him be."

Edmund steps in front of Flynn and I. Strange to be the one needing defense.

"You won't hurt him," Edmund says.

Brien smiles. "Why not?"

"Because you would not want me to hate you."

"Edmund. I can make you feel whatever I want."

Edmund winces. "Get out of my head."

"Come closer." Brien beckons with his fingernails like claws. When Edmund takes a step forward, I begin to rise, but Brien's gaze darts my way. "I really wouldn't," he says.

I remind myself Brien would not hurt Edmund, but it takes every bit of my resolve to not leap between them when he puts his hand on the back of Edmund's neck and presses their lips together. It's a lingering kiss, mouths open and demanding. Brien practically devours Patricia's blood from Edmund's lips—those flower petal lips that belong to me, that want no one but *me*.

My dark creature rises just as my sailor shoves Brien away. Brien's eyes widen, as does his grin. "You broke my influence."

Edmund steps back, wiping his mouth with the sleeve of his stained shirt. "You will leave now. Forever. Never come back here."

"I go nowhere without you, and I will kill all of them to keep you."

Flynn mumbles, which draws my attention to our human who has most certainly lost too much blood. I put my hand on his face, say his name, and he mumbles some more. Then, I wrap my fingers around his delicate throat and squeeze.

"Edmund!" I have no control over my movements as Brien apparently winds his way through my mind. "Make him stop! Quickly!"

I am too busy fighting myself to notice the silent fight behind me—not until Edmund falls to one knee, gasping for breath, and my grip on Flynn's throat finally loosens. God, I almost killed him.

Edmund stands on shaky legs. "You will not hurt anyone I love ever again."

Brien laughs, his hair a thick, dark halo around his head. "Who will stop me, dead man? Not you. You see what I can do to your beloved. I could make him do anything."

"You're wrong."

Brien smiles. "About you, I have been consistently right."

"No. You shouldn't have given me so much of your power, but you didn't know I'm not to be trusted with so much responsibility. I once lost a year's paycheck to a game of faro in the West Indies. Did a bit of prostituting on the side. Was actually a good career choice for me."

He must have a plan. Edmund is only this talkative when he's calm.

Brien chuckles over the story but then stops. His right eye twitches. "You're trying to influence *me*? That will only make you weaker."

"I don't have to be strong for very long."

"Andrew? Edmund!" I hear Felipe and Michelle down the hall. They rush toward us. They must smell the blood, but the library door slams shut and locks before they reach it. Under normal circumstances, they could use their immortal strength to open it. Apparently, these are not normal circumstances. I think Edmund is purposely keeping them out.

"This is going to hurt." He pauses. "I am sorry, Brien, but you shouldn't have threatened the ones I love."

Flynn begins to stir beside me, so I pull him into my arms. Next thing I'm aware of is the sound of tearing fabric and a shocked groan. I look up, and Brien's long nails are impaled into his right upper thigh.

"Edmund?" He gawks, mouth agape. "You wouldn't."

"I am indeed very good at bluffing. But not today."

Brien tears himself apart. I watch as leg separates from hip and he falls sideways to the ground. I soon turn away, though, surrounded by the sound of the Elder's angry screams and tearing flesh. He mumbles Edmund's name, begging, but no one told Brien men like my sailor and I do anything to protect the ones we love.

When the room gets quiet, I turn. Brien is but a torso with one arm and a head, resting in a massive pool of black gore. Edmund is on his hands and knees, arms shaking. They stare at each other.

"Edmund." Brien swallows with difficulty and lifts his remaining arm. "You must drink."

My darling actually falls face first into the rug, laughing. "It's so ridiculous. It's all so..." His laughter turns to tears. He sobs.

"Andrew," Brien says, "help him."

I drag Edmund to Brien's extended arm and push the hair back from his face. "Drink, my love."

"Drink, dead man. Then, finish it."

Edmund bites into Brien's skin and drinks what elixir is left but does not linger long. He sits back and stares at the horror he has wrought while Michelle and Felipe still pound at the door.

Brien puts his hand on Edmund's knee. "I was wrong about you. I thought men wanted power, deep down, but all you want is him." His gaze rests on me. "Andrew."

I hear the command, no influence required. I never expected to tear a vampire's head off, but needs must. We will burn the body later.

Edmund then wilts against me, fingers grasping for purchase on my shirt. I crush his trembling body to mine as he cries. His entire body heaves beneath the force of his grief. God, what will the nightmares be like now?

The door finally flings open. Michelle's fine shoes slide in Brien's remains, and Felipe gags into his hand.

She recoils when her foot comes close to the Elder's head. "What in God's name?"

"Everything is going to be all right," I say, and Edmund moves closer until he rests in my lap. He keeps pressing against me, climbing me. I fall backward beneath his weight. I hold him in my arms until he stops crying. It takes a good hour.

Chapter Fourteen

EDMUND STILL ISN'T talking when I lead him up to his mother's room. It is I who must take charge now. Michelle helps too, while Felipe seems content to get roaring drunk in the parlor. I've left them downstairs to help Flynn recover from Brien's attack by feeding the young man fruit. We sent Hallie away into the village to spend the night at the inn. She trusts Edmund enough to not ask questions.

I have rinsed most of the blood from his face and hands and changed his shirt. His suit is ruined. I would laugh at the irony—he's always been so fastidious about getting blood on his clothes—but I need him to speak first. I need to make sure he's still himself. Then, I will hold him to me and never let go.

I push him into Evelyn's bedroom and allow him space to walk toward her alone. She sleeps but appears to wake when he sits on the edge of her bed. I can't hear their whispered words, but I watch him help her drink from a glass of water. She smiles that so familiar smile.

Stockinged feet arrive at my side. Michelle left her blood-soaked shoes in the library with the corpses. I face her, but she watches Edmund. "It was rather brutal," she says.

"They deserved to die."

"Yes, well. Still."

I look back toward the haunted man who has seen so much. "Edmund has always been brutal."

Michelle hums and rests her hand on my arm. "Then, you are perfectly matched."

I nod.

"Felipe has prepared a fire outside. Join us."

"I thought he was content to drown himself in drink."

"From what you've told me, we must make sure Brien is really gone. When I told Felipe we needed to protect Edmund, he got right to it." She takes my hand and squeezes. "He is our family now."

I watch him say something to Evelyn that makes her laugh. She is not recovered, of course. She might never recover from Patricia's henbane, but there is still a chance, and Edmund clings to it—which reminds me...

"What of Patricia's body?"

"She was mauled by a wolf during her evening walk. We'll find her in the morning."

I sigh. I used to hate Michelle. I spent years hating her, and yet, she gave me my beloved. Now, she keeps him safe. She shields us all.

"Bring Edmund." She squeezes my hand, lets go, and walks back down the hall.

When I beckon for him, he kisses his mother on the forehead and pulls the blankets up higher around her. He gives her a last, lingering glance as we leave her chambers and make our way onto Heavenhill's front lawn. A fire already burns, practically my height, and Felipe stands next to a wheelbarrow, stacked with body parts.

He points at Edmund, a liquor bottle in hand. "You owe me, you crazy bastard."

I'm not sure Edmund hears.

Brien's burning body smells of nothing. I would have expected the stench of scorched meat, but the aroma is simply burnt wood, spicy and fresh.

Finally, Edmund speaks. He wraps his arms around himself and asks, "Do you still love me after what I've done?"

I stand by his side but don't touch him. "I said I would never stop loving you. I meant it."

"What happened to my mother is my fault. Of all I learned about myself today, I think that is the worst."

"She'll get better."

"Maybe." Flames dance in his eyes. "I can apologize, but I suppose I can never tell her the truth. About anything. Not even the stains on her rug."

"We're throwing away the rugs."

Bless him, he laughs.

I rest my hand on his upper back.

"What now, Andrew?"

"We get your mother well. Take her back to London, where you will be helpful with the trading company inquiry. Finish our business there." I shrug. "And then, who knows?"

He hugs himself tighter. "Michelle won't send me away?"

I glance toward her and Felipe. They lean against each other across the fire. They share sips from a bottle and watch us. "I think Michelle has learned that sometimes bad people have to die."

He shakes his head. "Never again. I will never kill again."

"Was it true what Brien said? Did you feel more powerful after?"

"Yes. It was too much." He glances at me and back into the flames. "It's quieter now that he's gone. I am myself again. What's left of me."

"We'll get through this."

"This is when I usually run," he says. "The moment I realize I need someone I leave them before they can leave me."

A gust of wind blows a wave of heat into our faces.

"But I can't imagine leaving you," he says. "Maybe one day we'll hate each other or grow bored. You'll tire of me. Maybe one day you'll leave, Andrew, but it doesn't matter so long as I know you're out there. That maybe I'll see you again someday. When he threatened to kill you… I would have murdered half the world to stop him. Does that make me bad?"

My dark creature purrs at his bloody admission, but I can control it now. I push that part of me away, subdue it, and put my arm around his shoulders. "I would anticipate nothing less."

He chuckles, and I rest my chin on his head.

"I wasn't expecting you, Edmund."

"I wasn't expecting me either. Thought I'd be dead by now."

I laugh into his hair. "You are."

"Oh, right."

"Hey, Duke Edmund, can we get raging drunk, please?" Felipe shouts.

"Yes! Fuck, yes." Edmund kisses my cheek and escapes my grasp. He walks around the fire and wraps his arms around Michelle and Felipe, my dear, old friends. Their arms envelop him, and they walk as a single entity back toward the house. "Andrew, come on," Edmund shouts.

I follow my sailor. I'll follow him anywhere.

Epilogue

IN MY THOUSANDS of years, I've never much paid attention to specific dates. Once one gets to be five hundred, most days simply flow into the next. I've had to learn to pay attention on occasion. For instance, there are Christian holidays like Christmas and Easter that people celebrate in abundance in America. There is a specific day in September, too, known as Edmund's human birthday, when I shower him with gifts.

Then, there is today: June 24, 2011.

I sit in our bedroom on the Upper East Side, an empty mug of blood on the bedside table. Vampires run most blood banks nowadays. With the advent of modern technology, we've become a surprisingly entrepreneurial race.

The usual traffic sounds of New York float like familiar music through the air as I watch the news. Handsome men laugh and cheer on my TV screen, raising rainbow-colored flags. I think of the velvet box I've hidden on the bookcase behind an aged copy of *Dorian Gray*.

I turn off the TV when I hear the front door open and close. Edmund shouldn't be home yet. When he left that morning, he said he would be working late, but I hear his voice. He's on the phone with someone.

Edmund has never stopped working. I had feared, originally, that he might bore of immortality. He's always had such an active mind, and living forever can be downright murderous to someone incessantly curious. So Edmund works. He's a scientist—a chemist, at present, although I'd be hard pressed to list the degrees he's earned over the years. He avoids photographs. He changes his name. He creates new identities every time we jump continents. He has won awards and altered the direction of history. He's no longer only my miracle but the world's, as well.

Then, there's me. I find contentment in simply loving him.

I hear him on the phone as I walk down the hall: "No, I'm not bringing the Porsche to Mexico. Are you bloody mad?"

Possibly the least surprising part of our century and a half together is Edmund's affinity for sports cars, matched only by his penchant for scuba diving and trips to exciting locations—a fancy resort in Cancun, for instance. He must be talking to Felipe in San Francisco. Every year, they go on a trip together, the two of them. So many years ago, I never would have expected them to become best friends.

"No, I won't," he says. "I don't care if it's a nude beach. That's not for everyone to see."

I turn the corner. He stands at our kitchen island, his black leather satchel on the countertop. He hasn't aged a day, and his fashion sense hasn't really changed that much—no matter the decade. Today, he wears an artfully tailored navy three-piece suit, no tie. His dark hair is an attractive mess; it must be windy outside. My mouth waters looking at him.

He notices me staring and smiles. "Yes, I will make it very clear to everyone that I'm in a relationship, you twat. It's not as if you have trouble pulling." He laughs. "You tell him, Michelle."

I lean my hands on the island next to him and nudge him with my hip.

"Hey, I just got home. I have to go." He kisses my cheek. "Yeah, see you next week. Love you guys." He hangs up and puts his cell phone on the counter.

"What are you doing home already?" I kiss him on the lips, and his hand lingers on my side. "I thought you had some big project you were working on."

"Oh, you know..." He toes at the floor.

"Edmund?" He's nervous. He's never nervous.

"I, um..." He licks his bottom lip and kisses me again, more forcefully this time. "I was watching the news."

"Me...too." I tilt my head.

We stare at each other.

Edmund reaches for the front pocket of his suit coat, and I cover his hand with mine. "You didn't."

He winces. "I might have." Pause. "Did you..."

I chuckle. "Wait. Just..." I hurry to the bookshelf in our living room and reach for Oscar Wilde. I palm the black velvet box, return to the only thing I have ever loved, and kneel.

He gawks. "Hey, who said you got to ask me?" He kneels too.

"Edmund!"

"No." He pulls a red velvet box from his pocket. "Equality. It's all the rage."

I chuckle, and so does he.

"I can't believe we both fucking did this."

I feel like I've done *this* before. I think back to a gaudy hotel room in New Orleans, the night when I asked him to spend eternity with me. I suppose we got married then, but now, it can be legal—no matter that our birth certificates are forged. Now, I can call him "husband."

I pop open my black box as he opens the red. "Edmund William Baines."

"My Andrew."

I smile.

"Marry me," we say at the same time.

"Yeah."

"Yes."

We don't even look at the rings before we hug. I breathe him in; he'll always smell sweet to me. I close my eyes and try not to consider all the times I almost lost him, but the images rush at me: cannibals, infection, despair, and guilt... We came so close to never getting here.

He pulls back, grinning. His eyes are the color of the Caribbean Sea. "So what'd you get me?"

"It's tungsten." And black and matches his hair. "It's supposed to be good for men who work with their hands. It shouldn't scratch or bend. Even your reckless experiments won't destroy it."

He slides it on his ring finger, a perfect fit. "Did you measure my ring size while I was sleeping?" He is indeed a heavy sleeper nowadays. The nightmares haven't haunted him in years.

"Might have." I shrug.

He stares at the ring on his finger. "Wish my mum could see."

All those years ago, Evelyn didn't last much longer, even with proper care in London. The Devil's-eye had done its work, although she did come back to her senses. She did beg Edmund's forgiveness—he equally begged hers—and they shared a few precious weeks as beloved son and mother. He even introduced me as his lover, and although Evelyn did turn a rather scandalized shade of pink, she took my hand and thanked me for making her son happy. Before she died, she made me promise to take care of him—a promise I've always kept.

Edmund holds the red box up for me. The ring is gold with a strange black stone in the center. "It's, well." He bites his bottom lip. "It's gold, but this is lava rock. Igneous rock. It's from a volcano on an uninhabited tropical island. I know ours didn't have a volcano, but I *erupted* a lot there, so—"

I maul his mouth with mine. He falls backward under the onslaught, and I land right on top of him. He grunts beneath my weight, but a second later, his hands are in my hair. His mouth opens wide under mine, allowing my tongue entrance, and he moans.

"Wait," he pushes me back, panting. Yes, he still breathes; won't give it up. "Put it on. I want to see it on you." He nibbles on my neck as I claw for the red box on the floor. I lean back, straddling his hips, and put the ring on my finger. Also a perfect fit.

"Did you measure *my* ring size while I was sleeping?"

Even on his back, he's smug. "Might've."

I stand and grab his hand, dragging him up. "Come on. I'm not fucking you on the floor."

Edmund's formal wear is always a lot of work to remove, especially since he isn't a fan of me tearing his bespoke suits. I've become a button expert over the years, though, so I have him naked in the space of thirty seconds. I was in pajamas when he got home, so I'm down to my skin in five.

Wearing nothing but wedding bands, we tumble into the center of our king-sized bed. I press his legs apart and kneel, kissing his toned chest and stomach. Vampires supposedly don't change, but Edmund swears by yoga. He practices once a day, and by God, I insist he's more muscular now than when we first met. His nipples are just as sensitive too. His back arches when I bite one.

"Need you now," he says. The bedside drawer opens by itself, and a flying bottle of lube hits me in the arm. Edmund doesn't use his abilities very often. I think he still fears Brien, even though the man is long dead. Edmund does clean the house using his mind, though. He perfected that trick after seeing *Mary Poppins* back in 1964.

I rub lube between my fingers—silicone-based, what a modern miracle—and run my fingers down the cleft of his ass. He rests back on the bed, waiting. The decades have taught him a modicum of patience. Which I effortlessly destroy by tickling behind his knees.

He twitches. "Don't."

I snicker and lick his belly button.

My fingers seek lower once again and find his entrance. I press one finger inside, then two. Edmund never needs much preparation. He still loves his pleasure with pain. We've even started dipping into the newly popularized BDSM culture.

"Please," he begs, breathless.

I pull my hands away. "Stomach."

He rolls over without question. I admire the long, electric eel scar that adorns his back before tugging his hips until he's on his knees in front of me. I press wet kisses down his spine and continue playing with his ass with my slick digits. He moans my name. I lick once over his hole, lube taste be damned, and Edmund keens.

"Fuck, fuck, do that again."

I acquiesce, and his entire body shivers.

"God, I'm going to come already."

I dig my fingers into his hips. "I won't stop if you do. I'll keep going until you come again. Hell, might even go for three."

He buries his face in a pillow, words muffled. "Shit, I believe you."

"You should by now."

I press into him, and he yells my name. I give a few playful thrusts before tugging on his hair. He gets the hint and lifts up onto his hands, which gives me the grip I need to wrap my arms around his chest and pull him up onto my lap. The deeper angle makes his head fling back, and I only just miss a skull to the face.

He leans his head against my shoulder as I fuck up into him. His mouth sucks on the side of my neck.

I try to slow us both down, but we're too keyed up, high on wedding bands and "husband." Maybe we'll make love slowly later, but not right now. Now, I want him undone in my arms. I thrust, and he lets me. He's a ragdoll in my grip—except for his cock. It stands straight up, hard as stone but covered in silk as I wrap my hand around it and stroke.

Edmund comes with a low groan. I run my hand up his chest and clasp his shoulder, tugging him down harder as I push up. Then, I join him. I bite into his shoulder with my human teeth as I finish, which makes him shiver some more.

I roll us onto our sides, curled together like enormous spoons. I kiss and lick at the back of his neck as he hums in contentment. "Let's fuck all day," he mutters.

"Don't want to go to the courthouse?"

"The lines will be atrocious. And Michelle and Felipe would be irate if we married without them."

I lick the soft skin behind his ear and am reminded of oceans and sea storms. Of course, we own a sailboat. We keep it docked nearby at North Cove Marina, and Edmund captains barefoot.

"Tell me you love me," he says.

"Love you."

We probably hold the record: longest monogamous relationship in vampire history. We broke our rule but once, when we finally slept with Flynn. He was a bit older by then, midthirties. We hadn't seen him in over a decade. After Brien, the young man was smart enough to get away from vampires. Imagine our surprise to find him in Paris.

He was still desperately in love with Edmund, but he was also ill. I smelled sickness on him, something serious. He wouldn't live much longer. Edmund must have sensed it too, because he kissed Flynn in the back of a Moulin Rouge dancehall, dragged him back to our apartment in the Latin Quarter, and gave him everything he'd ever wanted. Flynn remained in our apartment, in fact. Edmund cared for the man until the day he died. He comforted Flynn through the pain and told dozens of stories. I think our favorite redhead died happy in Edmund's arms.

My sailor has learned to be so good, he often makes me a better man by proximity. Edmund's dark creature has been silent since the bonfire at Heavenhill, but mine still lingers on occasion. Edmund is the only one who sees it, and even then, the creature is content with tying Edmund to the bed and fucking him blind.

His hand squeezes mine. "What are you thinking about?"

"Things past."

"Well, stop it. I'm here now."

I wrap my arm around his waist. "You were there then."

The side of his mouth twitches up in a smile. "I don't remember what it's like to be without you."

I squeeze him tighter.

Over a hundred years ago, all I wanted to do was escape an island. When a sea-soaked sailor washed up, all I wanted was him. Deserve it or not, my wishes were granted. Now, all I want is to be Edmund's husband, to wake to his face every morning until the world crashes and burns around us. I have escaped much in my life, but I will never escape him. My heart is his prisoner. Of that, I am glad.

About the Author

Sara Dobie Bauer is a bestselling author, model, and mental health / LGBTQ advocate with a creative writing degree from Ohio University. Twice nominated for the Pushcart Prize, she lives with her hottie husband and two precious pups in Northeast Ohio, although she'd really like to live in a Tim Burton film. She is author of the paranormal rom-com Bite Somebody series, among other sexy things.

In case you never want to miss a new release, sign up for Sara's newsletter on her website, follow her on Amazon, or join "Sara Dobie Bauer's Sexy Circle" on Facebook, where she geeks out about sexy stuff and sexy people.

Email: sara@saradobie.com

Facebook: www.facebook.com/AuthorSaraDobieBauer

Twitter: @SaraDobie

Website: www.saradobiebauer.com

Also Available from NineStar Press

Connect with NineStar Press

www.ninestarpress.com

www.facebook.com/ninestarpress

www.facebook.com/groups/NineStarNiche

www.twitter.com/ninestarpress

www.tumblr.com/blog/ninestarpress